A SECOND PROPOSAL

He drew in a deep breath. "I've missed this. Strolling around your yard, watching the girls play, sharing our opinions about goats and child rearing and birthday cakes."

Ach, she had missed it too. "All very exciting subjects, for sure and certain." Menno had been her anchor and her wall, someone to keep her grounded and bounce ideas off of at the same time.

He folded his arms across his chest and Joanna tried not to let his good looks unsettle her.

"Joanna, I have been needing to apologize to you for months. I badly botched my proposal, and I've regretted it every day since. I'm very sorry."

She tried to laugh it off, cuffing him casually on the shoulder. "I'm sure you'll do better next time."

Hope flickered in his eyes. "Will there be a next time?"

Her heart tried to claw its way out of her chest. "For sure and certain there will be a next time for you . . ."

The Amish Quiltmaker's Uninvited Guest

JENNIFER BECKSTRAND

ZEBRA BOOKS
Kensington Publishing Corp.
www.kensingtonbooks.com

ZEBRA BOOKS are published by

Kensington Publishing Corp.
900 Third Avenue
New York, NY 10022

All Kensington titles, imprints, and distributed lines are available at special quantity discounts for bulk purchases for sales promotion, premiums, fund-raising, and educational or institutional use.

Special book excerpts or customized printings can also be created to fit specific needs. For details, write or phone the office of the Kensington Sales Manager: Kensington Publishing Corp., 900 Third Avenue, New York, NY 10022. Attn. Sales Department. Phone: 1-800-221-2647.

Zebra and the Z logo Reg. U.S. Pat. & TM Off.

First Printing: July 2024.
ISBN-13: 978-1-4201-5612-6
ISBN-13: 978-1-4201-5613-3 (eBook)

10 9 8 7 6 5 4 3 2 1

Printed in the United States of America

Chapter 1

Joanna Yoder climbed out of the van followed by her three sisters, Mary, Ada, and Beth. Joanna wrapped both hands around the handle of the bag that carried her half-finished quilt squares. She looked up at the sky, breathed in slowly, and savored the smell of warm spring air and freshly cut grass. A lilac bush in full bloom grew on one side of Esther Kiem's porch. It was breathtakingly beautiful.

"Do you smell the lilacs?" said her *schwester* Mary as she shut the van door behind her.

Joanna nodded. "Hmm. Delicious."

"Lilacs don't smell delicious, Joanna. That's not the right word," Ada said.

Joanna grinned. Ada couldn't resist correcting her *schwesteren* whenever she got an opportunity. Ada was the eldest *schwester*, and being persnickety was her favorite hobby. She rarely spared sharing her opinion about anything.

"It's the right word if you like lilac ice cream, Ada."

Ada wrinkled her nose. "Does anyone like lilac ice cream?"

Their driver, Cathy Larsen, came around to the passenger

side of the van. "You have to have a sophisticated palette to enjoy lilac ice cream, and most people aren't as refined as you and I, Joanna. I eat lilac ice cream while I watch PBS."

"You like lilac ice cream, Cathy?" Beth asked, obviously not believing her.

Cathy shook her head. "I'm not fond of it, but sometimes you have to pretend if you want your friends to think you have good taste. That's why I drink herbal tea and go to the symphony. I have to keep up appearances."

Joanna laughed. "I don't have to pretend. I love lilac ice cream and lilac jelly."

Cathy pointed her finger in the air. "Mention that in casual conversation, and you'll get invited to a lot of fancy soirees."

Joanna laughed. "I'm not sure I want to know what a soiree is."

Cathy waved her hand. "It's just a party for snobby people."

A series of squeaks and loud thuds caught their attention. With Mary leading the way, all five of them trudged to the side yard where they found Esther Kiem vigorously beating a small rag rug against the house. She didn't see them as she lifted the rug above her head, squeaked in exertion, and brought the rug down against the brick. She'd obviously been taking her frustration out on the rug for quite some time. Sweat trickled down her face, and her breathing was heavy and ragged. Her two small children, Winnie and Junior, played on the grass not ten feet away, apparently seeing nothing strange about their mother violently slapping a rug against the wall.

"I think it's dead," Cathy said, just as Esther lifted the rug in the air again.

Esther flinched and turned, dropping the rug into the

grass when she saw her visitors. "I lost track of time," she said, a sheepish expression on her face. Small tufts of hair escaped from her *kapp* in every direction, and a thin stick of celery was tucked behind her ear. Esther always had something tucked behind her ear for safekeeping.

Joanna never knew what would be there next. To go along with the odd celery stick, three pastel quilting clips were attached to the hem of Esther's left sleeve, and a sky-blue binkie was hooked to her finger by its handle, like a giant ring made out of plastic.

Ada reached out and brushed a piece of lint from Esther's sleeve. "It looks like that's not the only thing you lost."

Esther gave Ada a defensive look. "It's always very productive to clean my rugs when I'm mad. I kill two birds with one stone."

"It looks like you've also killed the rug," Cathy said.

Esther was the dearest woman in the world, but she had a temper and a reputation for destroying things when she got mad. She'd broken four pickleball paddles over the years, de-leafed the bushes in front of her porch, thrown apricots against the house, and dented her own mailbox with a rock. The dent was still there, even though her husband, Levi, had tried to hammer it out.

"Aendi Ada!" Winnie, Esther's four-year-old daughter, threw out her arms and ran into Ada's embrace. Ada was one of Winnie's favorites.

Junior, the almost-eighteen-month-old, dropped his ball, toddled over to Joanna, and lifted his hands. Joanna hoisted Junior into her arms and gave him a big kiss on his chubby cheek. He smelled like baby shampoo and was just about the cutest baby Joanna had ever seen, with his light brown curls and coffee brown eyes that could have melted even the hardest heart.

Esther picked up her much-abused rug and gave it a little shake, as if to dislodge any remaining dirt that was still hanging on for dear life. "You didn't come all this way to watch me clean my rugs. Let's go in and talk about your poor *grossmammi* and her long-overdue quilt."

Ada took Winnie's hand. "Grossmammi Beulah is in excellent health. No need to worry about her."

Esther draped the rug over her arm. "I'm mostly concerned that you *schwesteren* were supposed to finish her quilt last year for her hundredth birthday."

Mary's eyes glowed with the light of unbounded happiness. "After Clay crashed into our barn, quilt plans got derailed."

Clay Markham, a professional baseball player, had been driving drunk and crashed his car into the Yoders' barn a year and a half ago. It was quite extraordinary, but he and Mary had fallen in love, Clay had been baptized, and Mary and Clay were married in October. Joanna had never seen anyone as happy as Mary, unless you counted Clay, who was so happy he wore a permanent smile on his face and looked like he was floating most of the time. He hadn't just crashed into their barn, he'd crashed into their lives, and everything had been turned upside-down and inside-out with him on the farm. He was famous, so reporters and fans and other curious people had regularly come onto their property to gawk or get an autograph or ask prying questions. It had been a disconcerting, crazy, turbulent year for all of them. In all the excitement, they had set Grossmammi's quilt aside.

Joanna couldn't even remember who had the original idea to make Grossmammi Beulah a sampler quilt for her hundredth birthday, but each *schwester* had chosen a quilt pattern several months ago. Ada was finished with her blocks. Beth hadn't even started hers.

Beth sighed. "It's *gute* Grossmammi is still alive. We have time to finish the quilt before she dies."

Ada puckered her whole face. "What a horrible thing to say."

Beth didn't seem concerned that Ada was about to have a stroke. "We're all thinking it. Grossmammi is old, but Lord willing, she'll last until we can finish her quilt." Beth was right, though she always had a clumsy way of saying things.

Ada was often too hard on Beth. She pinned her with an accusatory stare. "I've finished mine."

Beth sniffed into the air. "Joanna isn't finished with hers yet. I'm not the only one."

Joanna loved all her *schwesteren*, but she was especially protective of Beth. "I'm not even halfway done, and like Beth said, we still have time. Grossmammi Beulah still does calisthenics every morning."

Esther took a tissue from her apron pocket and swiped it across Winnie's nose. "Well, we don't have an unlimited amount of time. Let's go in and talk about your quilt."

Cathy set her gigantic purse on the grass. "First, I want to know if any more rugs or trees, or pots and pans are in danger. You could pull a muscle in a fit of temper, and it's no fun walking around on crutches for six weeks. I should know. I have a bunion."

Esther huffed out a breath. "It's Levi's cousin Menno."

Cathy's eyebrow traveled up her forehead. "I didn't know Levi had a cousin Menno. Is he the one in danger?"

"He's Levi's *dat*'s brother's grandson, so not a first cousin, but sadly, he and Levi are related. We got a letter from him this morning. His wife died exactly a year ago tomorrow, and he'll be here tomorrow with his two little girls for an 'extended visit.' He wants Levi to find him a job and a wife and give him a bed and three meals a day."

Mary's eyes widened. "He wants Levi to find him a wife?"

Esther strangled the rug in her arms. "Levi has assigned that task to me."

Ada harrumphed her disapproval. "I don't mean to criticize Levi, but that doesn't seem very nice."

Esther ground her teeth together. "Levi feels bad about it, but I know a lot more about the unmarried girls in the community than he does. He says it would be inappropriate if he tried to find Menno a wife. He'd raise more than one eyebrow and be the source of gossip for years."

Beth giggled. "He's right about that."

"You're not obligated to find Menno a wife," Joanna said. "He's a grown man, and if he can't find his own wife, he doesn't deserve to have one."

Esther's shoulders sagged. "He put all the details in his letter. His wife has been gone exactly a year, and now the next step in his life is to find someone else to marry. Menno is very determined, very methodical, and very serious about anything he puts his mind to. He doesn't want to waste time looking for a *fraa*. He wants us to make a list of all the likely candidates so he can pick a *fraa* quickly and get back home to plant his sugar beets."

"I don't wonder but the girls will line up to meet him." Joanna connected her gaze to Mary's, and they shared a wry smile.

Esther didn't catch on that Joanna was teasing. "I feel sorry for him, losing his wife and all, but I've got three quilts to make before the Memorial Day auction, and two children of my own. Menno will expect me to watch his girls while he works and courts some poor, unsuspecting girl. I told Levi I can't spare the time."

"*Jah*," Joanna said, righteously indignant for Esther's sake. "Menno should find his own *fraa*. It's not like plucking a can of corn off the shelf at the grocery store."

Beth's brow creased in confusion. "Why is he coming to Colorado to look? There are more Amish girls just about anywhere else."

Esther slapped the rug against the house again. "*Ach*. He lives in Baker, Idaho, which is even smaller than Byler, and he's coming here because Levi owes him."

Joanna tilted her head to one side. "What does Levi owe him?"

"Menno saved Levi from drowning as a teenager. His family had gone up to visit Menno's family in Idaho, and they went swimming, and Levi almost drowned. Menno saved his life. He pulled Levi out of the lake and even performed CPR, for goodness' sake."

Beth frowned. "What's CPR?"

"It means Levi's heart stopped, and Menno got it beating again. You can't just shrug off something that remarkable. I should be more grateful, but all I am is irritated." Esther puckered her lips as if she'd eaten a lemon. "And now I have to be polite and hospitable and accommodating. He's methodical, but he says he's not picky. He wants a mother for his girls, and he's got one month to find someone before he has to be back in Idaho. Levi is going to let Menno work with his carpentry crew while he's here. At least the job is settled, but the worst part is that I have nowhere to put him except in the quilt shop."

Esther's husband, Levi, had built a spacious addition on one side of Esther's house where she had opened a quilt shop. The room was full of quilts, and there was a display bed in the middle of the shop where Esther spread her most expensive quilts. It was the only extra bed, and apparently, Cousin Menno was going to be sleeping in it.

Esther slumped her shoulders. "I'm sure Menno's little girls are sweet, but they're two and three, and they're going to ruin my quilts."

"Could he stay with Levi's parents?" Ada wanted to know.

Pain traveled across Esther's face. "I thought about it, but Nanna starts another round of chemo this week, and I just can't ask them to take on one more thing."

Joanna shifted Junior to one arm and wrapped the other around Esther's shoulder. "Nanna is going to be all right. She's tough, and she has practically the entire state of Colorado praying for her."

Esther sniffed brusquely. "Lord willing. On top of everything, we're having *gmayna* here on Sunday. It's the first time we've hosted because we finally have a place big enough to hold services . . . if we move all the quilts out of the quilt shop. How am I going to clean the house and prepare for *gmayna* with Menno and his *dochters* underfoot?"

Cathy was practical and blunt. "You should tell him to go back to Idaho. I'll tell him for you, if you like. I'll drive him to the bus station if he pays me."

"Much as I don't want him here, I feel sorry for him. His wife is passed, his girls are young, and he's overwhelmed with taking care of them."

"He doesn't want a wife," Joanna mumbled. "He wants a babysitter."

Esther glanced at Joanna. "And someone who can cook and clean"—she fingered the celery stick behind her ear—"and do all the wifely duties."

Beth's jaw dropped as if her tongue had swollen too big for her mouth. Mary blushed like a beet, and Ada seemed to have smoke coming out of her ears. Joanna's throat felt scratchy like a burnt piece of toast. *Ach, du lieva.* Cousin Menno was shaping up to be the last man any girl in her right mind would want to marry. But Joanna knew better. There were many women willing to settle for almost any man simply because they were desperate to be married. Fortunately, she wasn't one of them.

"The wifely duties aren't so bad," Mary said, turning even redder than Cathy Larsen's shiny red jacket.

Esther cracked a smile. "Of course not."

Joanna didn't know anything about wifely duties, but she did know that neither she nor any of her *schwesteren* wanted to feel like a can of corn or a bag of flour, something random pulled off the shelf out of necessity.

"Wifely duties are *wunderbarr!*" Mary blurted out then clapped her hand over her mouth as if she'd just said something shocking.

Joanna grinned. She adored that Mary was so happy. Mary had experienced a lot of pain in her life, and she deserved every *gute* thing.

"No need to be embarrassed about that," Cathy said. "Do you think anyone would want to get married otherwise?"

Beth pressed her hands over her ears. "Can we not talk about this anymore?"

Ada seemed just as happy as anyone to change the subject. "What are you going to do about Levi's cousin, Esther?"

"I don't know. I feel like a terrible person, but I don't want him to come. On top of everything"—she paused and glanced at Cathy—"I'm going to have a baby. But don't tell anyone yet."

Everyone cooed and sighed and exclaimed their delight.

"When is it coming?" Ada asked.

Esther grinned and laid her hand on her stomach. "September."

"How are you feeling?"

"I throw up in the morning and feel rotten the rest of the day. That's why I don't think I can even be polite to Menno. I'm a candle spent on both ends." Esther sighed. "I have to help him. The sooner he finds a *fraa*, the sooner he'll leave." Her lips twitched upward. "I regret to inform you that three of you are eligible for my list. Only Mary is safe."

"Thank Derr Herr," Mary sighed.

Ada's eyebrows inched up her forehead. "If you put me on that list, I'll never speak to you again, Esther Kiem."

Joanna glanced at Beth. "None of us want to go on that list."

Beth nodded her agreement. "Who wants to marry an old man?"

Esther looked at Beth sideways. "Beth, Menno's girls are two and three. Menno is only twenty-seven. Joanna's age."

Beth's eyes flashed with amusement. "It looks like Joanna is the perfect age."

Joanna gave Beth the stink eye. "Somebody should wash your mouth out with soap."

Winnie kept asking to be picked up, and Ada finally lifted Winnie into her arms. "How can we help? We could make you some freezer meals for days you don't have time to cook."

Esther drooped with relief. "That would be *wunderbarr*."

Ada motioned to the *schwesteren*. "We can come on Saturday and scrub the whole place down for *gmayna*. I'm *gute* with toilets."

Esther laughed. "I'll gladly let you do that."

Joanna bounced Junior in her arms, even though he was almost eighteen months old and didn't really need to be bounced anymore. "How long did you say he would be here?"

"One month or until he finds a *fraa*."

Joanna glanced at Mary. "We need to do what we can to hurry that along."

Ada liked to make assignments. "Mary, you should be the one to make a list of all the women Menno could possibly marry."

Mary grimaced. "It doesn't feel right to put anyone on the list. Menno isn't truly looking for love. He seems more concerned about convenience."

Mary was right. Joanna wouldn't want to be put on that list without her knowledge and without knowing what Menno was really up to. "I couldn't care a whit about helping Menno, but if we find him a *fraa*, it will help Esther." In her head, Joanna counted up the single women she knew of the right age. Byler was a small place with a small Amish population. Joanna couldn't even imagine how small Baker, Idaho, must be. "There are only six I can think of. I suppose it would be okay to make a list if we warned all the girls on the list and got their permission."

Esther thought for a minute. "I feel *gute* about that."

Junior wriggled in Joanna's arms. She set him on his feet, and he toddled around the grass plucking dandelions out of the ground. They'd come up with a plan, but Joanna still felt very sorry for Esther. Joanna hated nausea worse than anything, and Menno and Levi expected poor Esther to care for four children and find Menno a *fraa* while she was afflicted with the throw-ups. It wasn't fair, and Joanna had half a mind to give Menno a scolding when he got there. "What would you think if I come every day while

Menno is at work and help you care for *die kinner*? You could get your quilting done, and I could help with some of the chores."

Esther's eyes flashed before their light dimmed. "I couldn't ask you to do that."

"You're not asking. I'm offering. It's only for a month."

"But, Joanna," Mary said. "What about your orders?"

Joanna ran a tiny bakery out of their house, and her potato rolls and fry pies were popular with the Amish and Englisch in the valley. She made six dozen potato rolls every week and four or five dozen fry pies. Customers came to the house every Wednesday and Saturday morning to buy her baked goods. Sometimes she did special orders, and on Friday mornings, she delivered three dozen fry pies to the bigger Amish bakery in Byler.

"I'll just rearrange my baking schedule a bit. I can make dough at Esther's house and come here a little late on Wednesday mornings after the customers leave."

"I can help," Beth said unenthusiastically. Plain and simple, Beth thought she was allergic to work, but she knew enough to volunteer so Esther wouldn't think she was lazy.

Joanna gave Beth's arm a squeeze. "If you help me with the fry pies on Wednesday nights and make Esther some freezer meals, that will be enough. You and Ada can help *Dat* with the goats and the alfalfa and keep the household running while I'm gone. It's only four weeks." She eyed Ada. "You'll have to take over the goat cheese."

Ada nodded. "You'll have to teach me. Beth will have to help."

Beth shrugged. "Okay."

Cathy clapped her hands and picked up her giant purse. "Okay, now that you've got Esther's problem solved, I hope we won't see any more battered rugs or broken golf clubs in your yard."

Joanna grinned at Esther. "You've broken a golf club?"

Esther blushed. "One. Clay had a whole set of clubs in the back of his truck, and I didn't think he'd mind if I swung just one of them against the wall. I didn't know it would be so fragile. One of those pesky reporters made me quite angry one day."

Clay was now Amish, but he had been a pro baseball player, and when he and Mary were dating, reporters had often harassed him at Mary's house and at Esther's.

Surprise popped all over Mary's face. "You broke his golf club?"

Esther chuckled. "He doesn't need clubs anymore anyway. So no harm done." She called to Junior. "*Cum*, let's go in and find out what still needs to be done on those quilt blocks."

"Mine are done," Ada said. "I made nine Bachelor's Puzzle quilt blocks."

"Do all your corners match?" Cathy asked.

"Of course they do," Joanna said. "Ada is meticulous."

Cathy shuffled toward the front door, and her neon pink nylon pants made a swishing sound when she walked. "Remind me of the quilt block you're making, Joanna. My memory is like a sieve these days."

"I'm making nine Sugar Bowl blocks, each with a different color palette. I thought it would look cute."

Cathy stopped short and gaped at Joanna as if she had said something very upsetting. "Wait a minute! Don't you remember what I told Mary about the magic of quilt blocks?"

Joanna drew her brows together. "Um, no."

"I told her that each square you make has a little magic in it."

"The Amish don't believe in magic," Ada said.

Cathy shook her head impatiently. "You Amish can be so stubborn, but it doesn't matter whether you believe or not. Do you remember the quilt square Mary chose?"

"I'm almost finished," Mary volunteered.

Joanna's gaze flicked between Mary and Cathy. Was she missing something important? "Um, she did the Drunkard's Path."

Cathy stomped her foot on the ground so hard, Joanna felt a vibration. "That's right, and do you remember what happened after Mary chose that particular quilt block to work on?" Cathy didn't wait for an answer. "A drunk driver crashed into your barn, and Mary ended up marrying that drunk driver. The drunkard's path led Clay straight to Mary."

Joanna gave Cathy a doubtful, encouraging smile. "*Jah*. It's *wunderbarr* when Gotte brings two people together."

Cathy rolled her eyes. "Of course it was God. And that quilt block."

Esther bloomed into a teasing smile. "Now, Cathy, don't you think you're overreacting a bit?"

Joanna agreed with Esther, but Mary was wide eyed. "It happened just like she warned me."

Cathy counted on her fingers listing all the reasons Joanna and Esther should believe in the miracle of quilt blocks. "You have chosen the Sugar Bowl quilt block. Cousin Menno is from Baker, Idaho. You are a baker. Bakers use sugar. Sugar comes from sugar beets. Menno grows sugar beets." Cathy was so flustered, she leaned against the house to catch her breath. "Joanna, you're going to marry Cousin Menno, no doubt about it."

"Let me reassure you that I will not marry Cousin Menno. He is looking for a *fraa*, any *fraa*, and I refuse to be just another can of corn."

As Cathy pulled a fan from her large bag and waved it in front of her face, Joanna stifled a smile. It was March, and it couldn't have been more than fifty-five degrees outside.

Cathy looked as if she were having a hot flash. "I agree that Menno is arrogant, thoughtless, and a little too sure of himself. I don't need to meet him to know he would be a very unsuitable husband, especially if he treated you like a can of corn. You're a sweet girl, Joanna, and I'd hate to see you stuck with that man for the rest of your life. To be safe, you should change your quilt block."

Joanna wasn't about to start all over again just to make Cathy feel better. "I've already cut out all the fabric."

Mary seemed to be taking Cathy's concerns seriously. "You could make Bright Star blocks, Joanna. Then you'd still be able to use your triangles."

Before Joanna could open her mouth to protest, Cathy clutched her chest. "That's the worst possible solution, Mary. Another name for the Bright Star quilt block is Idaho Beauty. *Menno is from Idaho*." She exhaled a heavy sigh. "You're doomed, Joanna."

Something about the way Cathy said *doomed* made Joanna want to laugh. She held it in by imagining Cousin Menno at the market shopping for canned corn and lima beans. What could she say to put Cathy's mind at ease? "I know what Menno is up to, and I won't be tempted in the least to accept an offer of marriage from him. I'm safe."

Cathy did not look convinced in the least, but she stuffed her fan into her purse and zipped it shut with finality. "I've done all I can. Your future is out of my hands."

Joanna laughed. "I don't know that my future was ever *in* your hands."

Cathy heaved a sigh. "True, but I always try to help where I can." She adjusted the glittery sun visor sitting on her head. "Alrighty then. Let's go into the house, have a cup of coffee, and plan Joanna's doom. Who's with me?"

Chapter 2

Menno Eicher sat at one of the two tiny round tables in the bakery, sipping *kaffee* and eating an exceptionally delicious doughnut. His two *dochters* sat on either side of him on regular sized chairs because the bakery didn't have highchairs. He kept a sharp eye on both of them so he could catch them if they teetered.

He had finally convinced Rosie to sit on her bottom, though she hadn't been happy about it. Her little feet dangled over the edge of her seat, and she sang a song to herself as she licked the glaze off the top of her doughnut and pinched little bits of dough from the edges to put in her mouth. Lily was much more obedient than her older *schwester*. She sat quietly, staring at the uneaten doughnut in her hand. Even at age two, Lily hated sticky fingers, and a glazed doughnut almost as big as her head must have seemed daunting.

"Here, let me help you." He took the doughnut and the napkin it was sitting on from Lily's hand and set it on the table. After grabbing a plastic knife from the dispenser behind him, he cut Lily's doughnut into bite-size pieces and handed her a single piece. "It's *gute*. You'll like it."

Lily daintily pinched the doughnut tidbit between her

thumb and index finger and popped it into her mouth. She grinned and reached out her hand for another piece.

Menno smiled. "*Gute?*"

"*Gute,*" Lily said, her mouth full of doughnut. She couldn't say many words, but she knew *gute* and *dada*. She'd never learned to say *mamm* or *mommy* or even *mama*. Suvilla had died two weeks after Lily's first birthday.

"Rosie, sit on your bottom, *sei so gute*."

Rosie pretended she hadn't heard him but slowly lowered her *hinnerdale* back to the seat and took another lick of her frosting.

Yesterday when he'd arrived in Byler, dread, sorrow, and determination had settled into Menno's chest like three fat elephants who'd invited themselves to lounge on his couch. Yesterday was the one-year anniversary of Suvilla's death, and the bishop had told him that the proper mourning period was one year and no longer and that if Menno didn't find a wife, he would become a burden to the church, his family, and Gotte.

Menno was nothing if not obedient. He lived his life by a strict set of rules, trying to seek Gotte's will and do it immediately because he didn't want to be a slothful servant. He wanted his life to be acceptable to Gotte and the bishop, so he tried not to make a mistake ever. Obedience was better than sacrifice, even though it got wonderful exhausting at times.

It would have been ideal if he'd been able to find a girl in Baker to marry, but Baker had a tiny Amish population—fewer than twenty families—and there was only one eligible girl in the whole district, unless he counted Eva Miller who was a forty-nine-year-old widow with two teeth in her mouth. Eva was nice enough, but even his mamm had agreed that Eva was too old. Two decades too old. The other eligible girl was Mayne Lapp, who was eighteen and writing to a boy in Ohio. Thank Derr Herr she was already spoken for because Menno would have felt obligated to court her, and she was way too young.

Eva was too old. Mayne was too young.

Menno had relatives in Ohio, Indiana, and Colorado, but looking for a wife in Colorado had appealed to him because it was closer to Idaho, and the Amish population here was smaller too. With fewer men in the area, surely there were women who hadn't been able to find a husband and were eager to get married. He hoped to find one willing to move to Baker.

He hated to impose on Levi and Esther, and that was why he'd given himself a one-month time limit. Surely he could find a suitable woman and convince her to marry him in four weeks. Lord willing, the arrangement would be convenient and beneficial for both of them.

Menno pulled his list out of his pocket. Across the top he'd written "With Gotte nothing shall be impossible." He'd neatly copied the numbers one through five down the left margin and put a task by each number.

#1 Find a wife

#2 Memorize the four gospels

#3 Buy Rosie some new shoes

#4 Order mulch

#5 Write to Mamm and let her know I made it to Colorado safely

Number two had been on his list for over a year, but he hadn't made much progress after Suvilla died because grief had made it so he couldn't think straight, and circumstances had made it so he had no free time for anything but caring for his farm and his girls. Time had dulled the pain of Suvilla's passing, and caring for the girls wasn't as time-consuming now they were a little older. He needed to start memorizing again. Surely it would please Gotte to see Menno studying the Word more often.

Menno handed Lily another piece of doughnut. "Rosie, sit on your bottom, or you'll fall over." Rosie glared at him as if she was barely tolerating his presence, but she wiggled her feet out from under her and sat down properly. He admired how easily his three-year-old could muster indignation, as if what he'd asked her to do was a terrible imposition. Her indignation made him want to chuckle, but also made him want to cry. Rosie needed a *mater*. He only hoped Gotte would lead him to someone kind and patient who loved children. His heart sank. It seemed too much to ask in such a short amount of time.

Menno rubbed his hand down the side of his face. He couldn't get used to not having a beard. Married Amish men wore beards, and when a man's *fraa* died, he usually kept his beard. Menno had shaved his face smooth, thinking it would be more appropriate when he started courting a girl. He didn't want girls to think a married man was interested in them, and since no one here in Colorado knew who he was, he wanted it to be obvious he was single. Would Gotte be displeased with his decision? *Ach, vell,* the bishop had approved, so surely Gotte would smile on his clean-shaven face.

The bell above the bakery door tinkled, and a young woman carrying two large cardboard boxes in her arms tried to push the door open with her elbow. The door was heavy, and she struggled to keep the door from closing on her. With one eye glued to his girls, Menno jumped to his feet and opened the door wider for the woman.

"*Denki*," she said, looking up and nearly blinding him with her brilliant smile and her bright blue eyes.

Menno's heart did a complete somersault. Did Gotte really answer prayers that quickly? Was this the girl Menno was supposed to meet? He pressed his lips together and willed his heart to slow down. For all he knew, she was married with four children and a very happy husband at home. It was foolish to get ahead of himself.

She slid the boxes on to the counter and took a deep breath. Still smiling, still glowing like an angel, she said, "I made extra fry pies today, and they wouldn't fit in one box. I should know better than to try to bring everything in on one trip. You saved my baked goods. *Denki*."

"You make fry pies?" he said, his tongue swelling up like a sponge.

"*Jah*. I bring them into the bakery every Friday." Her smile was so warm, so open, Menno couldn't look away.

An older Amish woman came from the kitchen and stood behind the counter. "Joanna," she said, "so *gute* to see you. We sold the last of your fry pies on Monday. Can you bring more next week?"

A tiny crease between her eyebrows marred Joanna's flawless skin. "*Ach*, I'm not sure. I'm helping my friend with a serious problem for a few weeks, and I'm going to have my hands full. I will try."

The older woman shrugged. "That's all I can ask."

Joanna turned back to Menno and gifted him with another bright smile. "*Vell*, I have to be going. *Denki* again for your help."

"Are you married?" he blurted out. It was the most awkward thing he'd ever said, but he was in Colorado to do one thing, and if Gotte had truly guided his steps here today, he had to seize the opportunity no matter how strange she thought he was.

She tilted her head, amusement playing at her full lips. "That's an odd question."

He cringed and screwed his eyes shut momentarily. "That didn't come out—I'm sorry. That's the dumbest thing I've ever said."

Two syllables of a giggle escaped her lips. "No need to apologize. It's flattering and sort of adorable." Her eyes were deep blue, like a cool summer lake, as she searched his face.

He didn't know what she was searching for, but Lord willing she'd find it—assuming she wasn't married, of course, which he still didn't know. He swallowed his embarrassment. "So . . . are you married?" He held his breath for the answer.

He felt a tug on his trousers and heard a small voice behind him.

"Dada?"

Ach. He'd gotten lost in Joanna's eyes and neglected his *dochters.* Turning, Menno laid a soft hand on Lily's golden head. How had she gotten off the chair by herself? "Coming, *heartzley.*"

Lily pointed at Rosie who had ripped what was left of her doughnut into small pieces and was throwing them on the floor around her chair.

Menno caught his breath, scooped Lily into his arms, and glanced back at Joanna. "Sorry. I need to—" He grabbed a handful of napkins from the dispenser, set Lily on her chair, and held out his hand to Rosie. "Are you done, *heartzley?*"

Rosie nodded, a sly and irresistible grin on her face, and handed Menno the remains of her doughnut. "I feeding the birds."

She was too cute to scold, and Menno could never be impatient with a three-year-old. He set the disfigured doughnut on the table, braced his hands on his knees, and leaned over so he was eye level with Rosie. She wouldn't look at him, as if she thought he'd go away if she pretended he didn't exist.

"Rosie girl," he whispered in a high-pitched voice. Then he walked his fingers lightly up her arm as if his hand was a spider.

When he got to her neck, she squealed and burst into delighted laughter. "Top it, Daddy," she said, slapping his hand away, leaving his wrist covered with sticky bits of glaze.

He chuckled. "This spider likes doughnuts. You'd better not throw pieces on the floor, or he'll come looking for them." He tickled her cheek.

She scrunched up her shoulders and leaned away from him giggling. "I feeding birds, Daddy."

Menno got down on his hands and knees and wiped up the doughnut fragments and sticky glaze as best he could. "Next time let's feed the birds outside. Please sit on your bottom." He stood and threw the dirty napkins in the trash.

To his surprise, Joanna was standing right where he'd left her, staring at Menno with an unreadable expression on her face.

Once again, his heart knocked against his rib cage as if it was trying to escape. "I'm sorry about that. These are my *dochters*, Lily and Rosie." He self-consciously fingered his jaw. "I'm a widower, but I shaved because—" He wasn't quite sure how to finish that sentence. Telling her he was looking for a wife and that she was the one he wanted to propose to seemed a little hasty.

She looked at him, then her gaze traveled from Rosie to Lily to his to-do list still sitting on the table. Her shapely eyebrows inched together as several emotions traveled across her face. She seemed at once startled, irritated, puzzled, and resentful.

What was she thinking? Was she close enough to read his handwriting?

Joanna took a deep breath, scrunched her lips together, and looked up at him, her expression now saturated with a mixture of exasperation and amusement. She stepped closer to the table, bent over, and shook Lily's hand, seemingly unconcerned that Lily's fingers were smudged with glaze. "Nice to meet you, Lily." She shook Rosie's sticky hand next. "Nice to meet you."

Lily and Rosie just stared at Joanna, probably as fascinated by her beauty as Menno was. She took a small water pitcher from the counter and poured some water on a handful of napkins, then knelt down and smiled at Rosie. She spread out her fingers and said, "Show me your piggies."

Rosie didn't ignore Joanna like she always did her *fater*. With her eyes shining, she spread her hands out in front of her, and Joanna wiped all ten fingers thoroughly with the damp napkin. Then she got more napkins and more water and wiped down Lily as well. Menno slid into his chair, mostly so as not to be in the way, but partly so he could get a better view of Joanna's face as she ministered to his children. She had to be the one! Gotte was so *gute*.

Joanna threw the sticky napkins away and grinned at Lily and Rosie. "All clean," she said. "Doesn't that feel better?"

Rosie nodded. Lily just kept staring at Joanna. She probably felt the same awe Menno was feeling. Here was the prettiest woman he had ever seen in an Amish *kapp*.

Joanna's mouth twitched playfully as she tapped her index finger to Menno's paper. "Going shopping?"

Menno picked up his list, folded it slowly so she wouldn't think he didn't want her to see it, and stuffed it into his pocket. "Um, *nae*. That's just the tasks I need to get done while I'm in Colorado."

She touched her finger to her smiling lips as if contemplating something very important. "Some lucky girl is going to be thrilled she's on your to-do list."

His pulse raced. Was Joanna hinting that she wanted to be the one? Because he wanted her to be the one too. Was it possible his business in Colorado could be settled in one day? It was too *gute* to be true, but with Gotte, nothing was impossible. He had tried to live a *gute* life. He had been obedient to the bishop. Gotte loved and rewarded those who kept His commandments.

Menno was so excited, he almost couldn't form the words in his mouth. "What . . . what do you think about my list?" What he really wanted to ask was, "Will you marry me?" but that would be foolish. He was in a hurry, not crazy. And smart enough to be patient.

"I didn't see canned corn on the list, but it goes with every meal, and it's convenient when you can't think of anything else to make for dinner. You should write it down." Her eyes danced as she folded her arms and waited. But what was she waiting for?

Menno flinched, pulled his list out of his pocket, and quickly wrote the number six at the bottom and *can of corn* next to it. Okay . . . Joanna was little odd, but it was nothing he couldn't work around. Either that or she liked corn an awful lot. He would have to remember that when they got married. Corn at every meal.

"But . . . what do you think of my list?"

She sighed as if she'd lost her patience, though she didn't lose her smile. "There are many girls who would be happy to make your list, but I'm not one of them."

His hope deflated like a leaky balloon. She wasn't interested? Not even a little bit? "*Ach.* Okay," he murmured. "Okay." His whole body was suddenly made of lead. He curled his fingers around his now-cold *kaffee*.

She tilted her head and gazed at him like a saint offering some kindness to a lowly sinner. "Your *kinner* are sweet, and you seem resolute. Lord willing, you'll find what you're looking for. I wish you all the best, Menno." She turned toward the door. "I'm sure we'll be seeing each other around Byler. It's a small place."

She pulled back her shoulders, and he watched her stroll out the door as if she hadn't just given him a thorough set down. He furrowed his brow. He hadn't remembered telling Joanna his name.

In Byler a little more than twelve hours and he'd already failed with one woman. Lord willing, he would have more success with another one. He scrubbed his hand down the side of his face. Why did the thought of any woman *but* Joanna tighten his chest?

Was he finished before he had begun?

Chapter 3

Joanna stepped onto Esther's porch and rapped on the door. *Ach*! How irritated she was!

Irritated with Menno Eicher, canned corn, and to-do lists, but mostly irritated with herself. She'd walked into the bakery this morning, and the sight of a handsome man had taken her breath away, as if she were some silly schoolgirl with a crush on one of the eighth-grade boys. Before she realized who Menno was, she had been almost giddy about the prospect of a new, wildly good looking, unmarried man in Colorado. Menno wasn't as tall as Mary's husband, Clay, but he had that same potent masculinity Clay possessed. He glided across the floor with a cougar's grace and bore himself with the confidence of a man who worked hard and conquered difficult, nearly impossible tasks on a daily basis. Yesterday she had been determined to dislike Menno, and today she'd almost fallen for him.

It was too aggravating, especially for a person who prided herself on being sensible and intelligent and unlikely to be fooled by tricks, even ones disguised in attractive packages.

And Menno was an attractive package. He had a square,

strong jaw and brilliant green eyes with a steady gaze, a man who could look you in the eye with the confidence of his convictions. His nose was too big but fit perfectly on his face, and his hair was the color of sunbaked wheat. Joanna had a weakness for muscles, and Menno had plenty of them, his arms thick and his shoulders broad.

Of course she knew better than to judge a book by its cover, but Grossmammi Beulah always said if you were going to fall in love with a man, he might as well be handsome.

It wasn't just Menno's countenance that had gotten Joanna's heart beating fast. Despite his list, he seemed like a truly kind man. He was quiet and gentle with his *dochters*, patient and loving, and he seemed eager to be helpful to Joanna. She'd seen more than item number one on Menno's list. He wanted to find a wife *and* memorize the four gospels? Who did that?

So now Joanna was annoyed because she wanted to adamantly dislike Menno, and she just couldn't do it. She still wanted to give him a scolding about imposing on Esther and Levi and about putting *find a fraa* on his to-do list, but she couldn't dislike him.

Esther answered the door with a toothbrush behind her ear and Junior in her arms.

Joanna gasped. "*Ach*, Esther, you've got toothpaste . . . everywhere."

Esther raised her hand to the toothbrush and felt around the bristles. "*Ach, du lieva*," she growled. "I've been throwing up all morning, and I put the toothbrush behind my ear just in case I needed it. I forgot I also put toothpaste on the brush." Light blue toothpaste was smeared across her temple, into her hair, and even on the tip of her earlobe. "What a mess."

Joanna laughed, knowing Esther wouldn't take offense. "*Ach, vell*, you smell minty fresh."

Esther handed Junior to Joanna. "He can go in his highchair."

They went into the kitchen where Winnie was coloring on a piece of paper. "*Hallo*, Winnie. *Vie gehts*?"

Winnie looked up from her paper. "I'm drawing a picture for my cousin Rosie. She's staying in the quilt shop for a few days." She moved her hands to show Joanna her artwork. It was a not-so-round head with two dots for eyes and a red smear for lips surrounded by spirals of golden hair.

Esther gingerly removed the bandanna from her hair, dampened a dishrag, and started working on the gloopy mess on the side of her head. "One Christmas I wasn't thinking and put a chocolate orange stick behind my ear. I didn't notice it until the chocolate started dripping down my face. It's a terrible habit, but Levi says it's one of the things he likes best about me."

"It's one of the things I like best about you too, Esther. It's fun to see what you'll tuck behind your ear next."

Esther cracked a smile. "You must all think I'm a little odd."

Joanna slipped Junior into his highchair. "Who wants normal friends? The odd ones are so much more interesting."

"I'm *froh* I can make things more exciting." Esther ducked into her bedroom and came back with a clean bandana tied around her head and nothing behind her ear. "Good as new, and I don't feel like throwing up anymore. I should make the most of it while it lasts." She propped her hands on her hips. "I don't know what I'd do without you. Are you still sure you have time to help me with Menno's *dochters*? I really can make it work somehow if you have more important things to do, and for sure and certain you have more important things to do."

"We'll make it work. More than once I've heard Cathy say we girls need to stick together. I can do some of my baking here, and I want you to be able to finish those quilts. Beth helped me make fry pies last night, and she didn't do half bad. The truth is, she's been needing to learn how to cook for a very long time, and I've been too lazy to teach her. Sometimes it's just easier to do it myself."

Esther grinned. "Don't I know it! Every time my *schwester* Ivy tries to put a stitch in one of my quilts, I'm driven to the edge of a heart attack. But I don't have the patience to help her be a better quilter."

"Lord willing, Menno will be gone in a month."

"He got here last night, and this morning he was up bright and early with his girls. He borrowed the buggy and took them to the bakery because he said he wanted to get out of my hair for at least an hour or so. He'll start work with Levi on Monday." Esther looked at the clock. "I'm not sure when he'll be back." She peered sheepishly at Joanna. "I think my judgment of him was too hasty. He's not quite what I expected."

Joanna felt her face get warm. "He's not quite what I expected either."

Esther's eyebrows traveled up her forehead. "What do you mean?"

Joanna huffed out an exasperated breath and rolled her eyes. "I met him at the bakery."

Esther caught her breath. "You didn't! What did you say? What did he say? Did you scold him about that list? What did you think of him?" She sat at the table and pulled Joanna to sit next to her.

Joanna couldn't help the laughter that bubbled from her throat. Menno was exasperating, but the thought of him made Joanna a little *ferhoodled*—much to her delight and dismay. "*Ach, du lieva*, Esther, I have to admit he is wonderful handsome."

Esther grabbed Joanna's hand. "Oh, *sis yuscht*, I knew you'd think so. Despite his many faults, he's not going to have any trouble finding a *fraa*." They both giggled like teenagers. "He's quite solemn and reserved, but he's not pompous or arrogant like we thought he'd be. He's considerate, and he apologized three times last night for imposing on me."

Joanna grunted her disapproval. "Well, he's still imposing, even if he feels bad about it. If he felt really bad about it, he wouldn't have come at all. I can't say he's completely blameless."

"*Nae*, you're right," Esther said. "And there is that troublesome list."

"Very troublesome."

Esther eyed Joanna intently. "But what did he say? What did you say to him?"

"He helped me with my boxes of fry pies and then asked if I was married."

Esther's mouth fell open. "He didn't!"

"He did."

"He's very determined to find a wife. I don't wonder but he thought to get started immediately."

Joanna laughed. "That's what I thought too. His list was sitting right out on the table with item number one written in big bold letters. Find a *fraa*."

Esther traced her finger along a seam in the table. "It's sort of sweet when you think about it."

Joanna lifted her chin. "It is *not* sweet. It's odd and insensitive and arrogant."

"But you said you liked odd."

Joanna made a face at Esther. "I like my odd friends, but I don't want an odd husband."

Esther laughed so hard she snorted. "I'm just teasing. It's definitely irritating that he's trying to find a *fraa* the way he'd pick a *gute* horse."

Joanna smirked. "He'd probably take more care finding a horse."

One of Winnie's crayons rolled toward Esther. She picked it up and put it behind her ear. "For sure and certain he was speechless when he laid eyes on you. You're wonderful pretty, Joanna. He probably settled on you as his future *fraa* the minute you walked into the bakery."

"It doesn't matter how pretty anyone thinks I am. Menno is looking for someone to marry. He doesn't care who."

Esther raised an eyebrow. "*Ach*, I'm sure he cares very much, especially now that he's seen you. You said he asked you if you were married."

Joanna held up two fingers. "Twice."

Esther nodded as if this didn't surprise her. "He seems too single-minded to give up on you. He'll think no one else is *gute* enough."

"Lord willing, I shut him down."

Esther's eyes got rounder. "What did you say?"

"He asked me what I thought of his list—twice. That man is persistent."

Esther's lips twitched upward. "You refused to answer him, didn't you?"

"I didn't want something rude or snarky to come out of my mouth."

Esther threw her head back. "What a word. *Snarky*!"

"I heard that one from Cathy. Just about everything she says is snarky."

"I agree with that." Esther propped her elbow on the table and fingered the crayon at her ear. "I'm dying to know what you said to him."

"I suggested he write down *canned corn*."

"You didn't!"

"I did. I was very polite about it. He had no idea what I meant." Joanna smiled at the memory of Menno carefully adding corn to his list just because Joanna had told him to. "Then I said, 'There are many girls who would love being on your list, but I'm not one of them.'"

Esther's eyebrows nearly flew off her face. "You are so brave. I never could have done that."

"You could have. I've seen you take on a bush with a pickleball paddle. I've seen you attack your house with a rug. You stood up to your *schwester* Ivy when she wanted to take Winnie away. You're the bravest woman I know."

Esther waved her hand in the air. "That's not brave. That just means I have a bad temper. What did Menno say when you told him you didn't want to be on his list."

"He drooped like a sunflower in the heat."

"I'm not surprised," Esther said. "For sure and certain he's already decided he wants to marry you."

"He'll get over it. There are plenty of cans of corn in the sea."

"You're more like a can of fancy tuna."

Joanna laughed. "Cat food."

Esther pulled a notebook from her junk drawer and opened it. "Mary helped me make a list of five girls who are willing to be introduced to him. I haven't shown him the list yet, but I want to help him."

Joanna nodded. "Of course. The sooner he finds a wife, the sooner he'll be out of your hair."

The corner of Esther's mouth curled upward. "Like toothpaste."

"Something like that."

"He's not what I expected, Joanna. That's why I want to help him. He just . . . he just seems young, too young to be so lonely." She looked at Joanna out of the corner of her eye. "He has a whole life of happiness ahead of him with the right girl."

"When you're lonely, any can of corn will do." Joanna narrowed her eyes and studied Esther's face. "I'm not sure I like that look. You're not suggesting I give him a chance, are you?"

Esther cleared her throat. "I'm not very *gute* at tiptoeing around things. I tried it with my niece Mattie, and it got me in a lot of trouble. So, *jah*, I think you should give him a chance. What would it hurt?"

Joanna hesitated. Menno was handsome, and before she had realized who he was, she'd been drawn to his eager-to-please smile and broad shoulders. "I appreciate your honesty."

Esther scrunched her lips to one side of her face. "But . . ."

"I'm almost twenty-eight years old, an old *maedel* for sure and certain."

"I was over thirty," Esther said.

"I know, but Levi could have married anybody he wanted. He chose you because he loves you. Menno desperately needs a wife. He doesn't care about marrying for love. He wants to marry for convenience, and any old *maedel* who's desperate to be married will do. I'm not desperate. I love my life. I get to be with my *dat* and my *schwesteren* every day, I can try out new recipes, and we have four adorable goats that keep me laughing. What more could I want?"

Esther pressed her lips together. "You have a *gute* life."

"And I'd rather not be a task on someone's list. Zeb Nelson proposed to me three years ago because he liked my potato rolls and needed someone to help him on the farm. Josiah Neuenschwander asked me to marry him during fellowship supper because 'he'd never known an old *maedel* to make such *gute* church spread.'"

Esther grunted. "*Ach*, Josiah is sixty-three."

"He thought I was desperate enough to marry a sixty-three-year-old. He was shocked when I refused him. I don't want to be the *convenient* choice. I don't want to marry a man whose only requirement for a *fraa* is her willingness to say yes to a marriage proposal."

Esther smiled wryly at Joanna. "That probably isn't his only requirement."

Joanna returned Esther's smirk. "True. He would probably rather not marry anyone over forty. What girl doesn't want such a romantic proposal? *You're the right age. I'm the right age. I need someone to take care of my children. Let's get married.*"

Esther laughed. "Okay, okay. I can understand your reluctance. I was an old *maedel* too once. It's one of the reasons I moved to Colorado."

Joanna stood and started filling Esther's kitchen sink with water. "I'm going to help you cook and clean and babysit *and* find Menno a wife. I want to make your life easier. I don't really care about Menno." Joanna squeezed some dish soap under the running water. It wasn't precisely true that she didn't care about Menno. She was irritated with herself for being drawn to him in the first place, but he was too handsome to completely forget. In the end, she didn't care who he chose to marry, as long as he did it quickly and left Esther in peace.

Esther grabbed a rag from the drawer, swirled it in Joanna's water, and wrung it out. She wiped the counters while Joanna washed the breakfast dishes. "Menno got here last night at about six. Cathy drove Levi to Monte Vista to pick him up at the bus station. As soon as Menno came in with the girls, he fashioned a barrier in the quilt shop out of some old cardboard boxes and put the girls to bed inside the barrier. He said it was so they wouldn't touch my quilts."

"You were worried about that."

"It was very thoughtful of him."

Joanna frowned to herself. It was hard to cling to her certainty when Menno behaved so well. She swallowed the lump in her throat and rinsed the plate in her hand. She'd have to let go of her pride and acknowledge that Menno had some *gute* qualities. That didn't mean she approved of his list or wanted to marry him, but it was just plain stubborn to hold on to her dislike after what she'd seen of him.

Someone knocked on the door. Esther threw her dishrag into the water. "That would be Menno." She glanced at Joanna. "Is it going to be awkward?"

Joanna glued her eyes to the plate she was washing. "Very awkward. For both of us, but mostly for Menno." She had nothing to feel embarrassed about.

He was the one with the list.

Esther opened the door. "You don't have to knock, Menno," she said. "You're our guest for a few weeks. Our home is your home."

Menno's two little girls, Rosie and Lily, ran into the kitchen, grinning and giggling as they got on either side of Winnie's chair and threw their arms around her like a long-lost friend. Winnie put down her crayon, slid from her seat, and gathered her distant cousins into a clumsy three-way hug.

"Neenee!" Lily said, which must have been how she said *Winnie*.

Rosie laughed and planted a loud kiss on Winnie's cheek. Winnie gurgled and smiled as she swiped her hand down the side of her face to wipe off Rosie's kiss. "Why did you do that?" she squealed, as if Rosie's kiss was the most delightful, funniest thing that had ever happened to her.

Joanna couldn't help but smile. Oh, the joy of sharing so much affection with another person! Her smile faded when Menno strolled into the kitchen carrying a pink cardboard box like the ones they used at the bakery. She quickly turned back to her dishes, quite sure that he hadn't seen her face.

"Winnie," Esther said. "Do you want to take Rosie and Lily outside to play?"

Rosie had made her way around the table to Junior's highchair. Out of the corner of her eye, Joanna saw Rosie caress his hand. "Can Juno go?"

Esther strode to the highchair. "Of course. Winnie, will you watch him outside?"

"I don't know if Lily is old enough to go outside without me," Menno said, his voice low and saturated with concern.

Esther pulled Junior from his chair and set him on his feet. "The entire backyard is fenced in. There's nowhere to go. Winnie can't lift the gate latch."

"Okay," Menno said.

Joanna heard the girls and Junior trundle down the back hall like a flock of ducks waddling their way to the riverbank. The door opened and shut and suddenly the kitchen was quiet except for the sound of Joanna zealously washing dishes.

Too quiet. She sensed Menno's gaze on the back of her head.

"It's you," he said. His tone was half puzzlement, half tension.

Joanna reluctantly turned around to face him, clasping

her dripping wet hands together in front of her. "Nice to see you again, Menno."

Was that a lie or the honest truth?

He was very nice to look at, so it was nice to lay eyes on him again, but she also didn't want him to be here, so maybe it was a lie?

A herd of emotions traveled across his face, and Joanna couldn't begin to guess if he was happy to see her or completely mortified. Or neither.

"J-Joanna," he stuttered. His gaze flicked from Joanna to Esther and back again. "This is an answer to prayer."

Joanna had no idea what he meant and no idea what to say.

Thank Derr Herr Esther jumped in. "Joanna mentioned she met you at the bakery."

Menno couldn't seem to take his eyes off Joanna. "Um, *jah*, we met," he said, as if it was more significant than just two people being at the bakery at the same time.

"It was a chance meeting," Joanna said, in case he thought she'd planned the whole thing.

He tilted his head and studied her face. "I don't believe in chance. 'All things work together for good to them that love Gotte.'"

Oh, *sis yuscht*, Menno was quoting scripture.

Esther strangled the edge of her apron in her hands. "What's in the box?"

Menno looked down as if he'd forgotten he was carrying anything. His lips twitched sheepishly. "I brought some fry pies home from the bakery. They looked so *appeditlich*, I couldn't resist. I bought half a dozen raspberry ones."

Joanna thought her face might burst into flames at any minute. Menno had bought six of her fry pies, even after she'd been rude to him? "Raspberry is my favorite," was all she could think to say.

"Mine too," Menno said. "My *mamm* has a small raspberry patch behind the house, and we get just enough raspberries every year to make a dozen pints of jam and a couple of pies. I adore them. Just adore them."

Why did Joanna have a suspicion he wasn't talking about raspberries anymore? *Ach*, *vell*, he couldn't sweet-talk her that easily. "There are dozens of girls who make better fry pies than I do."

Did she sound as churlish as she felt? Probably. Menno studied her face and clammed up like a horse resisting the bit.

Esther, bless her, was trying so hard to ease the tension in the room. "Joanna has graciously offered to help me take care of the girls while you're here."

Menno's dark eyebrows inched closer to the middle of his forehead. "Am I the serious *problem* you told the woman at the bakery about?"

Joanna's heart lurched. Menno was handsome, perceptive, and uncomfortably plainspoken. *Ach*, *vell*, she could be just as honest. "*Jah*. Esther can't do everything you've asked of her by herself."

Esther laughed nervously. "*Nae*, Joanna, it's okay." This coming from the woman who was beating a rug against the house two days ago.

Menno's expression darkened like a storm cloud. "I apologize. I thought it would be all right. I'm only here four weeks."

Esther shot Joanna an irritated look. "I already said it was okay."

Joanna pressed her lips together, sorry she'd put Esther in an awkward position. The entire morning had turned

into a tangle of awkwardness, like one of those hairballs
Ada pulled out of the bathtub drain every few weeks.
Joanna couldn't really blame herself. Menno had overheard
her telling Myra at the bakery that she was helping a friend
with a serious problem. Menno was smart enough to realize
the problem was him.

He sidled closer to the window, leaned against the pane,
and gazed out into the backyard. Joanna wondered if he
was so offended he couldn't look at her, until it registered
that he was keeping an eye on *die kinner*.

"I was so eager to get started that I didn't stop to think
I might be imposing on you," he said, not looking away
from the backyard.

"You're family. We're happy to help family, and Winnie
is thrilled to have two new cousins." Esther cleared her
throat and draped an arm around Joanna. "Joanna is a dear
friend. She volunteered to help."

Joanna was grateful Esther hadn't hung her out to dry,
but seeing the look on Menno's face, Esther's reassurance
was small comfort.

Menno's eyes were like looming thunderclouds, his
expression stormy. He shoved his hand into his pocket
and pulled out a handful of money. "I had been insensitive, and I'm sorry. I am happy to pay you both for babysitting my girls."

Esther protested loudly and strode across the kitchen.
She cupped both hands around the money and shoved it
toward Menno. "*Nae, nae*. I don't want your money. Please,
Menno, put it away. I feel like dirt."

Ach! If Esther felt like dirt, Joanna was a worm crawling under the dirt.

Menno's frown was practically etched into his face. "I
didn't mean to offend you or impose on you or expect

things that I shouldn't have. I am only trying to do Gotte's will, but it's harder than I thought it would be. I don't know what to do."

Joanna's gut clenched. For a brief moment, Menno looked younger than his almost twenty-eight years. This mess was her fault, and like it or not, she would have to fix it. She huffed out a breath. "Oh, *sis yuscht*, Menno. You've gone about this whole thing like a bull in a china closet. Learn something from it, apologize, and next time, have a little more consideration for other people's feelings."

His mouth fell open as if no one had ever talked to him like that before. "I apologize. Sincerely."

Joanna nodded. "That is *gute*. Esther and I both forgive you. Don't we, Esther?"

"Of course."

"But I hate to be anyone's problem," he said.

Just like Joanna hated to be anyone's canned corn. "*Ach, vell*. You're here now. You might as well stay. We've made arrangements to care for your children and find you a *fraa*. You don't want to let all our hard work go to waste."

He glanced out the window again and looked back at Joanna, his eyes warm with gratitude as if he trusted her completely. "That seems sensible. It's only for a month."

She wasn't entirely comfortable with that look. "I can't say that I approve of how you are going about finding a *fraa*, but I will try to be ungrudging. Esther and I really do want to help you." She didn't mention that her willingness to help was because she wanted to get rid of him. If he had a fiancée at the end of the four weeks, what would it matter?

His solemn self-assurance returned with full force. "*Denki*. Gotte said it's not *gute* for man to be alone."

"Memorize the four gospels" was on Menno's list, but he seemed to know a lot of the Bible by heart already. It was sweet and irritating at the same time.

Oh, *sis yuscht*. It was going to be the longest month of Joanna's life.

Chapter 4

Joanna sat through church without really listening to any of the sermons. She'd have to repent for her negligence, but Menno Eicher was just too distracting, and she couldn't help herself. He sat with his girls in the back by the *maters* with small children and was so tender and attentive to his *dochters* that Joanna couldn't look away. He was looking for a *fraa* to babysit his children, but he didn't seem to think of his girls as a burden like some *faters* did. At one point in the sermon, Rosie was wiggling on the bench, a sure sign that she needed to use the bathroom. Menno stood and took both his girls' hands and led them out of the room. When they came back, he put one girl on each knee and an arm around each and bounced them gently while the bishop spoke.

Joanna couldn't help herself. Menno was a fascinating stranger who defied all her expectations. She wanted to dislike him, but she just couldn't, despite his aggravating to-do list.

Then there was the fact of his troublesome good looks. No man had a right to be that handsome. She felt a little shallow for being drawn in by a handsome face but didn't try to talk herself out of it. Menno was only going to be there for a month, and she might as well enjoy the view while she had the chance.

The entire *gmayna* was crammed into Esther's quilt shop today for church. The display bed in the middle of the room had been moved out, along with most of the quilts, and benches had been moved in. Joanna, Ada, Mary, and Beth had been there most of the day yesterday, scrubbing floors and toilets, planting pansies, and pulling the few weeds that had popped up in the garden. Levi and Menno had cleared out the quilt shop, and Menno had touched up the paint on the quilt shop door. He'd been more of a help than a burden, and Joanna once again had to repent for thinking so badly of him in the first place.

Rosie whispered something to Menno, and again the three of them got up and left the room heading toward the bathroom down the hall. Joanna smiled to herself. *Gmayna* was a never-ending parade of *maters* taking out crying babies and *kinner* needing to use the bathroom.

After services, the room exploded into a beehive of activity. Men carried the benches outside to set up as tables for the fellowship supper. The day was warm enough that the deacon had decided they could take the meal outside. There would be much more room that way.

Joanna went into the kitchen to help the women with the simple meal. There was honey wheat bread with church spread, apple butter, and three kinds of jam. Joanna filled bowls with pickles and red beets, and Ada and Verla Ann Miller cut slices of cheese to go with the bread. The older men ate first because there wasn't enough room for everybody to sit at once. Then the younger men, the older women, younger women, and teenagers and older children ate. Joanna took two bowls of pickles outside and set them on one of the tables. Menno sat with his girls, coaxing them to eat, while the teenagers and older children milled around Esther's backyard.

Verla Ann Miller took a plate of cheese right to Menno's table and said something to him. He smiled up at her, and it looked as if he was introducing his girls. Verla Ann smiled sweetly and patted Rosie's head. Rosie scrunched her face like a prune and turned away as if she'd been stung.

Joanna had already noticed Rosie had a mind of her own.

After eating with her *schwesteren*, Joanna picked up her paper plate and headed toward the kitchen to help with the clean-up. Menno came up beside her and said hello. For some reason Joanna couldn't explain, she was so startled, she dropped her plate into the grass.

Without hesitation, Menno picked it up and took it to the garbage can next to the house. Smiling, he brushed off his hands and came back to her. "It's *gute* nothing is breakable." He produced a small package of wet wipes from his pocket, pulled a wipe from the package, and sponged off his hands. He glanced at her. "Do you want one?"

Hmm. He liked clean hands, and he'd come prepared. "*Nae. Denki*. Where are your girls?"

He pointed across the lawn where Winnie, Rosie, and Lily were plucking dandelions from Esther's grass. "I'm sure she'll appreciate that."

"I'm sure she will."

Menno pulled a piece of yellow notebook paper from his pocket, and Joanna recognized it immediately. "I want to give you an update on my list." He unfolded it. One side was completely filled with his neat, small handwritten notes. She wasn't surprised. Menno was serious about finding a *fraa*.

"You've been busy."

"I don't have much time."

"Have you found the girl you want to marry yet?" she said, without a hint of ridicule in her voice.

He gave her a vague smile, as if he knew something she didn't. "I'm getting close." He pointed in the direction of Esther's blossoming apricot tree. "It wonders me if you'll sit under the tree with me and help me sort out what I've learned so far."

Joanna glanced toward the house. "I should go help *redd* up. The other women will say I'm shirking."

He grinned. "They won't mind. They know I'm looking for a *fraa*. Maybe they'll think it's you."

Joanna laughed uncomfortably. "It's not me."

That mysterious smile again. "Oh, I know, but I don't mind keeping them guessing."

Joanna gave in, though she'd rather be doing dishes than helping Menno with anything. "Okay then, show me your notes."

They sat under the apricot tree, Menno positioning himself to keep one eye on his girls. He glanced at his list. "You and Esther were kind enough to go through this list with me on Friday. I made some notes. That night I put the girls to bed, asked Esther to listen for them, then went to Sadie Sensenig's house."

"You're very single-minded."

"I've only got a month." That wasn't much time to get a girl—even a desperate girl—to say yes.

"What did you think of Sadie?" Sadie Sensenig was the youngest girl on the list, only twenty-one. She was always ready for an adventure, even if the adventure was in the form of a handsome widower looking for a *fraa*.

Menno read his notes with a serious look on his face. "She is very sweet, but maybe a little young."

"I love Sadie. She's always cheerful, always laughing.

She and Beth are *gute* friends. She hasn't been baptized yet so she has a cell phone, which her parents aren't happy about."

Menno chuckled. "She showed me her cell phone and the hundred selfies she's taken. She also showed me some of her drawings. She's a very *gute* artist. Said she helped get her *schwester*-in-law, Mattie, elected to the town council."

"*Jah.* It was the most exciting thing to happen in Byler in a hundred years."

He rubbed his hand along his jaw. "I think I would have liked to see that."

Joanna tilted her head and studied his face. "Why did you shave your beard?"

"I thought it would be easier for the girls I want to court. I don't want anyone to mistake me for a married man dating an unmarried woman."

"That's wonderful thoughtful of you."

He glanced at his list again. "On Saturday night I killed two birds with one stone. I met both Lydia Herschberger and Naomi Zook."

"How romantic."

He eyed her as if he was trying to read her mind. "I don't need romance. I need a *fraa.*"

"Of course."

At thirty-seven, Naomi was the oldest woman on Menno's list, but she was a young thirty-seven, with bright, laughing eyes and her own house with a huge garden where she grew ten different kinds of tomatoes and raspberries. Lydia Herschberger was thirty-two, pleasingly plump, and very attached to her collection of stuffed animals. She had agreed to let Esther put her name on the list if Menno would agree to move her stuffed animal collection to Idaho if they married. Esther had made sure Menno knew about the stuffed animals before putting Lydia on the list.

"Naomi showed me her garden, and we talked about growing produce and the best kind of mulch to use in cold weather. She's got a whole bookshelf of gardening and farming books, and she said I could borrow them any time I wanted."

"What about Lydia?"

Menno nodded. "I didn't stay long, because I'm just trying to get an overview of all my choices, but I liked her. She has a very pretty smile and makes *appeditlich* snicker-doodles. I probably shouldn't have eaten four, but I wanted her to know I appreciated that she'd made them especially for me."

Joanna smiled to herself. "That's very kind of you."

"I almost forgot about Priscilla. On Saturday after we got the house cleaned up for *gmay* and before I went to Lydia's, I went to the Bent and Dent grocery store to meet Priscilla Weaver. I bought twenty dollars' worth of expired groceries just for a chance to talk to her." Menno folded and unfolded his list. "I've taken Priscilla off the list."

Joanna raised her eyebrows in surprise. "Why?"

"We won't suit."

"But why?"

"It's not appropriate to speak anything but kindness."

Well, that was interesting. "It is just as useful for me to know what you don't want in a *fraa* as what you do want."

"Do you remember what Jesus said about Nathanael?"

Joanna curled one side of her mouth. "*Vell*, I wasn't there, but I think I remember."

"He said, 'Behold an Israelite indeed in whom there is no guile.' I want people to say that about me, that I have no guile. So I'd rather not talk about Priscilla or any of the reasons she's off the list."

Joanna suddenly felt guilty for all the mean things she'd

said about Menno before she'd met him. *Ach, vell*, she couldn't take it back now, and she still felt the same way about his list. Joanna knew why *she* would take Priscilla off the list if she were Menno, but she was curious as to why Menno did. Priscilla was the prettiest can of corn on Menno's list. Maybe he actually cared what was on the inside.

"I won't think less of you if you tell me why Priscilla is off your list."

He ducked his head to hide a smile. "There are four girls left. Can we talk about them?"

She heaved a dramatic sigh. "I suppose, *Nathanael*."

He nodded. "A high compliment."

"I guess it is, but I'm partial to the Apostle Peter, who had trouble forgiving people and cut off somebody's ear."

Menno didn't even roll his eyes.

Joanna took the list from his hand. "Your handwriting is very neat. It looks like you got to meet Verla Ann."

Verla Ann and Mary Ann Miller were both in their twenties. Esther had originally put both *schwesteren* on the list, but Esther, Joanna, and Menno had all agreed that Menno should focus on Verla Ann because she was the oldest, and it would be terrible to pit the *schwesteren* against each other. Verla Ann was twenty-five, and of all the prospective wives, she seemed the most eager to find a husband.

A line formed between Menno's eyebrows. "I think Verla Ann would say yes right now if I asked her." He glanced at Joanna. "I hope you don't think that's arrogant of me. She seems willing."

Joanna didn't know why the thought of Menno getting engaged to Verla Ann annoyed her. Maybe because it confirmed all the criticism she'd made about Menno in the first place. If Verla Ann and Menno were willing to settle for the first person who came along, they deserved each other. "There's your solution right there. You could ask her to marry you tonight and have a fiancée with more than three weeks to spare."

He folded his list and put it back in his pocket. "*Nae*. I want more time to weed out the list."

Joanna pretended to be shocked. "Are you calling these girls weeds, *Nathanael*?"

Menno snapped his head around to look at her. "Of course not." He grinned when he realized she was teasing. "I have a pretty *gute* idea who I want to ask, but it's too soon, and I want to do more research. Is she willing to move to Idaho? Does she like children? Can I convince her to marry me? Will she make me a fry pie every day?"

It was Joanna's turn to be caught off guard. She formed her lips into an *O* and gave him a light shove. He winced as if she'd punched him in the stomach. "Don't even joke about that," she said. "I don't want to be on your list."

"*Jah*, you've made it very clear." His lips twitched upward. "But *would* you make your husband a fry pie every day if he asked?"

Joanna didn't like the way he was looking at her, as if she was part of his research. "Only if I loved him very much, and if he was willing to kill all the spiders."

Menno pulled a nub of a pencil from his pocket and wrote on the back of his list. "Must kill spiders."

He was quite aggravating, but Joanna couldn't help but smile. "You're wasting your time writing down anything about me."

He ignored her protest. "So, you don't like spiders?"

Joanna decided not to scold him. "They give me the creepy crawlies. I refuse to touch a spider."

"If you use your shoe, you don't have to touch them."

"I refuse to touch anything that has touched a spider.

Ada kills all the spiders at our house, and Pepper eats them."

"Pepper sounds like a very strange woman."

Laughter burst from Joanna's mouth. "Pepper is our dog."

"I'm *froh* to know you don't have a human living at your house who likes to eat spiders."

Rosie, Winnie, and Lily skipped toward Menno and Joanna giggling as if today was the best day ever. Rosie and Winnie shepherded Lily along because she was holding up the sides of her dress to form a little basket.

"Look, Daddy," Rosie gushed. They had filled the hollow of Lily's dress with dandelions.

Menno picked a dandelion from Lily's pile. "What pretty flowers! What are you going to do with them?"

Winnie threw another dandelion into the basket formed by Lily's dress. "We're going to make jelly. My *mamm* says dandelions are *gute* to eat."

Rosie looked curiously at the dandelions, plucked one from Lily's pile, and popped the yellow flower into her mouth. Both Menno and Joanna gasped, then Joanna grimaced. Just as she expected, Rosie's eyes got big, and her mouth twisted in distress. She immediately spit the dandelion out onto the grass. Squealing in alarm, she wiped her mouth and spit again and again.

Menno jumped to his feet. "I'll get you a drink, *heartzley*. Hold on." He ran into Esther's house.

Rosie kept up the squealing as tears ran down her cheeks. "Yucky. I no like." She sounded like a hundred squeaky doors being opened all at the same time.

Joanna wrapped her fingers around Rosie's arm. "It's okay, Rosie. It tastes bad, but it won't hurt you. Keep spitting it out until you can't taste it anymore."

Unfortunately, the crying spread like a virus. Lily

studied Rosie's face, and then her bottom lip trembled violently just before she released the corners of her dress and burst into tears. The impressive collection of dandelions fell to the ground. Winnie screamed, dropped to her knees, and gathered an armful of dandelions. Her screaming gave way to hysterical bawling. Joanna didn't know if Winnie was sad about the dandelion jelly or mad about the fallen dandelions. Or maybe she was simply crying because Lily and Rosie were.

Joanna did her best to comfort all three girls at once. She patted Rosie on the back, put her arm around Lily, and spoke what she hoped were comforting words to Winnie. "It's okay. We can pick them up and still make dandelion jelly. Don't worry, Rosie. Your *dat* will be here soon with a drink."

None of the three girls calmed down or even paused to take a breath. They made a horrible racket, and several pairs of eyes turned in Joanna's direction. *Ach*, *vell*, she wasn't the *mater*, and she was doing her best. Why should she care if everybody stared?

In less time than Joanna would have expected, Menno came running out of the house with a cup in his hand. He knelt next to Rosie and calmly put his arm around her. "Here. Get some water in your mouth then spit it out so it doesn't go down your throat."

Rosie took a drink between sobs and spit out the water. Joanna was impressed that a three-year-old understood enough to spit instead of swallow. Rosie took a swig and spit out the water three times. Menno pulled Lily into an embrace with his free arm while holding the cup for Rosie. Winnie seemed to forget that she needed to cry. She sat on the grass with her armful of dandelions and watched Menno give Rosie drink after drink.

Menno nodded reassuringly to Rosie. "Does your mouth taste yucky anymore?"

Rosie squeaked softly and shook her head.

"Okay," Menno said. "Now take a drink and swallow it."

Rosie did as she was told then smiled through her tears. Menno took out a bright white handkerchief, mopped up Rosie's face, and held it to her nose. "Blow."

Rosie blew her nose as well as a three-year-old could blow.

Then Menno wiped Lily's face and gave her a kiss on the cheek. "All better?"

"Lily dropped my flowers," Rosie said.

Menno cupped his hand around Rosie's arm. "She didn't mean to, and we can pick them up. Lily, do you want to hold them in your dress again?"

Lily held out her hand as if stopping traffic. "*Nae*," she said, sticking out her bottom lip.

Joanna grinned. The first time had ended in tragedy. Lily didn't want to be responsible for the flowers again.

Winnie managed to stand up with her load of dandelions. Without a word, she dumped the flowers in Joanna's lap.

Joanna flinched in surprise and giggled. "I guess I'll hold them."

Menno pursed his lips as if he wasn't sure it was okay to smile. "Um, sorry, Joanna. I can hold them."

Joanna pulled up a dandelion that was growing right next to her and put it in her lap. "I don't mind."

Winnie jumped up and down and clapped as if Joanna had just saved the world. Lily and Rosie giggled and jumped up and down too. Winnie took the *schwesteren*'s hands, and they skipped off to another corner of the yard to pick more dandelions.

Menno eyed her doubtfully. "Those dandelions are going to stain your apron."

"I have a jumbo-size bottle of bleach at home, and I know how to use it."

His look was warm and serious. "You make fry pies and know how to do laundry. Are you sure you won't reconsider being on my list?"

"Believe me, you don't want me on your list."

His lips twitched playfully. "Why not?"

"I'm afraid of spiders . . ."

"I can live with that."

"I won't move away from Byler, I make a mess when I bake, and I hardly ever make my bed."

He tapped his chin as if deep in thought. "I'd be willing to make the bed every other day."

She felt her face get warm. Menno was irritating beyond belief. "I'm not like Nathanael in the Bible. I'm sarcastic and resentful and rebellious. I've got guile coming out of my ears. In fact, people say I'm guileful."

"Is that a word?"

"It is now, and it describes me perfectly."

"*Ach, vell*," he said. "Every Nathanael needs the opposite of a Nathanael."

She huffed out a breath. She'd have to be blunt because Menno did not seem like the kind of man to give up easily. "I don't want to be on your list, Menno. Ever. It irritates me when you tease me about it. That's another reason you don't want me on the list. I'm easily irritated."

He must have finally believed she was serious because his eyes stopped dancing and his solemn expression reappeared. "I'm sorry, Joanna. I was trying to make a joke, but I'm not very *gute* at it."

"*Nae*, you're not."

Rosie ran to the tree and threw a handful of dandelions in Joanna's lap. Lily followed close behind with another handful. She gave one especially big dandelion to her *dat* and kissed him on the cheek. Both girls skipped back to the spot in the yard where Winnie was picking dandelions.

Menno smiled as if he wasn't sure he was allowed to. "You're doing a *gute* job holding the dandelions."

"*Denki*. I think I'm pretty *gute* at it." She felt a little bad about how she'd scolded him. "You do a *gute* job with your girls. They adore you."

He leaned back on his hands and stretched his legs out in front of him. "Until Suvilla got sick, I never appreciated how much work *maters* do at church. It's not easy keeping my *dochters* quiet during sermons and prayers. Lily is un-usually calm and deliberate, but she's also two, and sitting still during *gmay* is hard for all *die kinner*. Rosie is older but also more defiant, so I have to keep a strict eye on her during services. And she has to go to the potty a lot. Lily isn't potty trained, but I'm hoping my new *fraa* will be willing to potty train her."

Joanna looked away and concentrated on the dandelion pickers across the yard. It was just another reminder that Menno wanted a *fraa*, any *fraa*, as long as she was willing to potty train Lily and sit with *die kinner* during *gmay*. How much easier Menno's life would be when he finally got married. He was looking for a can of corn, and Joanna refused to be a can of corn. She tried not to feel bitter about it. She couldn't get mad at Menno. He had been honest with her—honest with everyone about his intentions. In return, she had been honest with him. She hadn't told him how irritated and resentful she was, but still, she felt they understood each other fairly well.

She swallowed her irritation. "Tell me if this is a rude question, but how did Suvilla die?"

A hint of pain flashed in his eyes, but he didn't seem unwilling to talk about it. "She had ALS, a very aggressive kind. I'm *froh* she didn't suffer for years."

"What is ALS?"

"It's a disease that affects nerve cells, like in the brain. She was diagnosed right after Lily was born. At first she had muscle spasms and tightness. Soon she couldn't walk. The church bought us a wheelchair, but toward the end, she couldn't move or speak or swallow." He bowed his head. "It was terrible. But because it is a progressive disease, we had a long goodbye. I'm grateful for that."

"Are you the one who took care of her?"

"It was my privilege to take care of her until the day she died. My *mamm* was there most every day too, and often my *dat*. Suvilla's *mamm* lives in Pennsylvania. She was there for two weeks at the end."

Joanna blinked back tears. Menno might have wanted a *fraa* to take on his children and the household chores, but he obviously wasn't lazy or trying to avoid his responsibilities. "That's very sad. I'm sorry."

He nodded, concentrating on the dandelion in his hand. "Gotte must have needed another angel in heaven. I accept His will. I'm grateful she's not in pain anymore. She died two weeks after Lily's first birthday. The visiting bishop was over to the house a week later."

"Visiting bishop?"

"Our district in Baker is too small to have our own bishop. Gary Neuenschwander visits us from Rexford, Montana. It's a long drive, so we don't see him often, but he does his best. Sometimes he calls the minister's business phone. We have one minister who conducts all the services."

"The bishop came to visit you after Suvilla died?" Joanna said.

"He told me to take one year to mourn Suvilla and then to find a *fraa* as soon as possible after that. He admonished me not to wait even one extra day after the year was up."

Joanna didn't like the sound of that. "That seems a harsh burden for the bishop to place on your head."

Menno's gaze was serious and fervent. "My only desire is to be obedient to Gotte. Obedience brings blessings, but strict obedience brings miracles. I got to Colorado a year to the day Suvilla died."

Joanna wasn't convinced, but she couldn't argue with his sincerity, his zealous desire to do the right thing. If every man acted with the same devotion, there would be much less heartache in the world. "So you're in Colorado out of obedience."

"*Jah.* I need to find a *fraa.* My girls need a *mater.* It's Gotte's will."

Joanna still didn't like it, but obedience was a slightly better reason than needing someone to do all the chores he didn't want to do. She still thought he was going about finding a *fraa* the wrong way, but she understood why he thought he needed one immediately. It was still outrageously irritating. "I don't wonder but you're lonely. Another reason to find a *fraa.*"

He slowly plucked the thin, yellow petals off his dandelion. "I'm too busy to be lonely. I moved in with my parents after Suvilla died and rented out my house to my cousin. *Mamm* helps with the girls, but I'm still farming, and I work as a lumberjack when I'm not on the farm."

Menno was a lumberjack? That explained the solid muscles that covered every inch of his body. Joanna cleared her throat and reminded herself how irritating and persistent he was. Who cared about muscles if there was fluff between his ears?

Rosie, Winnie, and Lily came to the tree with a handful of dandelions and threw them willy-nilly into Joanna's apron. Rosie frowned when she saw the plucked dandelion nub in Menno's hand. "Daddy, you broke it."

Menno quickly shoved the naked dandelion behind his back. "*Ach, vell, heartzley*, there are plenty of others."

Joanna couldn't help a smile when Rosie marched behind Menno and grabbed the dandelion from his hand. "*Nae*, Daddy. Fix it."

Menno, looking sufficiently contrite, brought his hand in front of him and handed Rosie what was left of the dandelion. "I'm sorry. We might have to throw this one away."

Rosie puckered her lips and shook her finger at her *dat*. "Don't do that ever 'gain." Obviously not outrageously upset, she threw the broken dandelion into the grass and ran off to play with Winnie and Lily.

Joanna laughed.

Menno cracked a wry smile. "Rosie reminded me of you just now. You got that same look on your face when you warned me not to put you on my list. It's adorable."

Joanna cuffed Menno on the shoulder. "Adorable or not, I'm deadly serious. And don't you forget it."

Menno raised his hands as if stopping traffic. "I'd be too afraid."

Joanna snorted and gave him the stink eye. Something told her he wasn't afraid of anything.

Chapter 5

CRosie bawled with such force, she sounded like a whole herd of cattle. She ran at Joanna as if she was being chased by that same herd of cattle and launched herself into Joanna's arms. "I smuchlin finnen grow!"

Joanna knelt down on the ground and gave Rosie a big hug and a sympathetic sigh, even though she had no idea what Rosie had said. It very likely had something to do with the finger she was holding aloft like a sailor testing the direction of the wind.

"I'm so sorry. Does it hurt?"

"Jaa-aa-aah," Rosie sobbed. "The door smash it."

The family's four goats, Fluffy, Blue, Smiley, and Apple, and Dat's dog, Pepper, gathered around them like curious bystanders staring at a car accident. Winnie and Lily also came running. Nothing stirred up excitement like an unfortunate accident. Lily wrapped her arms around Fluffy's neck and kept her eyes on Rosie's face.

Joanna took Rosie's hand in hers and smoothed her thumb along the back of Rosie's index finger. The tender skin on the pad of her finger bore a little white crease, but the skin wasn't broken, thank Derr Herr, and the fingernail looked as if it would be unhurt. "Ouch. Did you pinch it in the little door in the chicken coop?"

Rosie nodded, tears running down her face.

Joanna stuck out her bottom lip sympathetically, kissed the injured finger, and tugged Rosie in for another hug. She pulled a tissue from her apron pocket and dabbed at Rosie's nose, leaving a clean space just above her lip that had previously been smeared with dirt. They had been playing outside with the goats for a long time, and the three little girls were filthy. What would Menno say about that? No doubt, he'd have an opinion. He'd probably quote the scripture about clean hands and a pure heart.

Joanna curled her lips upward. Menno's habit of quoting scripture was really quite endearing, if a little excessive. She had taken to quoting her own scriptures when she wanted to ruffle his feathers and take his confidence down a notch or two. Of course, she couldn't quote scriptures word for word like he could, but she could paraphrase all day long, and her versions of certain verses always made him smile.

Winnie leaned in, and Rosie held her finger up for Winnie to examine.

"Do you want a Band-Aid?" Winnie said. "Joanna, she needs a Band-Aid."

Joanna looked at Rosie. "Do you want a Band-Aid?"

Rosie sniffed back more tears. "I need one."

Joanna stood up. "I'll go get a Band-Aid. You three stay here with Pepper and the goats. I'll be right back."

The family had four pygmy goats, an old horse, and a border collie named Pepper. Each *schwester* had named one of the goats. Fluffy was Beth's goat. Blue was Ada's. Mary had named Smiley, and Joanna's goat was a cute white goat with black feet and a black spot on her nose. Her name was Apple. The goats were lovable and curious, and Joanna made goat cheese every week from their milk. Pepper the dog was lively and loyal and very protective of the family. He barked at all strangers, growled at trespassers, and occasionally chased a reporter off their property when it was absolutely necessary.

Reporters used to visit regularly when Clay was still a pro baseball player, but they hadn't seen a reporter or a baseball fan on the farm for more than six months. Clay and Mary had bought the farm next door to the Yoder family, and the fans and press had started bothering him at his own place. He didn't mind the attention, unless it was directed at Mary, and her *dat* was *froh* that his alfalfa wasn't getting stomped on.

Joanna jogged into the house, nodded to Ada, who was at the stove finishing the soup, and pulled out the Band-Aids with cartoon dogs on the box that Ada had bought two days ago.

She'd said, "Children like Band-Aids with pictures on them. The plain Band-Aids aren't any fun." Ada wasn't usually the one who thought about things in terms of fun, but she had been right. A Band-Aid with a dog on it would make an injury feel better faster than a boring beige Band-Aid.

Joanna ran back outside, and her heart lurched. Menno knelt next to Rosie listening intently as she recounted in her three-year-old language how she'd hurt her finger.

He glanced up at Joanna. "They were out here all by themselves. Unsupervised." There wasn't an ounce of condemnation in his voice, even though she could tell he was deeply concerned. Menno was solemn and anxious about everything, but he was also unfailingly kind and even-tempered.

Still, Joanna got defensive because he *was* judging her babysitting skills. "I ran inside for a Band-Aid. I was gone two minutes, and I left Pepper in charge. The girls were perfectly safe."

The lines around his eyes deepened. "You left Pepper in charge?"

Joanna hooked her arm around Pepper's neck and kissed his furry head. "I was gone for two minutes, Menno."

"Long enough for me to come into the backyard and kidnap one of my children."

She scrunched her lips to one side of her face. "Why would you kidnap one of your own children?"

Menno's lips twitched, and he sighed. "I can't help it. I worry. And even though you're doing me a favor, I depend on you to take *gute* care of my girls." He put his arm around Rosie and kissed her finger.

Joanna tried not to let his words hurt her. She would never let any harm come to *die kinner*.

Rosie wiggled away from her *dat* and took Winnie's hand. "Do you want to pet the chickens?"

Winnie nodded, motioned for Lily to follow, and the three of them skipped toward the chicken coop, the hurt finger all but forgotten. Pepper and the four goats followed them. Four of the five chickens scattered when they saw the girls coming. Bitty, the white Leghorn, seemed oblivious to the mob marching toward her and pecked at the ground as if nothing was more important than finding her lunch.

Joanna smiled at the sweet sight of the animals following the little girls as if they were marching in a parade. "If anyone ever tried to steal the girls away, Pepper would rip out his throat. Don't ever doubt it."

A reluctant smile grew on Menno's lips. "You have quite a morbid imagination."

"I'm only speaking the truth." She pinned Menno with

an intense gaze. "I would never do anything to put your girls in danger. I hope you know that."

He kicked at a dirt clod at his feet. "My *mamm* says I worry too much."

"Jesus said you can't make your hair grow longer no matter how hard you worry about it."

"Actually, he said, 'Which of you by worrying can add one cubit unto his stature?'"

"I should know better than to try to quote scripture to you."

He chuckled. "*Jah*, you should." They both watched the little girls gingerly reach out their hands to pet Bitty. "They're going to get pecked."

Joanna nudged him with her elbow. "No worrying. You get pecked once, and you learn to be more careful. I hope you don't mind that I brought the girls over here today. I needed to make cheese, and Esther needed to quilt. She kept Junior, and I offered to take all the girls with me. They love the goats and Pepper. Ada and Beth helped me make cheese and watch the girls."

"I guess it's okay, but there's a lot more danger for them to find here than at Esther's house, and when they come to your place, they always return home filthy."

Joanna laughed. "I make sure they roll around in the mud before they go home, mostly to annoy you."

He reared back in surprise then smiled. "You don't need to purposefully try to annoy me. You do it without even thinking."

"Glad to know it's working."

"Cathy is waiting in the car. I need to gather the girls and go."

Joanna didn't want him to leave, though there was no *gute* reason for it. "They're probably starving. Ada made a big pot of soup, and I made a cherry pie. You're welcome to stay for dinner."

Menno bloomed into a smile. "Cherry pie. I love cherry pie. It's my favorite."

"Cathy is invited too."

"I don't know," Menno said. "She's on a gluten-free, dairy-free, egg-free diet."

"What can she eat? Air?"

"Air and carrots, I think." He glanced in the direction of the highway. "The girls would enjoy eating here again, though I don't want to impose on Cathy. She's been so kind to drive us around. Do you think she'd mind coming back to get us in an hour?"

Joanna was pleased he wanted to stay . . . for the girls' sake, of course. "Go see what Cathy has to say."

Menno jogged around to the front of the house. Joanna buttoned up her jacket and wrapped her arms around herself. The temperature was sinking with the sun. She'd need to get the girls into the house soon. She grinned watching Lily follow Bitty around the yard, as the chicken strolled and pecked at the ground, pretending there wasn't a little girl trying to catch her. But Bitty kept three feet of distance between her and Lily at all times.

Lily couldn't say much, but the wheels were always turning in her head. She was less of a follower and more of a silent observer to everything Rosie and Winnie did. She was cautious and careful and never seemed to jump into any activity until she thought seriously about it first— just like her *dat*. Rosie, delightfully headstrong, never did anything she was told to do unless she pretended it was her own idea.

Joanna folded her arms and sighed pathetically. She was growing attached, and it was going to be a little bittersweet when Menno found a *fraa* and left Colorado for *gute*. The problem was that Menno's *gute* qualities were very appealing. So much so that they outweighed his bad qualities by about a thousand pounds. She almost, *almost*, wished her name was on the list, even though she would never, ever consider marrying a man who put convenience and duty over love.

Today was Thursday. Menno and his girls and Winnie had eaten at Joanna's house twice this week already. It was easier to take *die kinner* to her house so she could do a little baking, and she always took Winnie with her. Winnie kept the younger girls entertained while Joanna baked, Ada cleaned the house, and Beth tended to the goats. Esther was wonderful grateful, and Joanna had spent some very pleasant days with the girls and some very pleasant evenings at dinner with Menno.

He was becoming too easy to like, what with his penchant for quoting scripture to his habit of helping do the dishes every night. He was seldom cross with his *dochters*, and he gave them all his attention and focus when he was with them. He was a little overprotective, but Joanna could forgive him for that. Some *faters* didn't seem to care about their own children.

Menno jogged around the corner of the house. "Cathy says to tell you that she is annoyed that this is getting to be a habit, but she forgives us and will come get me and the girls at six thirty."

Joanna laughed. "Thank Derr Herr for Cathy. I'm *froh* she likes to haul the Amish all around the valley."

"Well, she says she doesn't like it, but she likes hearing all the gossip when people think she's not listening."

"She doesn't want to come for dinner?"

Menno hooked his thumbs around his suspenders. "She says she can't eat anything but plain potato chips and protein bars, so she'd rather not be tempted."

"She's got more willpower than I ever had." Joanna strolled toward the chicken coop, and Menno fell in step beside her. "Do you think Rosie will come in without a fuss?"

"Not likely." Menno stopped and looked at her. His gaze was full of something Joanna didn't want to see. "I hope you know how much I appreciate what you're doing for me."

She glued her gaze to the chicken coop so she wouldn't have to look at his earnest expression. "I know, and you're welcome. It's only been a week, and you've only got three more to go."

"Three more to go," he said, with an edge of panic in his voice.

"That's . . . p-plenty of time," Joanna stuttered. Plenty of time if all you needed was a can of corn. "Would you . . . would you . . . my birthday is a week from today. Would you like to come to my party?"

He looked at her as if she'd just done an astounding magic trick. "Thursday is my birthday too. April fourth?"

Joanna caught her breath. "*Ach, du lieva.* No kidding? And you're going to be twenty-eight?"

His smile was five miles wide. "*Jah.* I can't help but think this is some kind of miracle. Like it was meant to be."

Joanna pretended she had no idea what *it* was, even though Menno was on the hunt for a *fraa*, and *it* was on his list in big, bold letters. She had to stop him before his enthusiasm ran away with his reason. "Let's make it a double birthday party. Esther and Levi are coming, and Cathy and her husband have also been invited. Mary and Clay will be there too."

Menno thought about it for a minute. "That's a whole

week away. Maybe I'll have made my choice by then, and I can invite my fiancée to the party."

Joanna pasted on a smile. "What a *gute* idea." It was a terrible idea. She didn't want Menno's fiancée at her birthday party. It would dampen the mood, for sure and certain. But then again, it was his birthday too. Of course he'd want his fiancée there to celebrate. Still, the thought set her teeth on edge.

"Rosie, slow down!" Menno called, one second too late.

Rosie had been chasing Pepper with the wild abandon of a three-year-old when she caught her foot on a protruding edge of sagebrush and fell hard on her hands and knees. Flat on her stomach and frozen in place, she howled like a pack of wolves until Menno scooped her up in his arms and held her tight. He tried to whisper comforting words to her, but she just howled louder. He had to lean away from her to avoid going deaf in that ear.

"*Ach*, poor Rosie," Joanna cooed. "Hold out your hands. Let me see your hands."

Rosie, who was tucked in her father's arms, stretched out her hands on either side of Menno's head. Joanna slid behind him to take a look. She gently brushed the grit from both of Rosie's palms and gave each hand a kiss, and Rosie's crying dwindled to a whimper.

"It hurts to scrape your hands, but it looks like you're going to be just fine." Joanna brushed some hair from Rosie's face.

"She's got blood," Winnie said, pointing wide-eyed to Rosie's left knee.

Joanna looked down. A tiny spot of blood oozed from Rosie's knee.

Unfortunately, Rosie caught sight of the blood and started screaming again. "I bleeding."

Menno kissed her on the cheek. "It's okay, *heartzley*. Let's go in the house and get you some Band-Aids."

"Ada might have a sucker," Joanna said. "Would that make you feel better?"

Rosie stopped mid sob and nodded. "I want red."

Menno turned his face from Rosie and whispered, "At least she'll come into the house without a fuss."

"I want a sucker," Winnie said.

Lily raised her hand. "Me."

Joanna giggled. "You want a sucker too?"

Lily hopped like a bunny. "*Jah*."

Joanna grinned at Menno. "Do you want a sucker?"

"I do, but I'm afraid it will ruin my dinner."

"You can have it for dessert."

They strolled slowly toward the house.

"I'd rather have a piece of pie," Menno said.

"If you're nice, you can have two pieces."

He looked at her like he thought she was the most beautiful girl in the world. It made her feel a little giddy.

"I'm always nice," he said.

She couldn't keep a wide smile from her face. "*Jah*, you are." It was one of her favorite things about him.

She was making her own list, and it was getting long.

Chapter 6

The next Thursday after work, Menno and Levi jogged up the Yoder's porch, and Levi knocked on the door. They were meeting everyone there since Esther and Joanna had taken *die kinner* over to the Yoders' earlier in the day to help Joanna's *schwesteren* get ready for the birthday party.

Levi smiled as if he had a secret.

Menno eyed him suspiciously. "What is that look for?"

Levi chuckled. "You have a lot of spring in your step tonight. And you whistled at work all day. You're really looking forward to this party."

Menno smiled to himself. Levi had no idea. "Of course. It's my birthday, and Joanna made a German Chocolate cake. What's not to be excited about?"

Joanna opened the door and practically bowled Menno over with her smile. He could have gotten a tan from that smile. She made a show of looking behind him, as if he were hiding something from her.

"No fiancée? I thought for sure you'd bring your fiancée." She didn't seem disappointed about the absence of one.

"You know very well I don't have a fiancée yet," Menno said. "We talked about it just yesterday."

Joanna laughed as if he'd said something hilarious. "We talk about it every day, Menno Eicher, and I get the feeling you're dragging your feet. You only have two more weeks."

Menno wasn't dragging his feet exactly, but Joanna was right, he wasn't working especially hard at courting Sadie Sensenig, Lydia Herschberger, Naomi Zook, or Verla Ann Miller because he'd already chosen a fiancée, and she was standing in the doorway looking especially radiant in that baby blue dress and crisp white *kapp*. His heart jumped around like a jackrabbit.

Esther had agreed to take the girls home after the party and put them to bed so he could have some time alone with Joanna. Although he hadn't told Esther he was planning on proposing, she had probably guessed his intention. She'd given him a sad sort of look like maybe she pitied him and had laid a sisterly hand on his arm.

"Just remember Joanna doesn't want to be an item on your to-do list," she had said.

Esther had it completely wrong. Finding a *fraa* was on his to-do list, but Joanna wasn't on the list. Surely Esther could see the difference. Lord willing, Joanna wouldn't mind moving to Idaho. They just hadn't had time to talk about such things, and Menno had been forced to sneak up on her gradually. She had told him early on that she wasn't interested, but what she had actually said at the bakery was, "There are many girls who would be happy to make your list, but I'm not one of them."

Menno took that to mean she might be interested but didn't want her name on the list. Surely she had changed her mind. She was twenty-eight years old, pleasant to look at, and in need of a husband. Gotte wanted Menno to get married. It was the perfect arrangement.

At their first meeting at the bakery, Menno had been

discouraged but not defeated. Gotte had brought both of them to the bakery that day. For sure and certain He wanted them to be together. If Menno had harbored any doubts that their marriage was Gotte's will, Joanna had been at Esther's house when he had returned home from the bakery that morning. Gotte couldn't have made it any clearer. Encountering Joanna twice on the same day in less than an hour couldn't have been a coincidence, especially since Menno didn't believe in them. Their chance meeting was Gotte's way of telling Menno that Joanna was the one chosen to be his future *fraa*. After that, Menno had gone to meet all the women on Esther's list with no intention of marrying any of them. Gotte had already picked Menno's *fraa*, and Menno would be ungrateful to reject the gift Gotte had offered him.

When he had found out they had the same birthday, it was as if Gotte was giving him a bigger shove in her direction. Could there be two people more perfect for each other?

It didn't hurt that Joanna was the most beautiful girl Menno had laid eyes on—prettier than Suvilla on the day he married her—or that Joanna's eyes were the color of Forget-Me-Nots in the spring or that her smile lit up a room like an electric light bulb.

"Dada!" Lily barreled past Joanna and out the door and launched herself into Menno's arms. Nothing gave him more joy than seeing how happy his *dochters* were when he got home from work every day. *Ach, vell*, Lily was always overjoyed. Rosie was a little less enthusiastic, as if hugging her dat was a chore.

Menno set Lily on her feet and knelt on the porch so he was more or less eye-to-eye with her. "How was your day, Lily-Billy?"

Lily giggled. "I not Biwwy."

Smiling as if she was happy to see him, Rosie pushed past Joanna and pressed her palms to either side of Menno's face. "Happy Birfday, *Dat*. We have cake. It's a million feet tall."

Rosie's hands were filthy, as were Lily's, with black dirt under their fingernails and dirt smeared along their knuckles. They'd obviously been playing outside with the goats and Pepper again. They stunk like the great outdoors.

Menno gathered both girls into his arms, lifted them off their feet, and growled like a bear. Lily giggled. Rosie squealed in delight. She had an ear-piercing screech she used often, and Menno was sure his hearing would be gone by the time he was thirty-five if Rosie didn't learn to be a little quieter. He should probably make a habit of wearing earplugs whenever he played with Rosie. Either that or plan on hearing aids before his fortieth birthday.

With his girls in his arms, Menno walked straight to the bathroom and helped Rosie and Lily wash their hands. The dirt under their fingernails didn't budge. He found a pair of clippers in the drawer, clipped their fingernails, then filled the sink with warm, soapy water and had his girls soak their hands. The girls soon got bored of standing at the sink with their hands in the water, and he dried them and let them loose. Their fingernails weren't much better, but he didn't want to hold up dinner.

Was being on time for dinner more important than clean hands? Did Gotte favor promptness or cleanliness? Menno had no idea. He strolled into the kitchen.

Ada held a pitcher in her hand. "Happy birthday, Menno," she said, with as much enthusiasm as if she were reading it right from the dictionary.

"*Denki*," Menno said. "*Denki* for throwing me a party."

"Don't thank me," she said, pouring water into all the

glasses at the table. "I didn't do anything I wouldn't have done on any other night of the week."

Ada couldn't abide praise or gratitude directed at her. Her humility was admirable, but it was also a little aggravating that she couldn't accept thanks for anything. Esther had not put Ada on Menno's list of potential *fraaen*, but she was only thirty-one, well within Menno's age range. Ada was thin and wiry, as if every muscle in her body was pulled taut with hard work. She was also very pretty—all the Yoder *schwesteren* were—but she wore her beauty uncomfortably, as if her appearance were a burden instead of a gift. Ada was a little abrupt, as if she was too busy for chit-chat or trivial conversations. And she *was* busy. Like the other *schwesteren*, Ada cared for the goats, cleaned the house, and worked the farm. She was also in charge of the family's finances, which meant budgeting, buying groceries and feed, saving money, and taking care of the taxes.

It wore Menno out just thinking about it, mostly because his life looked much the same way. He had bought a small farm and built a little house when he and Suvilla married. He ran the farm, watched over his finances, cleaned, cooked, and cared for his *dochters*. Some days he felt as if he were drowning in his responsibilities.

Ada didn't seem to like Menno. She was polite and even made him pumpkin chocolate chip cookies when she found out they were his favorite, but she clenched her teeth every time Menno walked into a room, and she kept her eye on him as if he were going to spread a virus every time he breathed.

Beth was more friendly than Ada, but whenever Menno was there, she made an excuse to be somewhere else. Mary was always so kind, but she seemed almost amused when Menno talked to her, as if she was laughing at a joke he hadn't heard yet.

Everyone gathered around the table, and Joanna's *dat*, Try, assigned everyone a seat. His name *Try* was short for *drei*, which meant *three* in *Deitsch*. It was a nickname because he was Mervin Yoder Number Three. Joanna had told Menno the nickname saved a lot of confusion.

Mary and her husband, Clay, sat on one side of Menno. Clay's beard was filling in somewhat. Menno looked forward to the time when he could regrow his beard. He felt almost naked without one. Clay was a big man, a solid pillar of muscle and bone. Menno had never seen him with anything but a genuine smile on his face. It was plain that Clay had a kind heart and a fierce loyalty to Mary.

Menno had met Clay at church last week and liked him immediately, even though his *Deitsch* accent was atrocious and his suspenders never seemed to fit right.

Englischers Cathy Larsen and her husband, Lon, were there too. Cathy's frown was permanent, unless she was irritated, then the sour expression would dig itself deeper into her face. She was probably eighty-four or eighty-five years old with a thousand wrinkles crisscrossing her face, but she moved and walked like a much younger woman. She bragged that she was in shape because of all the pickleball she played and all the quilts she sewed. She wore a T-shirt that said, "The only thing I love more than quilting is being a grandma."

Lon was a quiet, unassuming man who used a walker with tennis balls on the legs and took his tank of oxygen with him wherever he went.

Someone had set up a small table for the four *kinner*. There was even a little chair for Junior, though he didn't want to sit in it.

Joanna's *dat* assigned Joanna and Menno the chairs next to each other, and it was all he could do not to grab Joanna's hand under the table. It seemed Gotte was smiling on their union at every turn.

Try said, "*Handt nunna*," and everyone put their hands in their laps and bowed their heads.

Menno silently thanked Derr Herr for giving him two beautiful *dochters* and leading him to a *gute fraa* in an astonishingly short amount of time. Everything was falling into place, and he would be engaged and back in Idaho to plant his sugar beets sooner than he thought possible. Gotte had been efficient as well as faithful.

Menno heard Try's fork clink against his plate and quickly finished his prayer.

Joanna, Ada, Esther, and Menno all stood up. Joanna and Ada brought serving dishes to the table, and Esther made plates for Winnie and Junior while Menno filled two plates, one each for Lily and Rosie. It was a feast fit for a birthday. There was buttered corn and buttered noodles, plus baked chicken, Joanna's mouth-watering rolls, red Jell-O salad topped with whipped cream, and green beans with cream of mushroom soup. Joanna had made the beans specifically for Menno because she knew they were his favorite. Was there any better indication that she wanted him to propose?

Menno cut Lily's food into tiny pieces and handed her the plate. He already knew she wouldn't eat the Jell-O because she wasn't comfortable with a spoon, and she couldn't pick up a piece of Jell-O and pop it into her mouth without getting her hands dirty. Rosie would eat her noodles and one or two bits of corn, but Menno couldn't hope she'd eat anything else. She was a picky eater, and the more he tried to convince her to taste everything on her plate, the more she resisted.

Mamm had said not to fuss about it, that Rosie had access to plenty of food. If she got hungry enough, she would eat. After that, he'd given up trying to get her to eat anything.

After serving his girls, Menno sat down and served himself. This was an important day for him. Not only was it his birthday, but it was the first of many *appeditlich* dinners he and Joanna would eat together. It was truly a celebration.

Cathy dished herself some salad and stared at the cheese crumbles on top of the lettuce. "Is this goat cheese?"

"Yes," Ada said. "Joanna made it."

Cathy pinched a tidbit of cheese between her fingers and popped it into her mouth. "I can't eat cow cheese because I'm on a cleanse, but goat cheese is acceptable. It's too bad you need goats to make goat cheese."

Joanna dished up some buttered noodles. "That is definitely the first thing you need for goat cheese."

Cathy picked up a green bean from her plate and studied it. "No offense, but I'm not fond of goats. They're smelly, and they nibble incessantly. They nibble on my jackets and my purse and the hem of every blouse I wear. My silk blouse is dry clean only, and goat saliva is surprisingly hard to get out, not to mention goat hair. I've gone through three lint brushes since I met you Yoder sisters."

Joanna giggled. "How can you not like goats. They have such cute little faces, and they trot around the yard like children. And they're pretty *gute* at running strangers off. One time, they helped Pepper get rid of a reporter who was pestering Mary."

Clay and Mary looked at each other and smiled.

"One of my favorite memories," Clay said.

"Goats are adorable and fun, even if they smell," Beth said.

Mary nodded. "They're practically part of the family."

Cathy skewered a noodle with her fork. "Quilts are also adorable and fun, and they don't shed or poop or drool. I'll admit that one of my quilts has never run a reporter off, but I've also never had extra laundry because one of my quilts decided to lick me."

"Lord willing," Esther said, "your quilts will never try to lick you."

Clay poured himself another glass of water. "Menno, Joanna says you're going to be here for just two more weeks. We'll be sorry to see you go."

Menno set his fork down. "I'll be very sorry too, but I'll be back in October for the wedding, and I'll get to see you all then."

Everyone at the table fell silent as all eyes turned to him.

Clay's eyes danced with amusement. "So, you've found a *fraa*?"

"No—I mean, yes. I've found the one I want to marry, but we haven't made any arrangements yet." He glanced at Joanna.

The color had drained from her face. Esther's complexion had turned a pale shade of green. Mary's cheeks flamed bright red. Menno cleared his throat. He'd said something wrong but wasn't sure how to take it back.

"I thought you hadn't found anyone yet," Joanna said.

He could tell she was trying to keep her voice steady.

Cathy snorted. "I'm impressed. I didn't think you would find someone to say *yes*."

Clay cleared his throat. "So who's the lucky girl, and when are you getting married?"

Menno shifted in his chair. He probably shouldn't mention Joanna's name. "I haven't actually asked her yet."

Levi nodded, his eyes sparkling with amusement. "You probably shouldn't make plans until you've talked to her about it."

"That would be wise," Try said.

Menno frowned. Should he ask Try first? Maybe, but it just wouldn't fit into his schedule tonight. Lord willing, Try would forgive him.

Joanna also cleared her throat. There was a lot of throat-clearing going on. "You should have invited her to the party."

Menno had nothing to say to that. Even though he was sure Joanna would say yes, he should still ask. Every girl wanted to be asked. "What kind of cake did you make?" He knew the answer because he had specifically requested German Chocolate days ago, but he had to change the subject. Everyone was looking at him as if he'd lost his sanity.

Joanna gave him a weak and unenthusiastic smile. "German Chocolate."

"Is it gluten- and dairy-free?" Cathy asked.

Joanna grimaced. "Um, no. I'm sorry, Cathy."

Ada pointed to Cathy's plate. "I should have warned you. There's nothing on there that's approved on your diet."

Cathy narrowed her eyes. "What about the green beans with cream of mushroom soup?"

"Dairy," Lon mumbled.

"And the rolls?"

Joanna grimaced. "Flour and scalded milk. Sorry. I thought you knew. The buttered noodles are full of wheat and dairy, and the Jell-O has whipped cream on top."

"What about the buttered corn?" Cathy blew a puff of air between her lips. "Oh, never mind. I can see where I went wrong. At least the chicken is on the diet."

Menno eyed the chicken on his plate. It had a bread crumb crust and was swimming in cream sauce. Joanna ducked her head and slipped her hand over her mouth, but she couldn't hide the spasms that shook her shoulders as if she'd had a sudden attack of hiccups. Finally she gave up holding it in and laughed so loud, Lon and Lily both jumped in surprise.

Mary soon joined her, though she looked as if she felt guilty for laughing, even though she couldn't help it. "Everything's better with butter."

Soon everyone at the table was laughing, and Winnie and Rosie left their small table and stood by Menno, trying to figure out what the fuss was about.

He relaxed in relief. Thank Derr Herr for Cathy's gluten- and dairy-free diet. She'd saved him from a very uncomfortable situation. The girl should always be the first to know that a boy wanted to marry her.

The rest of the meal went more smoothly, mostly because everyone turned their attention to other things. Clay had hired some friends and some Amish men to help him build a regulation-size baseball diamond in his backyard, and it was the most talked-about event in the entire valley. He was going to hold weekly baseball pitching clinics during the summer, and he had been asked to coach the local college baseball team. With the bishop's permission, he'd said yes.

After dinner and cake and singing "Happy Birthday," everybody did the dishes, then Cathy and Lon drove Esther, Levi, and all *die kinner* back to Esther's house. Joanna had seemed more than a little surprised and extremely uncertain that Menno had planned on staying.

There wasn't anything he could do about her distress but propose quickly so she wouldn't be kept in suspense for a minute longer than she had to. He suggested they take a walk outside, and Joanna agreed. They strolled out to the chicken coop together and made sure the chickens were safely inside.

Joanna hooked the door shut. "It keeps out the coyotes and kangaroo rats."

"You have coyotes in the area?"

"*Jah.* They love to eat chickens. As long as we keep the goats securely in the barn and the chickens locked in the coop, we don't have a problem. The coyotes are a great nuisance to the sheep farmers. The kangaroo rats are less of a problem because the owls love to eat them."

"Owls?"

"There's an owl nesting in our barn right now. Have you ever heard him screech?"

"Maybe. Does it sound like Rosie crying?"

Joanna laughed. "Just like that."

"I'm sort of surprised Pepper hasn't killed all your chickens yet."

"Pepper has a lot of energy, but he's smart and protective, and Dat has trained him not to bother the chickens. He sort of treats them like children, same as the goats."

"The goats are wonderful cute, even if Cathy doesn't like them."

"They're our babies. We adore them." Joanna puckered her lips, and for one brief, dizzying moment, Menno imagined she wanted him to kiss her.

Then she made a kissing noise and snapped her fingers. "Apple, Smiley, time for bed." She slid the barn door until the opening was wide enough for a goat to slip through. Fluffy and Blue poked their heads out as if watching for their *schwesteren* to come home. "Stay inside, you two," Joanna scolded.

Apple and Smiley trotted around the corner and loped into the barn without argument.

"That was easy," Menno said.

"*Jah*, they're very obedient. Especially after dark if they hear coyotes prowling the pastures."

He grimaced. "Are they out there?"

"Probably."

He wanted to reassure Joanna that she would like Idaho because there weren't any coyotes, but there *were* coyotes in the rural areas. But there were plenty of other *gute* things about Idaho that he could use to entice her. The weather was beautiful . . . three months out of the year . . . and he was sure there were more trees in Baker than in the whole San Luis Valley. Surely that would impress her. She'd told him she didn't want to leave Colorado, but like so many other things she'd told him, he hoped she hadn't really meant it. Surely she would move to Idaho if it meant she could marry and have a family.

Menno bit down on his bottom lip. Lord willing, Joanna wouldn't miss Pepper and her goats and chickens too badly. Maybe Try would let her take Apple with her. Menno would be willing to build Apple her own pen if Joanna would be happier to have her goat there.

Joanna slid the barn door shut and hooked the latch in place. "We probably don't really need to latch the door. The goats have never gotten out before."

"You can't be too careful."

Joanna grinned at him. "*Ach, vell*, you *can* be too careful, but I'm not talking about anyone in particular."

"Doesn't sound like anyone I know." He stuffed his hands in his pockets and tried to take a deep breath. His heart knocked against his rib cage, even though he had no reason to be nervous. For sure and certain this was Gotte's will, and the whole thing would be settled and done in a matter of minutes. He stopped walking and nudged Joanna's elbow. She stopped and eyed him, frowning as if she didn't want to hear what he had to say.

Menno shoved his misgivings to the back of his mind. He'd come to Byler to find a *fraa*, and he wasn't going to let doubt enter his heart and derail him from his purpose. *Let not your heart be troubled, neither let it be afraid.* "I haven't been here very long, and I know this is wonderful sudden, but two weeks has been long enough to know that I want to ask you to marry me."

He expected her to gasp in surprise, jump up and down, and maybe cry some tears of joy.

Instead, she pressed her lips into a hard line and folded her arms across her chest. "Why?"

"Why?" His stomach lurched, and his lips got stuck on the word. "Why what?"

"Why do you want to ask me to marry you?"

"'It is not *gute* for man to be alone.' God wants me to marry again."

"Does He?" she said, with a flippant toss of her head. But then her voice cracked, and he thought he saw a hint of moisture in her eyes.

"*Jah*, He does. And He wants me to marry you. I always try to be obedient, no matter the sacrifice."

"No matter the sacrifice," she murmured. "You make it sound so romantic." She turned her face from him and gazed into the pasture beyond the chain-link fence.

Menno felt his frown all the way to his toes. He hadn't thought he'd need to convince her. "Can you see how Gotte orchestrated things to bring us together? I knew when I first laid eyes on you that you were the woman I was supposed to marry. 'It's not *gute* for man to be alone.'"

"*Supposed* to marry?" Her words were tinged with irritation.

How could she be irritated by scripture?

"I have two little girls who need a *mater*. I need a *fraa*, and you need a husband. You're a wonderful *gute* cook, and we're going to eat very well the rest of our lives. It's perfect for all of us."

She was silent for several seconds, the most uncomfortable moments of his life. She wasn't thinking of saying *nae*, was she? That was impossible. Joanna wouldn't go against Gotte's will.

A heavy stone settled in his gut. "I know you're close to your family, but I've got everything figured out. We'll come back to Colorado twice a year to visit. If you want, we could take Apple with us."

"Apple wouldn't like Idaho," she said softly.

That was better than a no. "Then we don't have to take her. You're right that she'd be happier here among her family. But we will see her twice a year, I promise. And they can be long visits. My cousin can care for my horse and farm while we're away." He tilted his head to get a better look at her face. "What do you say?"

She wouldn't look him in the eye. "Say about what?"

Something wasn't right, but Menno couldn't do anything but forge ahead.

Maybe she wanted him to get down on one knee. He hadn't gotten down on one knee with Suvilla, but maybe Joanna liked the romance of it. He knelt down and took her hand. It felt limp in his. "Joanna, will you marry me?"

She looked at him, her eyes full of so much longing it took his breath away. "Why do you want to marry me?"

"*Ach*, Joanna, I already told you. It's not *gute* for man to be alone. You are an old *maedle*. You need a husband."

"Verla Ann Miller needs a husband," she said. "Priscilla Weaver and Sadie Sensenig need husbands."

"But I'm asking you. You're here, I'm here, we've just eaten cake." He grinned. "The mood is right."

He couldn't coax a smile out of her. "How convenient that I just happen to be here instead of Verla Ann." Pain and irritation traveled across her face as she pulled her hand out of his. "I let myself—why did I let myself?"

"Let yourself what?"

"I knew this would happen. I am the silliest, blindest girl in Byler. Probably in the entire San Luis Valley."

His throat felt tight and thick. He stood up and tried to take both of her hands. She took a step back. "*Ach*, Joanna, I know why you're upset."

She took another step away from him. "I'm not upset. A can of corn doesn't have feelings."

He threw up his hands. "You are not a can of corn. Why do you keep talking about corn like it means something to me?"

"That's the point, Menno. Corn means nothing to you."

He growled. "You've lost me beyond all finding."

She pointed to his pocket. "Show me your list."

Menno's face burned as if someone had set a match to it. Reluctantly, he pulled the list from his pocket and handed it to her.

She unfolded it and showed it to him, as if he hadn't read it every day for the last three months. "This, Menno, is a to-do list."

"Of course it is."

"Do you know how humiliating it feels to show up on your to-do list?"

"You're not anywhere on that list," he protested.

"*Nae*, I'm not, because you don't specifically care about marrying *me*. You just want to get married. Any girl will do. It's like buying canned corn at the store. There are fifty cans on the shelf, and any one of them is just as *gute* as any other. Do you know how it feels to be just one of a dozen choices you could make? If you'd seen Verla Ann Miller at the bakery two weeks ago, you'd be proposing to her right now."

Menno doubted himself for a fraction of a second. Would he be proposing to Verla Ann? He couldn't imagine it. If Verla Ann made fry pies, surely they weren't as *gute* as Joanna's. Verla Ann's birthday wasn't on the same day as his. Verla Ann didn't have eyes the color of cornflowers or hair the color of stained, smooth maple wood. He felt Joanna slipping away from him, even though she hadn't taken a step.

He couldn't let her go. "That's not true, Joanna."

She exhaled and closed her eyes briefly. When she opened them, Menno saw nothing but regret and affection in their depths. She pointed to item number three on Menno's list. "Did you buy Rosie a new pair of shoes yet?"

"I-I haven't had a chance," he stuttered. He'd been working exclusively on item number one.

"Her old ones pinch her feet. On warm days, I let her go outside barefoot. You should get that taken care of before you go back to Idaho."

"*Jah*. They're, uh, they're really hard to put on."

She returned the list to him. "Do you have a ride home?"

A vise pressed into Menno's chest. Was this the end? "But, Joanna, what about getting married?"

One side of her mouth curled upward, and she exhaled a short, soft laugh. "I wish you all the best, Menno.

May Gotte bless you with a wonderful-*gute fraa*. Thank Derr Herr it will not be me." She turned and walked into the house, leaving Menno by himself staring at the closed door.

He felt the pain of a thousand sharp daggers and recognized the feeling.

It was what a broken heart felt like.

Chapter 7

Joanna startled awake when someone pounded on her bedroom door. "Joanna, time to get up. You've been lazy long enough."

"Go away." Joanna groaned, willed her heart to slow down, closed her eyes, then pulled the covers over her head and pretended it was still three o'clock in the morning.

It was unfortunate there were no locks on the bedroom doors. Ada had never done as she was told, and she threw open Joanna's door so hard it slammed against the wall. "I'm not going away. You're going to stop pouting and get up and make the cheese. I've got to take a delivery to Alamosa this afternoon."

Joanna stuck out her bottom lip, though she was under her sheets so Ada couldn't be shocked by the expression. "I'm not pouting. I'm taking some vacation days. Everybody deserves a vacation."

Ada tried to pull the sheet off Joanna's head. "There's no such thing as a vacation in this house. You've got to pull your weight, or you get kicked out."

Joanna tightened her fists around the fabric and rolled onto her side, taking the sheets with her. Ada would never get them from her now. "Beth has never pulled her weight, and she's still with us."

"What a mean thing to say!"

Oops. Joanna hadn't realized Beth was in the room. "Just kidding, Beth."

Someone sat on the edge of the bed. It was probably Beth because Ada didn't believe in sitting when there was work to be done.

"Not *just kidding*. I've milked the goats and mucked out the barn and made bread every day while you sat up here in your room reading romance novels and eating ice cream."

Joanna reached her hand from under the covers and grabbed her pillow, which she promptly put over her head. "They were Christian romance novels. Nothing wrong with that."

"I didn't say there was," Beth said. "I read romance novels, but four days' worth is a little indulgent, don't you think?"

Ada didn't stand for such froth. "More than a little indulgent. But you have a broken heart, so we put up with it. It's been four days, and now it's time to get over it."

Joanna sat up and pulled the pillow and the covers off her head. "I don't have a broken heart. Who said I had a broken heart?" She blew at a curly lock of hair that fell over her face. Her braid had completely disintegrated two days ago, and her hair was going to be a beast to brush. But really, why did she ever need to brush out her hair? She never planned on leaving the house again, ever, and her *schwesteren* wouldn't care how messy and tangled her hair was. She could put it into a messy bun on top of her head and let little critters make homes in it, for all she cared.

Ada stood with her hands folded watching Joanna as if she were an incorrigible child who wouldn't pick up her toys. Beth sat on the bed with a look of deep pity on her face. Joanna didn't like that Beth's pity was directed at her. She didn't want pity. She just wanted to be left alone. Forever. Just her and her tangled mess of hair and the mouse that lived in it.

Beth smoothed her hand down her dress. She was wearing the pink one today that Joanna loved so much. Joanna was too old to wear pink, but she loved seeing it on Beth.

"Menno was at *gmay* on Sunday," Beth said, oozing sympathy from every pore.

Joanna sniffed and swiped at her nose with her sleeve. "I can't imagine that he'd miss. He's so righteous. Has he found a *fraa* yet?"

Ada ran her finger along the top of Joanna's dusty chest of drawers. Joanna didn't care how dirty it was. She wasn't going to dust ever again.

"Oh, he's found a *fraa* all right, but she won't have him," Ada said.

Joanna scoffed. "She has too much self-respect for that."

Beth put her hand on Joanna's ankle, which was still under the covers. "He asked how you were doing."

"I don't wonder but he's very disappointed he has to start all over again with less than two weeks left in Colorado."

Beth glanced at Ada. "*Ach, vell*, he didn't waste any time."

What did Beth mean by that? Joanna pressed her lips together. She didn't care what Beth meant. Menno was just a man from Idaho who hadn't paid her anything to babysit his children for two weeks. She wasn't heartbroken, and she really didn't care what he was doing with his life. If he'd already found another girl to propose to, that was just another reason she should be grateful she hadn't said yes to him. In matters of love, no one wanted to be disposable like a roll of paper towels.

Ada opened the curtains, and Joanna squinted at the bright light. "*Cum*, Joanna. If you don't make the cheese, I'll have to do it, and you know I can't get the flavor right. Last time it didn't end well, and I had to throw the whole batch out."

Joanna resisted as long as she could then threw her pillow at Beth. "You want to tell me, so tell me."

Beth didn't flinch. Giving a wide-eyed, innocent look, she threw the pillow back at Joanna. "Tell you what?"

Joanna growled and glared at Beth. "You said Menno didn't waste any time."

"Why do you care?"

Joanna lay down and buried her head under the pillow again. "I don't care."

Ada grabbed Joanna's foot, which was out of the covers, and before Joanna knew what was happening, she'd been pulled completely off the bed. She landed on the floor with a thud and a grunt.

Surprise popped all over Ada's face. "I didn't think that would work."

A giggle burst from Joanna's lips, and she wasn't able to stop. Ada's expression was just too comical. Beth covered her mouth with her hand and was soon laughing herself. Ada smiled, shook her head, and sat down on the floor next to Joanna. Her sigh turned into a chuckle, which gave way to a hoot of laughter. They laughed until tears ran down their cheeks.

Joanna loved each one of her *schwesteren* for different reasons, but this was one of the things she loved most about Ada. Ada never gave up on anyone, and she never put up with foolish behavior when there was work to be done. Ada worked harder than anyone, and Joanna never fully appreciated that.

Joanna huffed out a long, pathetic breath. "You're right,

Ada. I've been feeling sorry for myself for long enough. A man like Menno isn't worth crying over. He certainly isn't worth three racy romance novels and a quart of ice cream."

Ada raised an eyebrow. "Racy romance novels?"

Joanna smiled sheepishly. "I may have sneaked some in among the Christian ones. If it makes you feel better, they were terrible, and I should probably make a kneeling confession at church next time."

Ada stood and pulled Joanna with her. "I wouldn't worry about a kneeling confession. I'm sure you're sorry, and that's the end of it."

"Where are those racy romances?" Beth asked. "I can throw them away for you."

Joanna laughed. "I'm sure you can, but Dat unknowingly took them out with the trash yesterday."

Beth's shoulders sagged in mock disappointment. "Too bad."

Mary floated into the room like an angel. "*Ach, heartzley,*" she said, giving Joanna a hug. "It's *gute* to see you up and about." She smoothed Joanna's hair out of her eyes. "How are you feeling today? I'm sorry you've had a hard time of it."

Joanna gave Mary a quick kiss on the cheek. "No need to beat around the bush. I've been acting like a baby, and I apologize."

Mary grabbed Joanna's brush from the chest of drawers, turned Joanna around, and started brushing her unruly hair. "You don't need to apologize."

"*Jah*, she does," Ada said.

Joanna giggled. "*Jah*, I do. I'm going to make cheese and then go to the bakery and see if they're out of fry pies. Then I'll milk the goats and clean the toilets to make up for all the days I've been slacking."

"I'll clean the toilets," Ada said. "I have a certain way I like to do them."

Beth had always been especially grateful that Ada insisted on cleaning the toilets. "Thank Derr Herr Ada likes to clean toilets."

Joanna winked at Ada. "It's one of your best qualities."

Mary worked through the tangles in Joanna's hair. "I don't know if you want to hear about Menno Eicher or not, but I've heard some news that I thought you might be interested in."

Beth straightened the sheets on Joanna's bed. "I was just going to tell her."

Joanna didn't even pretend indifference. "What happened?"

Mary grabbed Joanna's wrist and directed her to sit on the floor next to the bed. Mary sat on the bed and kept brushing Joanna's hair. "I saw Menno talking to Sadie Sensenig at *gmay* on Sunday."

Beth nodded. "We all did. He also talked to Naomi Zook, Lydia Herschberger, and Verla Ann Miller."

"The ones left on his list," Joanna muttered.

"Sadie says Menno made an appointment with each of them for a date this week." Beth counted on her fingers. "He's seeing Naomi tonight, Lydia on Wednesday, Sadie on Thursday, and Verla Ann on Friday."

Mary gave Joanna a wilted look. "He's determined."

Joanna's heart shouldn't have ached like it did. She'd rejected Menno for this very reason and was glad of it.

Ada sat next to Mary. "At least he's honest."

Joanna wrapped her arms around herself. "I'm surprised he didn't ask you for a date, Ada. And Beth too."

Beth blew air from between her lips. "Not even Menno would be that *deerich*."

Ada smoothed her hand down Joanna's hair. "*Nae*. He

wouldn't be that foolish, but he's single-minded. If Sadie, Verla Ann, Lydia, and Naomi reject him, we might be next on his list."

Joanna laughed, but there wasn't any happiness in it. "It's not as easy to buy a can of corn as he thought."

"We already know how hard it is to find a *gute* man," Ada said. "Mary got the only *gute* man in Colorado, and he was an Englischer."

Joanna was facing the other way so she couldn't see Mary's face, but she could hear the smile in her voice. "Clay isn't the only *gute* man, but he is for sure and certain the best man."

Beth sat down cross-legged and faced Joanna on the floor. "I think we should all do what Mary did. Find an Englischer, make him fall in love, then get him to convert."

"Not me," Joanna said. "I gave up finding a husband long ago. I'd rather make fry pies and bread the rest of my life than be married for convenience's sake."

Beth narrowed her eyes. "That's what I don't get. You said as much from the very beginning. You didn't want to be a can of corn. You didn't want to be on Menno's list. So why are you so sad?"

Joanna squared her shoulders. "I'm not sad. Who says I'm sad?"

"I do," Mary, Ada, and Beth said in unison.

Joanna rolled her eyes. Her *schwesteren* wouldn't let her get away with denying it. "Okay. I'm sad. There's no use dwelling on it."

Beth giggled. "You've been dwelling on it for days. In fact, you've been wallowing in it."

Mary fashioned Joanna's hair into a bun at the back of her head. "The goats miss you."

Joanna almost shook her head, but she didn't want to

undo all of Mary's *gute* work. "I've been out three times to see the goats. They're fine."

Ada patted her on the shoulder. "*We* miss you."

That was an uncharacteristic admission from Ada. She wasn't one for sentiment.

Joanna laid her hand on top of Ada's. "I'm sorry. I've been wonderful selfish not pulling my weight."

"It's not about doing your share of the work," Ada said. "You're the frosting that holds this family together. You keep us from fighting. You keep us laughing. You keep us sane. We need you."

Until Ada said them, Joanna hadn't realized how much she needed to hear those words. Ada was stingy with her emotions and even stingier with her praise.

A tear trickled down Joanna's cheek. "It's not entirely my doing. We need each other."

"*Jah*, we're *schwesteren*," Mary said. "We have to stick together."

Beth stood and pulled Joanna's *kapp* from the top drawer and handed it to her. "So tell us why you've been down in the dumps. You were dead set against Menno even before he got here."

Joanna twirled one of her *kapp* strings around her finger. "I thought there was no danger of falling in love with him because I disapproved of him so completely. He had a to-do list, for goodness' sake. He imposed on Esther's hospitality, he was overly confident he'd find a *fraa*, and he's too handsome for his own *gute*. He expected that women would be chasing him around Byler, begging to marry him. He's too arrogant by half."

"So what happened?" Ada said.

Mary took Joanna's *kapp* and pinned it in her hair. "Menno isn't arrogant. He's obedient. He told me several times that Gotte wanted him to find a *fraa*. He's trying to do his duty as he sees it."

Joanna's sigh came out more like a sob. "I know. He's *wunderbarr*."

Ada stood. She couldn't stay idle for long. "So he wasn't what you expected, and you fell in love with him."

Joanna shrugged. "Can you fall in love in two weeks?"

"Of course you can," Mary said mildly. "Menno fell in love with you."

Joanna snorted her derision. "As much as you can love a can of corn."

Mary stood, took Joanna's hand, and pulled her up. "Joanna, he loves you, for sure and certain."

"He was just in love with the idea that he found a *fraa* so fast."

Mary sighed. "You know that's not true. Deep down you know."

"I don't know, Mary."

Ada folded her arms around her waist. "You should. He came almost every night and stayed for dinner. He barely looked at anyone else but you. He ignored the rest of us unless we had something to say about you."

Joanna lifted her chin. "Because I was on his list. He thought I was the one Gotte had given him. Like Mary said, he's single-minded and obedient."

"Now you're just being contrary, Joanna," Mary scolded. Only she could make a rebuke sound sweet and affectionate. "Almost as soon as Menno got here, you told him you didn't want to be on his list. He had five other women to choose from, but he picked you even though you discouraged him. He loved you probably from the moment he saw you."

Ada nodded. "He was seriously annoying because he never wanted to be far from your side."

Beth got off the floor and put an arm around Joanna. "One time you left the room, and he picked up your apron and smelled it."

Ada made a face. "That's weird."

"Not weird. He likes how Joanna smells." Beth turned to Joanna. "You read romance novels. You know what I'm talking about."

Joanna scrunched her lips together. "It's weird and romantic at the same time. Maxim kept Elinor's hanky and smelled it every day in *Rapturous Regency Love*."

Ada groaned in disgust. "Nope. Don't want to hear it."

Joanna pressed her fingers to her forehead. "Was I— Was I wrong to refuse him?"

"Probably. You may never have another chance." Beth was too young to be tactful.

Joanna wanted to fall across the bed and cry, but if she lay down again, she might not get up for the rest of the day. Had she reacted too quickly and lost Menno forever? "His proposal made our marriage sound so practical. 'You need a husband. I need a *fraa*. My *dochters* need a *mater*.' That's what he said. I felt dispensable."

"*Jah*," Ada said. "He was very clumsy."

Mary wrapped her arms around Joanna. "Of course you weren't wrong. You love him, and he loves you, but he doesn't know he loves you. He still sees it as his duty to get married, and when he proposed to you, you were just one of many on his list, even though he denied it. He had his list of reasons why you two should marry, but they were the same list of reasons he would have used on any girl."

"That's right. He didn't give me one reason he wanted to marry *me*, except maybe for my cooking. He just listed reasons he wanted to marry."

"Don't you see, Joanna? He started out wanting to get

married, but after two weeks, he only wanted to marry *you.*" Mary's eyes filled with compassion. "I feel sorry for him. Maybe love didn't seem like a *gute* enough reason to marry, and he was forced to justify his choice in the eyes of Gotte. He came to Colorado with blinders on and couldn't see that the best reason, the *only* reason to marry is for love. He is determined to choose a *fraa* to be obedient to Gotte. *You* are determined to be loved."

"I wanted him to choose me, but I wanted him to choose me because he loves me, not because he needs a *fraa.*"

"Unfortunately, he's acting as if you're just one of the crowd. He's already looking for someone else." Ada was even less tactful than Beth.

Mary sighed. "What's funny is that he *did* choose you because he loves you. He just doesn't realize it. You did the right thing by refusing him. He needs to figure out you're not just another can of corn. He needs to realize how deeply he loves you, or he won't ever appreciate what he has."

"You're talking as if there's hope, but it's too late for me and Menno." Joanna pointed to Beth. "He's already dating Sadie and the others. He's already moved on. He's looking for another girl. He still wants a *fraa*, and it appears that any *fraa* will do."

Mary laughed softly.

Joanna pressed her lips together. "It's not funny, Mary."

"I'm not laughing at you. I'm just thinking about Menno, courting all these women, trying to talk himself into asking one of them to marry him. But he won't ask any of them, because he loves you. That love is going to torture him until he comes to his senses, realizes that he wants to marry for love, and tries to win you back. *Nae*, Joanna, I don't think he'll move on."

Beth clapped her hands in excitement. "How long

before he comes to his senses? Wouldn't a June wedding be *wunderbarr*? You should do fireworks."

"*Ach*," Mary said. "He's stubborn and single-minded. How long are you willing to wait?"

Joanna laughed when she really wanted to cry. "You have more faith than I do, Mary. Sadie is sweet and energetic. Verla Ann makes delicious Yankee bean soup. Naomi's produce is organic. And Menno has only two weeks left."

Someone clomped up the stairs, and Sadie Sensenig burst into Joanna's room as if she lived there. "Sorry," she said, panting like she'd run all the way from her house. "I hope it was okay I let myself in. I knocked twice, and no one answered, and Pepper didn't seem to mind that I walked right in."

Joanna stiffened. She had always adored Sadie, but the thought of Sadie becoming Menno's *fraa* made Joanna irrationally jealous. She couldn't help herself.

Unfortunately, Sadie made a beeline for Joanna and grabbed her hand as if they were best friends. "*Ach*, Joanna, I am appalled, just appalled. Menno is the biggest idiot in the whole world, even though it's a sin to say such things."

Joanna didn't know whether to wholeheartedly agree with her or feel defensive of Menno. He was the most *wunderbarr* man in the world. And also an idiot.

Sadie squeezed Joanna's hand so tightly, Joanna winced. "I don't know what to say, Joanna. Menno is wildly in love with you, but he's trying to court four other girls. It's just . . . There are no words. He's such an idiot."

Beth gave Sadie a hug. "*Jah*, he is. We all agree."

Sadie pulled Joanna into an unwelcome embrace. Joanna let herself be hugged, even if she wasn't sure what Sadie was up to.

"Everyone can see it," Sadie said, releasing Joanna and

putting her arm around Beth. "Menno loves Joanna and no one else."

Mary eyed Joanna. "That's what we've been trying to tell her."

Sadie blew air from between her lips. "But, really, how can you tell a man he's being idiotic? You can't, that's how." She pulled Joanna to sit on the bed.

Joanna felt like a yo-yo. She'd been up and down on that bed all day.

"I have a plan that is going to make Menno realize he loves you and only you. I just wanted to come over here and tell you not to despair. He is going to come crawling back to you, or my name isn't Sadie Sensenig."

"I don't want him to crawl," was all Joanna could think to say.

Sadie grunted indignantly. "He's got to crawl. That's the only way you'll know he's sincere."

"What is your plan?" Ada asked.

Sadie grinned. "I'm not telling because it's a surprise, but we're all agreed." Her smile faltered slightly. "Except Verla Ann. She refuses to go along with the plan, because she sort of kind of wants to marry Menno. But I'm not worried about her. Menno isn't an idiot."

Joanna nearly laughed. First Menno *was* an idiot, then he wasn't. She caught her bottom lip between her teeth. Verla Ann wanted to marry Menno? Did she have her own plan?

Beth seemed the most convinced and enthusiastic. "Isn't it *wunderbarr*, Joanna? Sadie is the best friend a girl could have."

Joanna gave Sadie a tepid smile. "I appreciate your help." Whatever it was and even if it didn't make any difference.

Joanna could tell Ada didn't want to throw cold water on Sadie's plans, but she spoke anyway. "You shouldn't get your hopes up, Joanna. No matter what Sadie does, Menno might very well marry someone else. He's very obedient, and he's very persistent. He gave himself one month to find a *fraa*. I think he'll barrel forward until he convinces one of those other girls to marry him."

Joanna squared her shoulders. "*Ach, vell*, then he doesn't deserve me." It was easy to say and heartbreaking to consider.

Mary put her arm around Joanna and led her away from Ada, as if trying to steer her from any thought of Menno marrying someone else. "We can trust Sadie. Mark my words. Menno is madly in love with you. He'll come back to you."

"Or we'll be attending his wedding to another girl," Ada mumbled.

Joanna tried to smile and burst into tears.

Chapter 8

Menno propped his elbow on the table and rested his forehead in his hand, not even making an effort to appear cheerful. His head throbbed, his heart ached, and his gut felt as if it were permanently clenched with anxiety. He needed to snap out of this malaise before his date tonight with Naomi or she'd never be convinced of his sincerity.

I really want to get to know you better, Naomi, but the thought of dating you makes me tired and gives me a terrible headache.

Esther set a plate of scrambled eggs on the table next to the crispy bacon and pitcher of milk.

"*Handt nunna,*" Levi said. Everyone but Levi Junior put their hands in their laps and bowed their heads for silent prayer.

Menno bowed his head, but not even the smell of *kaffee* and bacon could whet his appetite. He thanked Derr Herr for the food, for Esther and Levi, and for helping him find a *fraa*. That last thing hadn't happened yet, but Menno thanked Gotte for it anyway even though the excitement had worn off, and finding a *fraa* felt more like a chore.

He tried not to let himself be overcome with discouragement, even though he'd lost all hope of finding an acceptable *fraa*. He'd wasted two weeks on Joanna, but the thought of asking anyone else to marry him gave him a stomachache. Still, he knew the duty he owed to Gotte and the bishop, and his girls needed a *mater*. He wouldn't give up, even if he wanted to.

Levi picked up his fork, and everyone raised their heads and started to eat. Menno served Lily and Rosie some eggs and one piece of bacon each and poured them an inch of milk in each of their glasses. "Esther, I just want to tell you again how grateful I am to you for letting me stay here. I know it's a terrible imposition, but I felt Gotte calling me to come here. I hope I'm not too much of a burden."

Esther smiled as if she felt sorry for him. It was the same expression she'd worn ever since the disastrous birthday party. "I must admit I was afraid it would be hard to have you here. But you do dishes and hang quilting racks in my shop and muck out the shed and prune apricot trees. You're very nice to have around."

Levi snickered. "You've made her see how sorely lacking I am as a husband."

Esther scooped a spoonful of eggs onto Junior's tray. "*Ach*, Levi, don't be silly. You always work very hard, though Menno is the better painter."

One side of Levi's mouth curled upward. "I think that was a compliment."

"Of course it was, *heartzley*. You can't be the best at everything."

Levi shrugged. "I suppose not. I need something to keep me humble. It might as well be my painting skills."

Esther and Levi loved each other so much, it was almost unbearable. Menno did his best to ignore it. "I just hope you know how much I appreciate it."

Esther nodded. "I know, and you're welcome."

"Since I've lost my babysitter"—he cleared his throat—"since I've lost my babysitter . . ."

Esther poured herself a glass of milk. "I'm more than happy to watch your girls, Menno. It's only for two more weeks, and Winnie adores them. Sincerely, I don't know what any of us are going to do when you're gone." She picked at the eggs on her plate. "I don't mean to speak out of turn, but Rosie and Lily should grow up near their cousins. It wonders me if you wouldn't want to move down here someday. If you marry a girl from Byler, I'm sure she'd rather live here than move up there, especially if she has goats or dogs or . . . other pets."

Menno held his breath and studied Esther's face. Who else had goats and a dog? Was she talking about Joanna on purpose or just making a general observation? Her expression was unreadable, and he didn't have the energy to guess. "I couldn't abandon my parents. My *schwester*, Hannah, moved to Iowa when she got married. Mamm still mourns it."

"Joanna has goats," Rosie shouted.

Lily clapped her little hands and grinned, a piece of bacon half in, half out of her mouth.

Winnie giggled. "Smiley tried to eat my shoe."

The corner of Esther's mouth twitched slightly. "We all love Joanna's goats."

"I want to see the goats," Winnie said. "Mamm, can we visit the goats today?"

Lily clapped again. "*Jah*. Goats. We want goats."

Menno nearly joined in the clapping. At that moment, rational or not, he wanted to see Joanna more than he wanted to do anything else in the world. It made no sense. She'd made it very clear she didn't want to marry him, but he felt like he was starving without her.

Esther glanced at Menno. "Today is not a *gute* day to see the goats, Winnie." She gave Menno a sad smile. "For sure and certain the girls love Joanna. She's very special."

"*Jah*," Menno said, his voice cracking in a hundred places. Joanna was like a bright light in the darkness. Her smile was a balm, and her fry pies were better than medicine.

Someone knocked on the door, and Menno jumped to answer it so Esther and Levi wouldn't be inconvenienced. It was the least he could do for all their hospitality.

Verla Ann Miller stood on Esther's porch with a picnic basket hooked over her elbow. Her face lit up like a light-bulb when she saw Menno. She was a pretty girl, petite and wiry, with a shock of yellow curls sticking out from under her *kapp*. "*Hallo*, Menno. How nice. You're just the person I came to see."

What did she want? Their date wasn't until Friday.

Verla Ann stepped smartly into the house and marched down the hall to the kitchen. Menno followed close behind.

"*Hallo*, Esther. *Hallo*, Levi," she said, as if it was the most natural thing for her to be there at breakfast time.

"*Guter mariye*, Verla Ann," Esther said, obviously surprised about a visitor at seven in the morning.

Verla Ann pointed to her own ear and then to Esther's. "You have a stick behind your ear."

Esther pressed her hand to the side of her head. "It's a bamboo skewer for my fruit kebabs this morning." She pointed to the plate holding a row of colorful fruit threaded onto four skewers.

"Very pretty." Verla Ann set her basket on the counter, then bent over, propped her hands on her knees, and looked at Rosie. "*Hallo*, Rosie," she said loudly, as if Rosie was hard of hearing instead of just young. Verla Ann turned to Lily. "*Gute mariye*, Lily. You both look as if you got a *gute* night's sleep last night. I'm *froh*. Sleep is so important for *die kinner*."

"*Jah*, it is," Menno mumbled, because no one else at the table seemed inclined to reply.

Verla Ann didn't seem to care that she'd created a stir. She cheerfully opened her basket and pulled out a loaf of white bread. "I made this yesterday, and I thought you might enjoy it."

She handed it, not to Esther, but to Menno. He took it, wondering what she wanted him to do with it. Should he pull it out of the plastic bag and take a bite? "*Denki*. It looks *appeditlich*."

"It's my *mamm*'s recipe. We've been baking bread together for ten years. I also make delicious soups and"— she pulled a jar of bright orange jam from the basket— "apricot jam. I made this myself last fall. Low sugar recipe."

Menno must not have been responding correctly since Verla Ann frowned at him and brusquely set the jam on the table. She took the bread from Menno, slid it out of the bag, and cut a thick slice off one end using one of Esther's knives. "Do you like the butt of the bread or an inside piece?"

"Uh, the butt, I guess."

Verla Ann opened the jam, found a butter knife in one of Esther's drawers, and slathered apricot jam a quarter-inch thick on the bread. She pulled a small plate from the cupboard, put the bread on the plate, and handed it to Menno. "Try it. It's a low sugar recipe."

She watched Menno like a hawk watched a mouse. Levi stared at Menno as if he were extraordinarily amused about something. The lines around Esther's eyes deepened.

Menno took a hardy bite because that was obviously

what was expected of him. It was fluffy, melt-in-your-mouth bread, and the jam was a perfect combination of sweet and tangy. "Very *gute*, Verla Ann. *Denki*."

Verla Ann was as pleased as punch. "My secret family recipe." She cut four more slices, smothered them with jam, and handed them out to the rest of the people at the table. Winnie, Rosie, Lily, and Junior each got half a slice. Esther and Levi got their own whole slice.

"What do you say?" Menno asked.

"*Denki*," Rosie and Lily repeated together.

"*Denki*, Verla Ann," Winnie said.

Verla Ann got more animated. "*Du bischt wilkumm*. I know you'll love it."

Lily hated to get her hands dirty, so she quietly stared at her bread without daring to touch it. Menno took his knife and cut Lily's piece into eight square pieces. Lily used her fork to pick up the first piece and pop it into her mouth. For a two-year-old, she was very good with a fork.

Rosie and Winnie picked up their bread and each took a bite. Rosie made a face. Apricot was not her favorite flavor, but Menno had taught her to be polite, so she swallowed the first bite without complaint, set her bread on her plate, and took a sip of milk. Winnie and Junior both seemed to like their bread, though most of the jam ended up on Junior's face instead of in his mouth.

Esther looked as if she had a sour stomach. "It's *appedetlich*, Verla Ann. How nice of you to come all this way to give us a taste."

Verla Ann nodded in satisfaction. "I don't bake a lot of desserts and sugary treats like some people. My specialty is hearty, stick-to-your-ribs food. Everyone wants seconds, and no one ever leaves my table hungry."

Menno's face got warm. He'd be thick indeed if he couldn't see that she was trying to impress him. Oh, *sis yuscht*! Menno wasn't prepared for an attack. Verla Ann needed to be patient like everybody else.

Verla Ann pointed to Rosie's plate. "Try another bite, Rosie. You don't want it to dry out."

Rosie picked up her piece of bread and watched Verla Ann out of the corner of her eye. Seeing that Verla Ann wasn't paying attention, Rosie set the bread to the side of her plate, as if hoping Verla Ann wouldn't notice it there.

Menno finished his bread, and Verla Ann immediately cleared his small plate. "Now, I've come to see how I can help you."

"Me?" Levi said, with a hint of laughter in his voice.

Verla Ann put the rest of the bread back into the plastic bag. "*Jah*, when all is said and done. Menno, you're in need of a babysitter because Joanna just dropped those girls in your lap."

Menno tensed at the sound of Joanna's name. She hadn't dropped them in his lap. He'd dropped them in hers.

"*Jah*," he said, not sure why he was irritated that Verla Ann knew so much about his life.

"I would like to take the burden off Esther and care for your children while you are working."

"You . . . you want to babysit my children?" Menno should have been overjoyed.

Her generous offer took a great burden off Esther, but every cell in his body rebelled against such an obvious solution. His girls didn't know Verla Ann, and she didn't know them. Did Verla Ann sense his hesitation?

"I'm very *gute* with children. I'll make them nutritious meals every day without extra sugar. I don't believe in spanking children, but I do use the time-out chair. I don't know if you've ever heard of that, but it's a *gute* discipline tool."

Menno glanced at his girls. Lily was gingerly eating

another piece of bread, her little fingers wrapped around her fork, her pinky finger sticking in the air. Rosie was making faces at Winnie. They were so young. Did they even need discipline?

Esther seemed less than enthusiastic. "But Verla Ann, it's right in the middle of the school year. You couldn't possibly babysit Menno's girls." She glanced at Menno. "Verla Ann is one of the schoolteachers."

Menno silently expelled a tight breath. He wouldn't have to tell Verla Ann *nae*.

"Not anymore." Verla Ann folded her hands in front of her. "I met with the school board last night and told them I'm quitting. My *schwester* Mary Ann will take over for me until the end of the school year."

Esther cried out in surprise. "Verla Ann! But . . . why did you do that?"

Menno knew the answer, and his heart dropped to the floor.

Verla Ann's expression was soft and mushy when she looked at Menno. "I told them I won't be coming back to teach in September."

Esther's dismay seemed to multiply. "You're not teaching next year?"

"I'd rather help Menno with *die kinner*. For as long as he needs me." Her eyes were full of an unspoken tenderness that made him want to jump from his seat and run out of the room.

"*Ach*, Verla Ann, don't quit your job for me. I'm only here for another two weeks."

Verla Ann didn't even flinch. "Who knows what the future brings? I want to be ready."

This wasn't happening. If Verla Ann quit her job, he'd feel an obligation toward her that he could never repay, never wanted to repay.

Again she looked at him as if he made the sun rise in the morning. *Ach, du lieva*. He didn't want her to look at him like that. He needed a *fraa*, and it appeared that Gotte was providing him with a *fraa* without Menno having to do any work. But wasn't that what he'd thought about Joanna?

He pressed his lips into a hard line. He just couldn't propose to Verla Ann right now. He needed time. He barely knew her. Surely Gotte wouldn't be displeased that Menno wanted to get to know the girl before they married.

He swallowed the bitter taste in his mouth, feeling like he was stuck between a rock and a hard place. Esther needed help. It would be very selfish to think only of himself when she was doing so much for him already. He had a chance to ease her burden, and he should take it. Verla Ann was the perfect solution. Surely Gotte had arranged it. "That's very nice of you, Verla Ann. I will gladly take you up on your offer."

Esther pulled the bamboo skewer from behind her ear and snapped it in half.

Verla Ann exploded into a smile like a bright sparkler on the Fourth of July. "*Wunderbarr*. We're going to be so *gute* together." She cleared her throat and looked down. That must not have come out the way she had wanted it to.

"But only for two weeks," Menno said.

Verla Ann leaned in. "Come again?"

"Take a two-week vacation from school, but don't quit your teaching job. It sounds like your *schwester* would be okay with you coming back. You are already sacrificing too much of your time for me. It wouldn't be right."

"Of course it's right. I've never been more sure of anything in my life."

And Menno had never been more mortified. "Maybe, but I do not want to feel responsible for you. If you quit your job, I'll find another babysitter for my girls." He tried to say it kindly, but she was being pushy. He had to be a little pushy back.

"Oh, Menno," she gushed. "You're always thinking of others before yourself. I'll talk to the school board. Surely they haven't hired someone else yet for September."

"Lord willing," Esther murmured. She balled her napkin in her fist. "You need to babysit here at my house. Winnie is very attached to Rosie and Lily, and I love having them around."

Verla Ann pursed her lips. "I suppose I could do that." She didn't look all that happy.

And neither did Esther.

"Then it's all settled."

Verla Ann seemed to regain some of her enthusiasm. "I can start right now. You men head to work, and Esther and I will clean up the dishes and the children."

Menno's gut clenched. Why did he feel like he was suddenly out of control of his own life?

He had no one to blame but himself.

Chapter 9

Menno's hair was still wet when he hitched up Levi's buggy and headed to Naomi Zooks's house. He maybe should have taken Levi's bike instead, but he didn't want to show up sweaty to Naomi's house and didn't want to ride the bike home in the dark.

Menno had rushed home after work where Verla Ann had greeted him at the door as if she was his *fraa*. She'd taken his jacket, hung it on the hook by the door, given him a report about the girls, and left without another word. The girls seemed happy enough with a new babysitter, and the stone that had been sitting in Menno's stomach all day didn't seem so heavy.

After Verla Ann left, he had eaten dinner and taken a quick shower so he wouldn't offend anybody. Esther had sweetly agreed to put the girls to bed so that he could see Naomi tonight. He'd chosen her as his first visit, because Naomi was thirty-seven, mature, pretty, and—he had to admit—more likely to say yes than one of the younger women on his list. In other words, older, less picky, and less likely to be offended by a man just trying to do Gotte's will.

He slowed the horse to a trot, not in any sort of hurry to

get to Naomi's house. Gotte wanted him to get married. The first step to getting a *fraa* was finding someone to say yes. He thought Gotte had put Joanna in his path, but she'd said no. What else could he do but move on to someone else? Wasn't that Gotte's will, even if Menno wasn't especially eager to marry anybody else?

The only thing he knew how to do was keep moving. Maybe he was moving backward, but for sure and certain he would go nowhere if he wasn't in motion. Just keep moving and hope Gotte would guide his steps, wherever they took him.

Naomi's house was nestled behind a rare grove of trees just off the main highway. It was a small, two-bedroom house with green shutters, white siding, and four solar panels on the roof. Many of the Amish in the area used them to run their lights, heat their homes, and warm their water. Solar power was off the grid, and there was plenty of sun in the San Luis Valley. Naomi had a whole share of irrigation water, and she used it to generously water what Menno heard was a beautiful garden behind her house. It was the middle of April, so the surrounding shrubs were just shooting out new leaves, and a small patch of crocuses peeked their heads out of the soil.

Naomi stepped out onto her porch and waved to Menno as he guided the buggy to the front of the house. He parked it in the warmth of the late afternoon sun and set the brake. He felt as droopy and tired as the dormant grass in Naomi's front yard. His enthusiasm for courting Naomi had abandoned him a mile back, but he slid out of the buggy and walked toward her.

She wore a wide smile and a twinkle in her eye that Menno couldn't interpret. Was she happy to see him? Overjoyed? Expecting a proposal? *Ach*! He hoped not. He wasn't up to proposing to anybody tonight, except maybe Joanna, but that was a dead hope.

Naomi seemed genuinely glad to see him. "I made some rice pudding. Would you like some?"

"Sounds *appeditlich*," Menno said.

The smells of cinnamon and cream met him as he followed her into the small living and kitchen area. He sat down at one of the stools at the bar, and Naomi dished up two bowls of steaming rice pudding.

"I hope you like raisins. It's feels almost like a sin to make rice pudding without raisins."

"I love raisins. My *mamm* never makes rice pudding without raisins."

Naomi sat next to Menno, and they talked about Idaho and Rosie and Lily while they ate. She asked about his sugar beets, and he asked about her potatoes. It was a pleasant conversation, but he didn't feel much emotion at all.

How did Joanna manage to be so interesting all the time? When he was with her, everything in the world seemed exciting, from barn owls and coyotes to goat cheese and canned corn.

They finished the rice pudding, and Naomi stacked the bowls in the sink. "I know this is supposed to be a date," she said, her eyes dancing merrily, "but I could really use some help prepping the garden before it gets too dark to see."

"Of course," Menno said. "We can talk while we work."

Naomi's garden was a formidable acre of land already plowed in rough rows and surrounded on all sides with posts and netting nine feet high to keep out the deer. Two pairs of garden gloves sat on the back porch next to two shovels and two shiny new hoes. She picked up the gloves and handed Menno the larger pair. Each of them picked up a hoe and a shovel.

"Who put up all this netting for you?" he said as they strolled into the small opening between two posts.

"Freeman Sensenig and three other men came last spring and put the whole thing together for me. My *dat* paid for the materials and the delivery. I was so tired of the deer eating my plants, and they can jump almost anything lower than nine feet. Last week a fawn got one of her feet stuck in the netting, and she kicked me something wonderful before I could untangle her."

"You've already plowed your furrows."

Naomi nodded. "Ben Kiem and Wally Bontrager broke up the soil last fall, and Freeman Sensenig brought his horse and plow a couple of weeks ago to give me some rows. Lorene Glick and her whole family offered to come over in May to help me plant. Will you help me move the hoses into place? I use a drip system, and once the plants are in, the hoses need to be moved regularly."

Menno helped Naomi move hoses for almost half an hour, then they repaired some raspberry trellises and used their hoes to break up large dirt clods. It was backbreaking work, and Menno was sweating before the hour was up. He really hadn't needed that shower earlier. He was sure he smelled worse than he had all day.

After breaking up the soil, they pulled the weeds that had already started to grow. Naomi was a fast and insistent weeder, pulling weeds and moving forward so quickly that there was no time to talk. There was barely time to breathe, and all that passed between them was an occasional glance to make sure they didn't knock into each other while they traveled around the garden. Menno considered himself a hard worker, but he had never seen anyone like her. She put her head down and worked like a bulldozer, pulling weeds right and left until it got too dark to see.

She called it quits fifteen minutes after Menno would have. They were both panting heavily as they trudged back to the house.

"I have two hats with lights that I wear when I have to weed at night," she said.

He couldn't see her face very well, but he tried to make out her features in the dark to see if she was serious. "Do you want us to do more weeding?"

"I wish we had time, but there are things that need to be done in the house that I can't do myself. How long can you stay?"

Menno stumbled over his answer. "Uh, I'm not sure. I have to get up early with the girls. I should probably leave no later than ten." He should probably leave no later than *now*, but he didn't want to disappoint Naomi. Apparently she had plans.

Naomi nodded in resignation as if she'd expected his answer. As if ten o'clock was too early but she would have to accept whatever he could give her. "I should have had you patch the leak in my roof first thing, because you can't do it now in the dark without risking a fall. *Ach, vell,* we'll just make the most of the time we have left. I don't wonder but you could come back tomorrow after work if you have some spare time."

She took his gloves and shoved them into a bucket by the back door. "I make jam from my raspberries and put up dozens of jars of salsa and spaghetti sauce every fall. I sell a lot of it at the variety store. Englischers love anything made by the Amish. I'm building shelves in the basement for all the bottles of food I'm planning to can. Ben Kiem made all the measurements for the shelves, and Simeon Beiler cut all the wood. Now I need help putting everything together. Do you know how to use an electric drill? I'm going to build the shelves clear to the ceiling."

It sounded like *Menno*, not Naomi, was going to build her shelves clear to the ceiling. He smiled to himself. She was not inclined to waste one minute of time, hers or anyone else's. He was glad to help, but this was the oddest date he'd ever been on. He glanced quickly at the clock on the wall before she led him down the stairs.

It was nine o'clock. He had an hour, and something told him Naomi would expect a lot of finished shelving by the time he left.

She turned on the battery-operated standing light in the basement. Someone had already started on one set of shelves. She quickly pointed out where all the shelves would eventually go and shoved an electric drill into his hand.

Menno worked as fast as he could, but he'd already weeded Naomi's garden and spent a full day building cabinets. He was beat.

After an hour, he'd completed one level of shelving. It wasn't much, but he was *gute* with his hands, and it would stand as long as the house did. Naomi finally admitted defeat, and they trudged up the stairs together just as her clock struck ten.

She pointed to the kitchen sink. "I need a new faucet, and the drain is slow. The window in my guest room squeaks, my front door sticks, and there's a hole in one of my chairs that needs patching. I suppose those can wait until your next visit."

Would there be a next visit? For sure and certain Naomi wanted him to come again, but she seemed to be interested in Menno less as a husband and more as a handyman. For some reason, the thought made him want to laugh out loud.

He couldn't get out of there fast enough but should probably be polite and at least say goodbye. "*Denki* for the rice pudding. I loved it." He purposefully didn't say anything about coming back tomorrow. He didn't want to promise anything he couldn't deliver, and he had a date with Lydia Herschberger.

Naomi reached out and brushed some sawdust from his shoulder, her eyes dancing as they had when he'd first arrived. "Menno, you are a *gute* man, and you have proven yourself a hard worker. My *mamm* says that's the most important quality a husband can possess. I know you haven't made up your mind, and you have several girls to choose from, but if you decide to ask me to marry you, for sure and certain I will say yes."

Menno woke up with a splitting headache and a sore back. He sat up in bed, the bed sitting in the middle of Esther's quilt shop, and ran his fingers through his hair. How long had it been since he'd had a *gute* night's sleep? Last night he'd been unable to sleep out of sheer shock. He'd actually accomplished what he'd set out to do and in less than three weeks from arriving in Colorado. He'd found someone willing to marry him. So why didn't he feel happiness or satisfaction or even a sense of accomplishment?

He had known the answer before he'd even asked it. He didn't want to marry Naomi Zook, and it wasn't because she had worked him to death yesterday. She was an industrious, sturdy, intelligent woman, with her own house and a green thumb, but she wasn't the one. It was as simple as that.

Did Gotte want Menno to marry Naomi? She was willing and able, and that used to be Menno's only qualifications for a *fraa*. Was he like the lukewarm servant that Gotte threatened to spit out of His mouth?

Soft morning light filtered through the curtains hanging over the only window in Esther's shop. Menno glanced at the little sleeping nook he had made for his girls out of sturdy cardboard boxes. They slept partitioned off from Esther's quilts so they wouldn't touch them, and they could only get out when Menno lifted them from the space in the mornings. Esther had been so kind to let them stay with her. He didn't want her quilts getting dirty.

He got out of bed and gazed at his little angels sleeping peacefully in their little *dollhouse*, as Rosie called it. He was jealous of how easily they could sleep without a care in the world. Surely he would sleep better if he could learn to trust Gotte with his whole heart.

Every morning but Sunday and Monday the cardboard boxes and all their things had to be moved out of the quilt shop. It was open five days a week, and customers came to look at quilts. Few tourists found their way to the San Luis Valley, but the number was growing all the time. Clay Markham, famous pro baseball player, now lived in the valley, and a few curious Colorado Peaks fans stopped by the quilt shop every weekend, probably because Clay had listed Esther's quilt shop as his permanent address. It was sneaky and *gute* for business.

Menno quickly made up the bed in the middle of the room and arranged a pile of quilts on top of it. When people came to look at quilts, Esther would often use the bed as a display to show off the patterns. Rosie and Lily were awake by the time he finished packing his few clothes and toiletries in his travel bag. He helped the girls dress and sent them down the hall to the kitchen. Breakfast smelled *appeditlich*. Wednesday mornings it was buttermilk pancakes with apricot syrup.

Esther truly was an angel sent from heaven. Menno didn't know how he was ever going to repay her for her kindness. Lord willing, Verla Ann would make things easier.

Before heading to breakfast, he took down the girls' cardboard petition, slid the flattened boxes into the back hall, and swept the entire floor. He opened the curtains, dusted the shelves, and tidied the little bathroom Levi had added when he'd built the addition onto the house.

After breakfast, he and Levi were going to lay some pipe for plumbing in the shed where Levi kept the horse and a couple of chickens. Then they were installing cabinets in a house in Alamosa in the afternoon.

Esther set a stack of hot pancakes on the table just as Menno walked into the kitchen. "It smells *wunderbarr*, Esther," he said.

She turned and smiled. A pink-striped straw was tucked behind her ear and two binkies were clipped to her dress at the shoulder. "*Denki*. It's one of my favorite recipes." She poured more batter onto her griddle. "The girls and Junior are already finished, and they went into Winnie's room to help her make her bed and clean her room. We'll see how that turns out." Her smile faded. "I suppose Verla Ann can fix it when she gets here. Levi is already starting on the trench for the water pipe."

Menno helped himself to three pancakes. "I'm sorry I slept in. It was a late night. I'll hurry and finish."

Esther propped her hands on her hips. "Give yourself a minute. You've run around like a headless chicken ever since you got here."

"I want to make myself useful."

"You've made yourself plenty useful, so don't fuss about that. You got home extra late last night. How was Naomi's house?"

Menno caught his bottom lip between his teeth. "It was, uh, fun."

Esther eyed him as if she thought he was lying. "How do you mean *fun*?"

He poured a generous amount of syrup onto his pancakes. "Well, we ate rice pudding, moved hose, fixed trellises, broke dirt clods, weeded the empty garden, and built shelves."

Esther laughed as if that was the funniest thing she'd ever heard. "*Ach*, Menno. I should have warned you, but it's not anything you can prepare for."

Menno narrowed his eyes at Esther. "What do you mean *warned* me?"

She wiped the moisture from her eyes. "Naomi is a dear, dear soul. I love her to pieces, but she is a bit demanding. She can't do all the work herself, so she wheedles free labor out of all the men in the *gmayna*. She's not afraid to ask, and we don't begrudge helping out a neighbor. It just gets to be a bit much sometimes, as if it's an expectation instead of a *gute* deed. At one time or another, every man and woman in the *gmayna* has helped Naomi with a project. Whether it's planting seeds or installing solar panels, she knows how to get work out of people. Levi jokes that she needs eight househusbands just to keep up with all the work she wants done."

Menno stifled a smile. He didn't want Esther to think he was poking fun at Naomi. "I can see that."

"I don't blame her. I can't imagine what it must be like to live alone and be responsible for everything in the household. I'm blessed to have Levi to share the load. Naomi is as smart as a whip. She knows how to get what she needs."

"I admire that quality."

"So do I." She grinned. "In small doses."

They heard the back door open, and Levi came down the hall into the kitchen with a funny look on his face. "Menno, there is someone here to see you."

"Who is it?'

"Go see for yourself. She doesn't want to come in, and she doesn't want anyone to see her so she came around to the back of the house."

"Who is it?"

Levi swiped his hand across his mouth to erase a smile. "Menno, quit asking. Go see."

Menno was more than suspicious. Why was Levi so amused? "My pancakes will get cold."

Levi looked as if he was on the verge of uproarious laughter. "Aren't you curious?"

Menno couldn't say no to that. He reined in his irritation before he did something unnecessary like smack the table and demand Levi quit teasing him. He stood up and ambled down the hall, hearing Levi chuckle behind him. With his curiosity about as high as it could go, he went out the back door. Menno's life was getting stranger and stranger.

And stranger.

Priscilla Weaver stood next to the apricot tree wearing a pastel lavender dress with a crisp white prayer *kapp* and a smear of soft pink lip gloss on her lips. Menno couldn't have been more stunned if Esther had thrown a rotten egg at his head. Priscilla was the only girl he'd crossed off his list, and he'd done that after knowing her for half an hour.

She held a small bouquet of wildflowers tied together with a piece of twine and smiled and batted her long eyelashes when he walked down the back porch steps.

Was she wearing mascara? And did he want to get close enough to find out?

Ach, vell, he couldn't really hold a reasonable conversation from fifteen feet away. Five feet was a *gute* distance. Not too close, but close enough to hear everything she had to say. "*Vie gehts*, Priscilla?"

Priscilla bloomed into a gorgeous smile. "You remembered my name."

How could he forget? She'd made quite an impression on him when he'd met her at the Bent and Dent grocery store. Not a *gute* impression, but an impression just the same.

She gazed at him as if she adored everything about him, and Menno actually glanced behind him to see if maybe she was gushing over someone else. Priscilla just stood staring at him, and she didn't seem inclined to speak.

Menno didn't want to be rude, but his pancakes were getting cold. "Can I help you with something?"

She puckered her shiny pink lips and sighed. "I think I can help *you* with something, Menno. Esther came to me three weeks ago and told me Levi's cousin was coming to town and that he was looking for a *fraa*. She asked me if I was willing to be on the list of possible girlfriends." Priscilla brushed a strand of hair from her face with her graceful hand. "People always want me on their lists. I had five boys interested in me before I turned eighteen. I had a marriage proposal on my nineteenth birthday." More lip puckering. More eyelash batting.

She stood in full view of the kitchen window, and no doubt Esther and Levi were peeking out from between the curtains. What were they thinking? Would one of them have the presence of mind to come out and save him?

"I was reluctant to say yes to being put on Esther's list. Old ladies are always trying to convince me to meet their ugly grandsons or ancient nephews. But Esther's my friend, and I wanted to help her out. You can imagine my surprise when I met you. You aren't old or ugly, and you have a strong jawline. You can always tell about a man by his jawline."

Menno suddenly very much regretted shaving his beard.

A tiny indent marred the space between her eyebrows. "You came to the Bent and Dent to meet me, and you haven't spoken to me since then. I decided you were just being stuck up because of where I work. But Sadie said you're still looking and really serious about finding a *fraa*." Priscilla kept her feet planted and swiveled her body back and forth as if trying to give him a better view of her figure. "So here I am."

Menno stretched a tight smile across his face. "*Ach.* I see." What could he say, without being rude, that would induce her to go away as quickly as possible?

It was obvious Priscilla knew how pretty she was. Menno had only needed minutes at the Bent and Dent to figure that out. She held herself like a princess and strutted like a peacock. But Menno didn't like princesses or peacocks, and he had no patience for people who thought they were better than everyone else. Priscilla was close to thirty, and he didn't want to be uncharitable, but he knew the reason she wasn't married yet. She fancied herself superior to just about everyone in the San Luis Valley, most especially the boys.

Did she think Menno was worthy of her?

He sincerely hoped not.

"It wonders me if you're too shy," Priscilla said. "Most

boys are too bashful to even ask me on a buggy ride. They don't think they're *gute* enough, and most of them aren't." She stepped forward and handed him her bouquet of flowers, her eyes shining like stars. "Menno, I'm willing to move to Idaho and be your *fraa*. Will you marry me?"

He swallowed down the wrong throat. He fisted his hand and covered his mouth and coughed and coughed like a barking coyote. Priscilla watched him in alarm, her eyes getting wider and wider the longer he coughed.

Was she offended or concerned?

Menno held a finger in the air, giving her the *just a minute* signal then doubled over and coughed some more.

She sidled closer to him and slapped him on the back a few times, trying to help him dislodge the stone she must have thought he was choking on. He took a deep breath and finally got control of himself, even though he had no idea what he was going to say to her. She'd just proposed to him, and though he had no intention of saying yes, he felt sorry for her. It took an immense amount of courage to propose to someone, even if you were Priscilla and had enough confidence to fill a wagon.

"Priscilla, I'm flattered. I truly am."

She stuck out her shiny bottom lip. Flattery was looked down on by the Amish. It meant an appeal to someone's vanity, and vanity was the next-door neighbor to idolatry. "I didn't set out to flatter you. I'm trying to help you out. We only live to help our fellow man." She certainly had an expansive view of helping her fellow man, if agreeing to marry someone was akin to helping someone plow his fields or doing the dishes after supper.

If he said no, would he regret it later? Was Priscilla the only girl who would say yes in the end? *Ach, vell,* Naomi told him that she would say yes, but should he keep his options open? Would he rather marry Naomi or Priscilla?

Neither.

He had been silent for too long. He covered his hesitation with another cough, and Priscilla flinched, as if afraid she'd have to give him CPR. "I appreciate the proposal, Priscilla. But I can't tell you yes until I meet with all the other girls on my list. I'm still deciding." An unpleasant realization punched him in the gut, and he finally had ears to hear himself. He sounded like he was picking a pumpkin or a can of corn, not a *fraa*. No wonder Joanna had refused him. If he had been Priscilla, he would have squared his shoulders and marched away, hopefully with his dignity still intact.

Was this what Joanna had felt like? Had his proposal humiliated and embarrassed her? Had he been so wrapped up in his list that he'd hurt her feelings?

Of course he had.

Priscilla tilted her head as her brows inched together in confusion. "Well . . . who else is on your list?"

He could hear Joanna's voice in his head. *Who else is on your list? Four other cans of corn, that's who.* "It's not important."

"I'd say it's very important since you're going to marry one of us. I'd like to know who the competition is."

He cleared his throat. "I don't think you can call it a competition. I'm looking at Sadie, Lydia Herschberger, Naomi Zook, and Verla Ann Miller," he said, and it truly did sound like he was reciting a grocery list. His face got warm, especially since it felt like a lie. If he was honest with himself, he didn't want to marry any of them, and he was realizing just how much he wanted the one not on his list.

Priscilla's confusion seemed to deepen. "I don't mean to be rude, but I'm prettier than all of them. Naomi is old, and Lydia has a speech impediment."

"I'm . . . I'm . . . 'the Lord looketh on the heart.'"

To his surprise, Priscilla laughed. "I guess He does, but every man wants a pretty *fraa*, whether he will admit it or not."

Menno wanted to say, "Pretty is as pretty does," but that was rude and wouldn't change how he or Priscilla felt. "There are more important things than being pretty."

"I'm a better cook than Verla Ann, and Sadie has a cell phone and giggles all the time. I have never had a cavity, and I know how to sing harmony. I once grew a three-hundred-pound pumpkin that I displayed at the county fair. The newspaper came."

Menno couldn't begrudge Priscilla her list of accomplishments. He was fond of lists, but he was just beginning to see how useless and hurtful they could be. "I'm still looking around, Priscilla. I can't explain it more clearly than that."

It was obvious she didn't like his answer. She frowned with her whole face and narrowed her eyes into slits. Even the flowers in her hand seemed to droop. "I got all dressed up for you, Menno Eicher. You have a lot of nerve, thinking you can keep me waiting indefinitely while you go off gallivanting around the town."

Menno had no idea what *gallivanting* meant, but it sounded painful. It also made her sound incredibly intelligent. He liked intelligent women, but he didn't like snobby ones. He would definitely marry Naomi above Priscilla. Naomi would work him to death, but if Priscilla were his *fraa*, he'd feel the need to apologize to all the neighbors.

"I'm sorry, Priscilla. It's probably best not to expect

anything from me. I don't think you and I will ever marry. It's plain we wouldn't suit, and you don't like gallivanters." He didn't know if that was a word, but it sounded impressive and hard to argue with.

"For sure and certain I don't like gallivanters." She threw her flowers on the ground, and a tiny sob escaped her lips. "From the very beginning I thought your list was silly and rude, as if you thought of us girls as different pairs of shoes waiting to be bought at the store. But I wanted to do Esther a favor. I shouldn't have let her put me on the list."

Menno felt bad that Priscilla was upset, but he felt even worse that he had ever made a list. "I'm sorry if I've hurt your feelings, Priscilla."

She, who just moments before had seemed on the verge of crying, sucked in a breath and straightened herself to her full height. "You haven't hurt my feelings. A man like you is not worth the water in my tears. Don't you even care how pretty I am? Don't you even care that I spent eight dollars on lip gloss? It took me an hour to pick wildflowers, and I even ironed my dress because I thought you would like it. Thank Derr Herr I didn't paint my fingernails like Ruthie told me to. Dat would not have approved."

"For what it's worth, I wouldn't have approved either."

She held up her hand to stop him. "I don't really care what you have to say."

Menno gave up trying to make her feel better or trying to explain himself. He deserved her lecture. He'd made a mistake with that list, and she'd spent eight dollars on lip gloss. She had every right to give full vent to her emotions.

He heard the back door open and close and glanced behind him to see Esther ambling across the lawn. "Priscilla, how pretty you look! Won't you come in and have some pancakes?" She had a plastic knife behind her ear and a small bottle of maple syrup in her hand, as if she'd come outside so fast, she hadn't had time to put it down. "And is that lip gloss? My, it's a beautiful color."

Priscilla obviously wasn't in any mood for friendly conversation, but she attempted to be polite. "*Denki*. It's Pink Sunrise, and it was eight dollars. I bought it for special occasions. You're welcome to use it any time you want. You're my dear friend, and dear friends do favors for each other, even if they don't want to." She glared at Menno. "Even if people are rude and don't care about cavities."

Menno almost raised his hand to mention that he cared about cavities but didn't want to get into a debate about dental hygiene.

Esther stayed calm and expressionless, even though she was probably wondering what cavities had to do with lip gloss or Menno. "So. Would you like a stack of pancakes?"

Priscilla stuck her nose in the air. "I wouldn't eat pancakes if Menno were the last man on earth," she said, as if delivering the ultimate insult. She kicked the bunch of flowers at her feet, and they sailed into the air and hit the side of Esther's house.

Priscilla had a *gute* foot. She should put that on her list of talents.

The back door opened, and Winnie, Rosie, Lily, and Junior burst out of the house. Lily, Rosie, and Winnie ran down the steps while Junior turned around and crawled down, putting himself far behind the others. Lily and Rosie ran at Menno full speed, and he scooped them into his arms, glad for the distraction since Priscilla was scowling at him. Winnie hugged her *mamm* and motioned for the other two girls to follow her. Menno set them on their feet, and they gathered Junior, linked hands, and made a circle around the trunk of the apricot tree.

Menno's heart lurched when Verla Ann followed *die kinner* out of the house. He was standing there with Priscilla as if they were having a secret meeting. What would Verla Ann think?

"Rosie, Lily, you naughty girls," Verla Ann scolded as she marched down the stairs. "Don't go outside again unless you ask me first." She stopped short when she saw Menno. "*Ach*, I didn't know you were still here." Her eyes nearly popped out of her head when she caught sight of Priscilla.

Priscilla folded her arms and narrowed her eyes. "What are you doing here?"

Verla Ann's spine stiffened so fast, Menno could almost hear it snap into place. "I'm babysitting Menno's *dochters*. What are you doing here?"

"Aren't you supposed to be in school?" Priscilla wanted to know.

"Aren't you supposed to be at the Bent and Dent?" Verla Ann replied.

Rosie found Priscilla's flowers. She waved them over her head, then plucked the blossoms off each stem one by one. Priscilla gasped, chased Rosie around the yard, and grabbed them away from her. Priscilla may have kicked her flowers across the yard, but apparently, she still wanted them.

Surprise popped all over Rosie's face, then she screamed as if Priscilla had stolen her favorite blanket instead of a bunch of wildflowers.

Menno didn't like that Priscilla had yanked a bouquet of discarded flowers away from his three-year-old *dochter*. "There's no need to be rude. All you have to do is ask nicely." He squatted next to Rosie and put his arm around her shoulder, even though that brought his ear dangerously close to Rosie's mouth. Hearing aids. He was definitely going to need hearing aids within a decade.

"Ask nicely?" Priscilla said, the indignation rising off her skin like a bad smell. "How dare you tell me to ask nicely? I asked very nicely, and you treated me like an idiot."

She probably meant that he was an idiot, not that she was one. Menno bit down on his tongue so he wouldn't laugh.

Rosie was screaming, so naturally, Lily had to cry too. Junior toddled across the lawn to see what was wrong with Lily, fell flat on his face, and started wailing. Esther ran to Junior and picked him up. A dribble of blood seeped from his bottom lip. Naturally, Winnie screamed because of the blood. Verla Ann tried to talk Lily out of crying, and Priscilla's gaze flicked from Verla Ann to her wounded bouquet of wildflowers.

Levi came out the back door carrying a toolbox and a pair of work gloves. He took one look at the chaos of the backyard and tiptoed back into the house.

Suddenly, Cathy Larsen came around the side of the house. Looking unruffled, she pulled a sucker out of her huge purse and handed it to Rosie. "Who wants a sucker?" she said.

"I do!" Winnie forgot what she was crying about and skipped to Cathy to get her treat. Lily did the same.

"No suckers," Verla Ann shouted. "They've just had breakfast."

Everyone, including Cathy, ignored Verla Ann. Menno didn't mind if Cathy passed out suckers. Rosie had descended into blessed silence.

Cathy handed Junior, still in his *mater*'s arms, a green

sucker. Cathy puckered her wrinkled lips and cooed at Junior. "Poor little thing. It looks like you cut your lip."

Junior whimpered softly, but he seemed to forget all about his fall when he popped the sucker into his mouth.

"You shouldn't use sugar as a bribe," Verla Ann said.

"Sometimes a bribe is absolutely necessary." Cathy popped a sucker into her own mouth. "Do you want one, Esther?"

"Sure."

Cathy gave Esther a sucker, and Esther tucked it behind her other ear for safekeeping. Now she had a plastic knife on one ear and a sucker on the other. She was prepared for just about anything.

Cathy half shut one eye and looked at Priscilla. "I don't know you, but do you want a sucker?"

Priscilla didn't say anything, but she held out her hand, and Cathy gave her a pink one. Priscilla ripped off the paper and stuck the sucker in her mouth, then tossed what was left of her wildflower bouquet on the ground and stormed away. Lord willing she could have a *gute* life and get her money back for that lip gloss.

Cathy eyed Verla Ann, who was glaring resentfully at her, obviously annoyed that she was handing out suckers to innocent children. "Can I tempt you with a purple one, Verla Ann? Grape is the best flavor."

Verla Ann twisted her lips into a pout. "*Nae, denki.* You might as well be handing out cavities."

Menno sincerely hoped Priscilla wouldn't get a cavity from her sucker. It would break her perfect teeth record.

Rosie pointed to Menno. "Daddy needs a sucker."

Cathy paused and looked at Menno as if she hadn't noticed him standing there. "Your daddy doesn't deserve a sucker. He has to prove himself first."

Menno's mouth fell open. "What do you mean by that?"

"You have a long list of faults, Menno Eicher, most of them involving Joanna Yoder, and I don't have time to sort them all out right now."

Verla Ann narrowed her eyes. "What about Joanna Yoder?"

"What about Joanna Yoder?" Menno repeated.

Cathy threw her sucker wrapper back into her purse. "I've been watching you, and it's been surprisingly entertaining having you here in Colorado. I like watching the acrobatics you've done to work through that list of yours."

"Acrobatics?"

"You dance and squirm trying to make that list conform to God's will, as if you can do your duty by making a check mark." As she studied his face, there was disapproval in her eyes and maybe something akin to kindness. "You can't nicely fit people into a set of plans or write them down on a list and expect them to do what you want. People don't work that way. *God* doesn't work that way. As soon as you learn that, you'll earn a sucker. Don't disappoint me."

Chapter 10

Menno was still smarting about not getting a sucker when he rode Levi's bike to Lydia's house that evening. Cathy was in her eighties, so she had a lot of experience and had probably gathered some wisdom along the way, but maybe she didn't know as much as she thought she did.

She'd told him he couldn't write things down on a list and then expect people to do what he wanted. She said that wasn't how Gotte worked.

But it was exactly how Gotte worked. Gotte made lists all the time. What were the Ten Commandments but a list? What was the Sermon on the Mount but a list?

Cathy had said Menno couldn't make people fit nicely into a set of plans, but he'd already had one woman tell him she was willing to marry him, and Priscilla had out-right proposed. It seemed like his plans were coming to-gether even better than he could have hoped.

His heart felt like an icy lump of coal. The only person who'd refused to fit nicely into his plan was Joanna. She had been at the top of his list from the very beginning, but since she had refused him, he was forced to find women who were willing to go along with the plan. So far, he'd been wildly successful and completely miserable.

He'd come home from work this afternoon and eaten dinner with Esther, Levi, Verla Ann, and *die kinner*. Esther said she'd put the girls to bed so Menno could go on yet another date.

He hated missing so much time with his *dochters*, but with a little more than a week left, he could only concentrate on the task at hand. He would make it up to them after he'd checked *finding a fraa* off his list. In the meantime, his girls would be okay. They'd be even better when he found them a *mater*. All this time away from them was for a greater purpose.

He sure could have used a sucker right then to clear his head.

Menno leaned his bike against the scrubby tree in front of Lydia's house then knocked on the front door. Lydia lived with her parents and seven siblings on an expansive, immaculate property with a ranch house, two large barns, and three storage sheds. Each building had yellow siding and white trim, and there wasn't a piece of sagebrush to be found on the whole place. He counted seven horses, three buggies, and several solar panels. The Herschbergers were well-off for Amish folk.

Lydia answered the door wearing a baby pink dress and a shy smile. Her *mamm* and *dat* and three siblings stood behind her, gazing out the door expectantly, as if Menno was the most interesting thing they'd seen in their entire lives. Lydia was in her early thirties, but she seemed much younger. She had silky brown hair and wide hazel eyes that made it look as if she were permanently surprised. She had a round face and a flawless, creamy complexion.

She talked with a slight lisp, reinforcing the illusion of extreme youth. "Menno Eicher, we've been expecting you. Please come in."

Lydia's *mamm* and a younger *schwester* giggled softly.

"*Jah*," her *mamm* said. "We've been expecting you."

Menno suddenly felt very awkward. They were looking at him like an item in a museum display case.

Lydia pointed to her family members crowded into the entryway. "This is my *dat*, Gary, my *mamm*, Eva, my *schwesteren* Fern and Millie, and my *bruder* Enos. I'm the oldest by twelve years, then *Mamm* and *Dat* suddenly started having all these kids."

Eva giggled again, her face turning bright red. "*Ach*, Lydia, Menno doesn't need to know all that. We sound like a pair of rabbits."

Lydia joined her *mater* in the giggling. "You do not, Mamm. Menno has two children. He understands about these things." She turned and smiled sweetly at Menno. "Do you want to see my stuffed animals?"

"Okay," he said, trying not to sound hesitant.

Esther had told him that Lydia wanted her stuffed animals moved to Idaho if they married. He was willing to do it, of course, but it seemed like a strange request. How attached was she to her toys?

Lydia led the way down the long hall to her bedroom, with Menno, Eva, Gary, Millie, Fern, and Enos following close behind. It felt like a parade.

Nothing could have prepared Menno for the sight that met him in Lydia's room. It looked as if a fur factory had exploded. Floor to ceiling shelves covered one whole wall of the room. Naomi Zook would have gone head over heels for all that shelving. Each shelf was laden with an impossible number of stuffed animals of all kinds. There were all sizes and colors of teddy bears: white, brown, black, pink, fluorescent green, multi-colored. Some had bows around their necks, others held purses or flowers or stuffed hearts. There was every imaginable kind of zoo animal and some creatures that Menno couldn't name. All shapes, all sizes, all colors.

In another corner of the room sat a pile of stuffed animals, six feet high and three feet deep. If Menno pulled one from the bottom of the pile, the whole thing would collapse and bury him in an avalanche of fluffiness. He'd never seen anything like it.

Eva nudged Lydia's arm. "Show him your Beanie Babies."

Lydia pulled a long, shallow box from under one of the twin beds, placed it on the bed, and opened it. Inside were dozens of smaller animals, each with a heart-shaped tag attached. "These are my Beanie Babies. Some of them are worth hundreds of dollars as collectibles. Of course, I would never sell them, unless my family was starving to death and I needed the money for food."

Millie reached out to touch one, and Lydia squeaked her disapproval. "Please don't touch them. They lose their value if they have handprints on them."

Menno wasn't sure how a handprint would show up on a furry stuffed animal, but Lydia obviously knew more about these things than he did. How would Lydia react if they were married and Rosie wanted to hold one of her bears? Would he have to dedicate a padlocked room to Lydia's stuffed animals? Did he have the space?

Ach, *vell*, at least Lydia came with some financial security. They would never starve as long as they had a Beanie Baby to sell.

Lydia and her family gazed lovingly into her box for a few minutes before Lydia closed the lid and slid the valuables back under the bed. She stood up straight and brushed her hands down her dress. "Should we have some pie?"

"How fun!" Eva squeaked. "We've got cherry pie and ice cream."

Menno tried to act excited about cherry pie, but Lydia's stuffed animal collection had thrown cold water on his enthusiasm for anything, not to mention the fact that her family was still eyeing him like a circus performer. "I love cherry pie," he said, forcing some lilt into his voice.

"We know," Eva said. "Joanna told us."

Menno's heart leaped out of his chest. "Joanna told you?"

Lydia nodded. "I asked Joanna what I should make for our date. She says cherry pie is your favorite."

Eva's eyes twinkled. "Lydia made it herself."

"I helped with the crust," Millie offered.

"And Millie helped with the crust," Eva said. "Lydia made the ice cream too. We have a solar-powered ice cream maker. Benny rigged it up for us."

Gary motioned down the hall. "Benny is our inventor. He's in the barn tinkering with the harrow. It's got three broken tines. We took it out last week, and the ground is still fairly hard."

"He invented a door for our chicken coop to keep dogs and coyotes out," Eva said.

"Fern and I made the cookies," Millie said. "They're molasses crinkles. Dat's favorite."

Menno soon realized that he didn't have to speak a word. The Herschbergers were talkative and enthusiastic about their farm, their family, and their interesting lives. All he had to do was nod occasionally and raise his eyebrows in surprise, and they were perfectly happy to talk.

Like a flock of sheep, they moved into the great room with a huge kitchen and a large open space perfect for church services. Eva invited Menno to sit on the couch. Lydia plopped next to him and grinned as if she'd just done something reckless. Menno didn't mind. He was here for a date, and he needed to decide if Lydia would make a *gute fraa*.

She smelled like baby powder. Did he like baby powder? Joanna smelled like sugar and cinnamon or sometimes a fresh spring morning or a rich cup of *kaffee*. She just . . . she just always smelled perfect. Menno drew in a deep breath.

"What about in Idaho?"

Menno snapped out of whatever daydream had absorbed him. "Uh, what was that?"

Gary leaned forward. "I said, do you use solar panels in Idaho?"

"There aren't enough sunny days to make it worth the money."

"We get lots of sun here in the San Luis Valley. It's about the only thing that there's plenty of. Water is scarce and so are trees and Amish people."

Fern and Millie served pie and vanilla ice cream to everyone. Menno felt full just looking at his plate. They'd given him at least a fourth of the whole pie and two huge scoops of ice cream. Would he be too stuffed to pedal home after the date?

Everyone stared at him in anticipation when he took a bite of his pie.

Ugh, could things get any more uncomfortable? He closed his eyes as if savoring his bite and groaned with pleasure. It was maybe a bit of a performance, but it was obvious what the Herschbergers expected. They all smiled as if none of them had ever been so happy.

"It's wonderful *gute*. Just the right combination of sweet and tart, and the crust is so flaky. How do you get your crust so flaky?"

Lydia smiled coyly and looked at him from under her

eyelashes. "It's my own secret recipe. Nobody knows how to make it but me."

Eva beamed at Menno. "She hasn't even told me. Lydia's husband is going to be the luckiest man in the world, to get that *appeditlich* crust whenever he wants. You haven't tasted anything as delicious as Lydia's chicken pot pie."

Gary took a bite. "And Lydia don't just make pie. She's the only girl I know in the valley who makes yummasetti."

"With a whole stick of butter," Lydia said.

Enos smacked his lips. "I like butter."

Gary wasn't finished. "She also makes melt-in-your-mouth butter chicken and butternut squash soup. Friends ask specifically for her butter cookies when they're sick."

Menno was sensing a theme here. The Herschbergers were a family that appreciated butter. "It all sounds *appeditlich*."

Eva patted her husband on the arm. "Now, Gary, life isn't all about food. Lydia has so many talents, it's hard to list them all. Her quilting stitches are the smallest in the valley, she sews all her own clothes, and she loves children. She taught my baby nephew how to use a spoon. And she reads her Bible every day."

It might have been hard to list all Lydia's talents, but Eva was doing a pretty *gute* job of it. Menno tried to nod in all the right places, but all he could think about was how Joanna hated spiders and the way her nose crinkled after Ada mopped the floor. Joanna hated the smell of Pine-Sol, and Ada insisted on using nothing else.

Joanna would have taken pity on him and given him a sucker this morning. She sneaked suckers and fruit snacks to Rosie and Lily when she thought he wasn't looking, and she couldn't resist running the back of her finger down Lily's soft cheek whenever she got a chance. As far as he knew, Joanna had never taught anyone to use a spoon, but that wasn't all that high on his priority list. Kindness was high on his list, as was *gute* humor, courage, a bright mind, and a strong will. Joanna had everything he wanted.

Menno wanted to kick himself for not telling her so when he had the chance.

They were all looking at him again, and he realized someone had asked him a question. How long had it been since he'd stopped paying attention? He leaned forward. "Come again?"

Gary drew his brows together then spoke loudly and slowly. "I said, how old are your *dochters*?"

Menno sat up straighter. "Rosie is three, and Lily just turned two."

Eva seemed delighted. "Lydia can teach them to talk."

"Um, they both already talk quite well. Lily knows at least thirty words, and she's a little parrot to Rosie. And she understands everything I say."

Eva's smile lost its luster. "*Ach*, *vell*, I'm sure Lydia would still be a great help as a tutor."

Did children need tutoring on how to talk? It seemed to just come naturally, like learning how to walk or feed yourself. Lily had learned several new words in just two short weeks at Joanna's house. She'd learned the names of the dog and all the goats. He smiled to himself. She called Joanna "JoJo." He loved how Joanna lit up like a lantern whenever Lily tried her name.

". . . it must be hard."

Menno sprouted a sheepish smile. He needed to quit thinking of Joanna and pay attention. "What was that?"

Gary narrowed his eyes. "Are you losing your hearing?"

Menno cleared his throat. "Not that I know of."

"You don't seem to hear very well. Either that or you're not listening." Gary's gaze intensified.

Eva didn't lose her smile, but she gave her husband a look that silenced him right quick. "I guess what I'm trying to say is that it must be hard rearing two little girls all by yourself. You need a partner. You need a helpmeet."

Gary nodded. "'It's not *gute* for man to be alone.'"

Menno's thoughts exactly, but it was also not *gute* for a man to be with the wrong woman. He was beginning to realize finding a *fraa* wasn't like picking a can of corn from the shelf.

Eva set her plate on the floor at her feet and propped her elbows on her knees. "Lydia would make you a fine *fraa*. How about it? Do you want to marry her?"

The proposal hit Menno right between the eyes, but luckily he'd just swallowed a bite and had nothing to choke on. He was glad not to repeat his earlier coughing fit. His gaze connected with Lydia's. She smiled and simpered and looked as if she would burst her buttons with excitement. It was a *gute* thing she didn't have any buttons.

Menno was struck dumb. He'd been proposed to twice in the span of ten hours. It was the strangest day of his entire life.

Lydia nibbled on her bottom lip. "I'll give each of your girls one of my Beanie Babies as a wedding present."

A Beanie Baby wasn't quite the inducement Lydia obviously thought it was because he could go buy a Beanie Baby for much less trouble than getting married.

Everybody was looking at him again. He would have to screw up his courage and speak, or Gary would think he was deaf and Lydia would think he didn't want to marry her. *Ach*, *vell*, he didn't want to marry her, but the longer he was silent, the more likely it was she'd get her feelings hurt.

"Lydia—" or should he talk to Eva? She was the one

who had proposed. "Lydia and Eva, I am flattered—"
Nope. Priscilla had found that word offensive, and he'd
rather offend as little as possible. "I mean, Eva, I'm hon-
ored that you want me to marry your *dochter*—or rather,
it's a high compliment that you would choose me out of all
the men in the valley—"

"There aren't that many single men in the valley," Enos
interjected.

Menno pretended he didn't hear, which wasn't too hard
to pull off since Gary thought he was deaf anyway. "I'll
keep your very generous proposal in mind, but I am not
ready to settle on a specific woman just yet." He felt kind
of bad for that half-truth. But was it really a half truth?

He wanted to settle on Joanna, but she didn't want him,
so it probably wasn't a half-truth after all. Was there any
man as pathetic as he was?

They stared at him as if he'd grown antlers, Eva with
that serene smile on her face, Lydia with her bottom lip between her teeth, Gary with his head tilted to one side, probably wondering if Menno had heard the question at all.

Menno shifted on the couch and cleared his throat. "I
haven't decided yet, but you are definitely in the running.
That pie was delicious." It sounded horrible, even to him.

Lydia stretched a smile across her face. "You take all
the time you need. I'm not one to rush Gotte's timing."

"But don't you have to be back in Idaho next week?"
Gary said.

Menno casually took a bite of ice cream. "I still have a
week."

"A week?" Gary said, as if it was the lamest excuse in
the world.

It was.

Menno stuffed the rest of his giant piece of pie into his

mouth and chewed vigorously. "I"—chew, chew, chew— "I really should"—chew, chew, swallow. "I should be going. It's a long ride home, and I've got to be up early with the girls." Feeling as if he'd just swallowed a whole cow, he set his empty plate on the side table and shot to his feet as if the house was on fire.

Eva and Lydia shot to their feet as well and shepherded him to the door, all the while cooing and simpering as if he was the bishop or an apostle or something.

"Come back anytime you want," Eva said.

Lydia nodded. "If you come back tomorrow night, I'll make a batch of cherry fry pies."

It was the wrong thing to say. Fry pies reminded Menno of Joanna, and he was trying not to make comparisons. Of course, everything reminded him of Joanna. How could Lydia have known? "I can't come back tomorrow. I have a date with Sadie Sensenig."

If Lydia's jaw hadn't been attached to her face, it would have fallen on the floor. "Sadie? But she told me—" Lydia balled her hands into fists and stomped her foot. "Don't believe a word Sadie says. She's only in it for herself."

Menno had no idea what Lydia was talking about, and he really didn't want to find out. "It's been fun. *Denki* for the pie and ice cream. They were delectable."

Delectable? That was a fancy word, but he instinctively knew he needed something grand to placate Lydia and her *mater*.

Lydia's face transformed immediately. She gave Menno a wide, doe-eyed smile. "*Ach*, Menno, you are the sweetest boy in the world. I just adore you."

"Uh, *vell*, *denki*. Lord willing I'll see you again soon."

He shouldn't have said that because he wasn't really looking forward to seeing Lydia again ever. Not that she wasn't a pleasant sort of girl, but Joanna had ruined him for everyone else. He growled inwardly. He'd have to get over this fascination with Joanna if he had any chance of choosing a *fraa* in the next seven days.

Surely he had enough willpower to resist Joanna Yoder.

Chapter 11

Menno's deep sigh rattled his whole body. He had two more dates to go, and he seriously didn't know if he could stand it much longer. He parked Levi's bike against Sadie's house and waved to Freeman, Sadie's *bruder*, who was planting in the vast field that surrounded the house and barn on three sides. Sadie's family grew potatoes while most other Amish families in the area grew alfalfa and raised sheep. According to Freeman, the San Luis Valley was an ideal place to grow potatoes. It had that in common with the entire state of Idaho. Menno could see himself growing potatoes if he ever moved to Byler.

Why would he move to Byler?

He knocked on the door, and Sadie answered, a wide smile on her face and a cell phone in her hand. "You're just in time! Enos and Millie will be here any minute."

Menno sucked in a breath. "Enos and Millie Herschberger?" Lydia's *bruder* and *schwester*? Whose *mater* had proposed to him just last night?

Sadie tapped her thumbs on her phone screen in rapid succession. "Everybody will be there at six. Enos is picking us up."

"I'm sorry. What's going on?"

Sadie glanced up from her phone and gave him a look of puzzlement. "You asked if you could come over, and I'm assuming you meant a date."

"That is what I meant."

Her eyes flashed with amusement. "*Gute.* I wanted an exciting date, not one of those nights where you eat cake and sit staring at each other. *Die youngie* are gathering at the park to watch the sunset and go ice blocking. I thought that sounded like a fun date."

Die youngie? Menno didn't want to do anything with *die youngie*. He was a twenty-eight-year-old widower with two small daughters and a farm to care for. "Um, what is ice blocking?"

Sadie looked horrified. "You don't know what ice blocking is?"

Menno shook his head.

"You get blocks of ice from the grocery store, take off the plastic, and put a towel over the top. Then you sit on the block and ride it down the hill. It's like sledding where you bring your own snow. It hurts your tailbone, but the pain is so worth it."

Menno couldn't think of anything he'd rather do less. "I didn't bring any ice."

Sadie tapped on her phone again. "Don't worry about that. Vernon Kanagy is bringing ice for everybody. Do you have four dollars?"

"Four dollars?"

"To pay Vernon for your ice."

Menno searched his pocket. He had a ten-dollar bill and one twenty. "Does Vernon make change?"

Sadie stuffed her phone into her apron pocket but immediately pulled it out again. "Don't worry about it. You can pay for mine too."

Menno gazed down the road, dreading the appearance of the Herschbergers' buggy. "I don't know if Enos and Millie are going to be happy to see me."

"Why? Did you offend Lydia last night?"

"How did you know about that?"

Sadie stared at her phone and grinned absentmindedly, as if she was just barely holding in her mirth. "You set up four dates at church on Sunday. Naomi was Tuesday, Lydia was Wednesday, I'm tonight, and Verla Ann is on Friday. If you followed the schedule, you went to Lydia's house last night."

"I don't think I offended her, but she proposed, and I just couldn't say yes when I still had two dates left . . ."

Sadie looked up from her phone as her eyebrows nearly flew off her forehead. "She proposed?"

Menno really didn't want to talk about it, but he'd let slip too much already. "I guess it was her *mamm* who proposed on Lydia's behalf. Enos and Millie were there. They didn't say anything, but I don't think I gave them the answer they were hoping for."

Sadie waved her phone in his direction. "*Ach*, they don't care. You've got forty girls on your list. They shouldn't expect you to fall in love with Lydia on the first date."

"I don't have forty girls on my list."

Sadie went back to examining her phone. "It's just an expression. You know, when they use the number forty in the Bible, they mean a lot or many."

Menno paused long enough to be impressed. He knew that fact about the number forty, but it was quite unexpected that Sadie knew it. "It's an exaggeration. I've only got four girls on my list."

"Five," Sadie said.

Menno frowned. "Five? Did Cathy tell you about Priscilla?"

Sadie's head snapped up, and she dropped her phone. "What?" she shouted.

Menno took a step back. "You said *five*."

Sadie picked up her phone and brushed the dust off the screen. "Joanna is number five, Menno. Not Priscilla. What happened with Priscilla?"

He pressed his lips together and took another step back. Sadie thought Joanna was number five?

Fire leapt into Sadie's eyes. "So help me, if Priscilla messes up my plan—" She seemed to think better of whatever she was about to say and smiled sweetly as if she hadn't just yelled at him. "You might as well tell me, because I'm very curious, and if I don't hear it from you, I'll march right over to the Bent and Dent in the morning and ask Priscilla to tell me everything."

"We aren't supposed to gossip."

Sadie snorted with laughter. "We Amish live to gossip. Do you want me to hear your version of the story or Priscilla's?"

Menno huffed out a frustrated breath. "Priscilla came over yesterday morning. She wore eight dollars of lip gloss and asked me to marry her."

For the first time since he had known her, Sadie was completely speechless. Her eyes were as round as dinner plates as she opened her mouth then closed it again. She looked a little like a fish gasping for water, but he would never tell her that. It didn't seem like a very nice thing to say.

She finally found her voice. "Did you . . . did you tell her yes?" She said *yes* as if it were the vilest word in the whole dictionary.

Menno pressed his fingers to his forehead. This was the strangest, most uncomfortable conversation he'd ever had, and he'd had some strange ones in the last week. "What do you think?"

Sadie was offended at the very question. "I know what I think, but I have to ask just in case you've gone crazy all of a sudden."

He refused to speak ill of anyone. "Priscilla is a sweet girl, but—"

Sadie snorted again. It was a very unattractive sound. Did he want to marry a girl who made rude noises?

"Priscilla is a sweet girl," Menno continued, "but I am not the man for her."

Sadie formed her lips into an *O*. "I bet she was pretty mad."

"It's not for me to say. I hope we parted on *gute* terms."

More snorting. "For sure and certain you did." Sadie eyed Menno with a tiny hint of respect in her expression. "You're more popular than even I could have imagined, but it all seems to be working out." She tapped on her phone again. "So Lydia and Priscilla want to marry you, but you couldn't say yes, huh?" Her tone was smug. "Why not?"

Menno had been asking himself the same question ever since Naomi said she was willing to marry him. What was the matter with him? Was Gotte wondering the same thing? "I want to go through everyone on my list just to be sure I choose the right woman."

"That is not the reason, and you know it."

He tried to hide his surprise at her attitude. "I don't know anything, Sadie."

Her expression was a mixture of innocence and deviousness. "I thought you didn't care who it was as long as you found somebody willing to say yes."

"I never said that."

She eyed him skeptically. "But you were thinking it. That is, until you met Joanna. Then you suddenly got picky."

Anger and hurt bubbled up inside him. Why did Sadie think she could be his judge? "Joanna said *nae*."

"Why does that have to be the final answer?"

Sadie was immature and aggravating, but she was making Menno doubt himself even more than he already did. "Because Gotte wants me to find a *fraa*, and I have less than a week left."

"You're putting a lot of pressure on yourself, when all you have to do is pick from one of several options and move forward." Sadie's lips twitched upward. "You're no fun to tease, Menno. So serious all the time."

"I'm serious about finding a *fraa*," he replied resentfully.

Sadie pressed a button on her phone and once again slid it into her pocket. She folded her arms and looked at him, utterly exasperated. "Okay, then, let me make it easy on you. If you ask me to marry you, I'll say yes."

She might as well have hit him over the head with a garden hoe. "You will?"

"For the proposal, I want a bouquet of red roses and a box of chocolates. But not the chocolates with weird pink and green fillings. I want the *gute* kind with nuts and caramel and coconut. Do you know the kind I'm talking about? In the hunter green box with gold lettering."

Menno held his breath as a wave of nausea hit him. He didn't know if the inclination to pass out or throw up was stronger.

Once again, Sadie pulled her phone out of her apron pocket and tapped on the screen with her thumbs. "What could be keeping Enos and Millie? The ice is going to melt."

Chapter 12

This was a very, very, very bad idea, and Joanna had known it from the moment Esther had suggested it three days ago. But she also really, really, really wanted to see Menno, if even from a distance. He was leaving for Idaho in less than a week, might very well be engaged by then, and would be strictly off-limits to Joanna's daydreams. She was like a thirsty woman who needed one more drink of water before heading into the desert.

It was still a very bad idea.

Then again, it wasn't just about Menno. Tonight she would get to spend some time with Rosie and Lily, and she missed them almost as much as she missed him. She missed Rosie's ear-piercing scream and Lily's aversion to dirt. She missed sticky hands and the sticky kisses and passing out Band-Aids on a daily basis. She missed the way Lily silently observed everything and seemed wise beyond her years. She missed Rosie's enthusiasm for goats and chocolate chip cookies. And she missed their *dat* like she missed the sunshine on a wintry day.

Joanna stood by the mailbox and gazed down the road. Cathy would be there any minute, and Joanna was going to get a lecture about her quilt square and how she shouldn't have picked the Sugar Bowl quilt block because now she'd brought an unnecessary amount of trouble and tribulation to Byler. She'd heard that lecture twice from Cathy already, and she just didn't want to hear it again.

Cathy drove her van down the road, made a U-turn, and stopped right in front of Joanna's mailbox. Joanna climbed into the passenger seat and buckled herself in.

"I can't believe you're doing this," Cathy said as she put her van into DRIVE and sped up the road.

"It's nice to see you too, Cathy."

She raised an eyebrow and shot Joanna a sour look. "Good friends can skip all the pleasantries and get right to the heart of the matter."

Joanna stared straight ahead. "Esther and Levi are going to Walmart, and Menno has a date with Verla Ann. I'm happy to babysit."

"I'm driving Esther and Levi to Walmart, and Esther's cooked up this whole thing just to get you over there to see Menno. You know that, don't you?"

Joanna heaved a sigh. "I know. But it's not like we're spending the evening together. He's going on a picnic with Verla Ann."

Cathy sniffed in the air. "A picnic. In the middle of April. I hope they take their coats and hats and space heaters."

Joanna's heart hurt like a bruise. "I just want to see him one more time."

She must have sounded extra pathetic, because Cathy's expression softened from cross to solemn. "I don't blame you. He's very handsome. But may I point out that absence makes the heart grow fonder?"

"I don't know why you would say that. Maybe out of sight, out of mind is truer."

"I have a lot of experience with romance, and right

now, Menno is surrounded by eager women, but he's pining for you."

Joanna didn't believe it for a minute. "How do you know that? Have you and Menno had a deep conversation recently?"

"No. He wouldn't be able to tell me what he's thinking even if I asked him. Menno doesn't know his own mind. That's why you've got to give him some time. Quit moping around, and let him work it out."

"I suppose, but what will it hurt to go over and say hello?"

Cathy took a turn a little too fast, and Joanna sucked in a breath. "Priscilla Weaver was over there the other day."

Joanna's heart lurched. "At Esther's?"

"I went to help with some quilting, and Priscilla and Verla Ann were both there. I think Priscilla had just proposed to Menno."

Joanna nearly choked on her own tongue. "Surely you're mistaken. Priscilla would never do that. Amish girls don't . . . do that."

"Well, she did it, and I guess Menno said no. I had to give her a sucker to calm her down."

Joanna was astonished beyond description. "I-I don't understand."

"You said it yourself. Menno is very handsome, and Priscilla saw an opportunity. I'm surprised he didn't say yes. Didn't you say he didn't care who the girl was? That any wife would do?"

Joanna couldn't wrap her head around such news. "Yes, but Priscilla isn't on his list. He took her off weeks ago."

Cathy gave Joanna a sideways glance. "Maybe I've misjudged him. If he's set on getting a wife, why would he turn down a perfectly good offer of marriage?"

"I-I don't know," Joanna stuttered. Menno hadn't wanted Priscilla in the first place. He wasn't so desperate as to marry just any can of corn.

They arrived at Esther's house, and Cathy stayed in the van. "Tell Esther I'm here. I hope you have a nice time with Menno and Verla Ann. I'd say, 'Give them my best,' but I'm saving my best for you. Hopefully you'll all get what's coming to you."

Joanna slid out of the van and resisted the urge to slam the door behind her. What did Cathy know about romance?

And why was Joanna so irritated about their conversation? She knew the answer without even pausing to think about it. Cathy had given her a sliver of hope, and it would just make things that much more painful in the end.

Joanna's heart leaped like a bunny when she spied Winnie, Rosie, and Lily with their noses and hands pressed against Esther's large picture window. They disappeared from view, and then the front door flew open. All three girls exploded from the house squealing and laughing, smiling widely with their arms outstretched. Joanna knelt, gathered them into her arms, and held on tight. *Ach*, she'd missed the hugs.

This hadn't been such a bad idea after all.

A high-pitched, stern bark came from the direction of the front door. "Girls, you do not run out of the house like a herd of wild animals." Verla Ann clapped her hands twice. "Please wait patiently on the porch for your visitor to come to you."

"It's okay," Joanna said. "I don't mind. I love the greeting."

Verla Ann ignored Joanna. "Girls, don't make me ask twice."

Lily looked stricken with a sudden cold, and Rosie

drooped like a daisy in the heat. They slumped their shoulders and shuffled their feet back to the porch.

Winnie stayed where she was. She cupped her hand over Joanna's ear and whispered, "I don't have to obey Verla Ann. Mamm says she's not the boss of me."

Joanna's throat tightened. "It's really okay, Verla Ann. They're just happy to see me."

Verla Ann softened around the edges. She patted Lily affectionately on the head. "I'm trying not to be overly strict, but if children don't learn *gute* manners when they're young, they grow up to be unruly teenagers. Menno is too busy to make sure *die kinner* learn their p's and q's. I'm happy I can be of help."

Joanna hesitated. She hadn't once thought of teaching Rosie and Lily their p's and q's when she babysat them. Had she neglected something important?

She took Winnie's hand, and they walked into the house together with Verla Ann and Menno's girls leading the way. Joanna's heart galloped at the thought of seeing Menno again, but only Esther and Levi were in the kitchen, washing up the dinner dishes. Junior sat in his highchair playing with a stack of blocks, and a picnic basket sat on the table.

Esther turned from the sink and gave Joanna a delighted smile. "*Ach*, Joanna, I'm so *froh* you decided to come. Levi and I have put off Walmart long enough."

Rosie and Lily grabbed on to Joanna's legs and looked up at her with those wide, innocent eyes. It seemed they had no intention of letting go.

"Lily has a secret," Rosie said.

Joanna gasped. "A secret? What is it?"

Verla Ann cleared her throat. "*Nae, nae,* Rosie. Not yet."

Gazing up at Joanna, Rosie grinned, pressed her lips together, and shook her head. "Not yet."

Joanna glanced at Verla Ann. "What do you girls want to do tonight when your *dat* leaves?"

"Can we go see the goats?" Winnie asked.

"*Nae*. It will be too late."

"Read the strawbewwy book," Rosie said.

Winnie and Lily cheered.

"The strawberry book," Winnie shouted.

Joanna smiled to herself. Rosie had found *Flicka, Ricka, and Dicka and the Strawberries* at Joanna's house under a stack of old children's books, and Joanna had given the book to the girls as a gift. She had read it to them at least a dozen times. It was their favorite. "For sure and certain we'll read the strawberry book."

Levi finished wiping the table and lifted Junior down from his highchair.

"Does he need a diaper change?" Joanna asked.

Esther took off her apron. "Not until bedtime unless he poops. You know where the nightgowns and the toothbrushes are?"

"*Jah*," Joanna said. "We'll be fine. We'll have a *wunderbarr* time. Maybe we can make some popcorn."

Lily threw her hands in the air. "Popcorn!"

Verla Ann straightened the chairs at the table. "Don't let them talk you into staying up past their bedtime, no matter how many times they want to read that book. They get grumpy if they don't go to bed on time. You have to be firm, or they'll take advantage of you."

It grated on Joanna's nerves how Verla Ann acted as if she was already the girls' *mater*, but that was a petty emotion, and Joanna felt immediately sorry for it. She winked at Rosie. "*Ach, vell*, it is a special night. We might have to stay up a little later and eat popcorn and ice cream and play Hide and Seek."

Esther grinned. "Oh, how fun."

The little girls, and even Junior, cheered and jumped up and down.

Verla Ann shushed them and pinned Joanna with a firm gaze. "It's tempting to bend the rules because you want the girls to like you, but I hope you'll honor my wishes tonight. Menno doesn't need a cranky pair of toddlers to deal with tomorrow morning."

Joanna gave free rein to her irritation and decided she didn't care how cranky the girls were tomorrow. She was in charge, and they were going to have fun tonight, no matter what Verla Ann wanted. She would never know.

Unfortunately, Joanna had been so righteously indignant with Verla Ann that she'd forgotten to be on guard for Menno. He suddenly appeared from the back hall, and she lost the ability to breathe. His hair was damp, he was freshly shaven, and he wore a crisply ironed cream-colored shirt that accented his warm green eyes.

Ach, she hated that he was so handsome.

His surprise at seeing Joanna was obvious. He flinched, and his smile grew like an autumn sunrise. It was the most beautiful thing she had seen since their disastrous birthday party.

"Joanna." Her name hung in the air like a song. He cleared his throat and glanced at Esther. "I didn't know you were coming."

Joanna tried to act as if she didn't love Menno to her very bones, but it was a difficult task. Just in time she remembered that she was only a can of corn to him, and he would just as soon marry Verla Ann. "I'm babysitting tonight."

He looked around the room. "Everybody?"

Joanna's gaze flicked in Esther's direction. Joanna had agreed to babysit, but this had been Esther's idea, and Esther would have to explain.

"*Jah*, everybody," Esther blurted out. "Levi and I have to go to Walmart, and I didn't want you to have to cancel your picnic with Verla Ann. Joanna is the only one I trust with all four of *die kinner*."

Menno shifted his feet uncomfortably. Was he ashamed that he had a date with another girl a week after proposing to Joanna, or was he simply embarrassed he hadn't found a *fraa* yet after he'd been so adamant about his list? "*Denki*, Joanna. That's so kind of you."

Rosie tugged on Menno's trousers. "Daddy, can we stay up late and eat ice cream?"

Menno gazed at Joanna, his eyes glowing with their own inner light. "Of course. It's a special night."

Verla Ann clapped twice. It sounded like a whip snapping. "Rosie! Don't ask your *dat* when I have already said *nae*."

Rosie lifted her chin so high, she looked like a turkey standing in the rain. "You not the boss a me."

Verla Ann clamped her mouth shut, clasped her hands together, and gave Menno a glare that could have curdled milk. *Ach*! It could have curdled water.

He held out his hand, flicking another look in Joanna's direction. "It's okay, Verla Ann. It's only natural that she would come to me for permission for something like this. I appreciate that you're teaching my girls *gute* manners. *Denki* for being so patient."

Menno truly was without guile, and Joanna felt ashamed of herself for having unkind feelings toward Verla Ann. Joanna gazed at him with renewed affection and grace. He had a list and he'd treated her like a can of corn, but he was kind and patient and good-natured. She loved him, but she didn't deserve such a *gute* man. Maybe it was for his own good that she'd said *nae*.

It was probably true, but she found no comfort in the thought.

Verla Ann burst into a smile. "Of course you're right. I want to do a *gute* job caring for your girls, and sometimes I get a little too eager."

Esther glanced at Joanna, and they made an unspoken connection. It seemed they were of the same mind about Menno and Verla Ann, even though Joanna had no right to judge his choices. She had refused his proposal. He was simply doing what he thought Gotte wanted him to do.

Menno couldn't seem to pry his eyes from Joanna's face, even though he was talking to Verla Ann. "You are doing a wonderful *gute* job. I appreciate everything you've done for my family yet."

Verla Ann soaked in his praise. She nodded to Lily. "Should we tell your *dat* the surprise?"

Lily grinned. "I potty trained!"

Menno's mouth fell open. "You . . . you're what?"

Verla Ann clapped, much less violently this time. "She's potty trained. We've been working on it this whole week."

Menno knelt down next to Lily, and a look of pain flitted across his features. "You know how to go to the toilet?"

Lily giggled. "I can!"

He looked up at Verla Ann. "How did you manage that? I didn't even know."

"You've been gone most of the week," Esther said, sticking a yellow pencil behind her ear. "I helped Lily at night, but Verla Ann gets all the credit. She's been very persistent."

Verla Ann lowered her head. "It was nothing. She was ready, and I wanted to do something that would make you happy."

"This makes me very happy," Menno said. He gave Lily a warm hug. "I'm so proud of you."

"Pride is a sin," said Verla Ann, who looked as proud as anyone.

Menno nodded thoughtfully. "Then can I say I'm pleased? For sure and certain this makes things much easier for me."

Joanna's heart sank. She couldn't compete with that. Potty training was completely beyond her skill level. Then again, why did she want to compete with Verla Ann? Menno would choose her or he wouldn't, no matter what Joanna did or didn't do.

Verla Ann sat on the floor opposite Menno and took Lily's hand. Rosie sidled behind Menno and wrapped her arms around his neck. Joanna couldn't stand it. They looked like a cute little family all together like that. Agreeing to babysit had been a very, very, very bad idea.

"Menno, you'll have to watch her closely tomorrow since I won't be here," Verla Ann said. "Set a timer and take her to the toilet every hour, whether she says she has to go or not. And be prepared for accidents. They always happen at the first." She raised her eyebrows "Unless . . . do you want me to come over? I wouldn't mind spending the whole day here to help with Lily."

Esther stiffened like hard cement. "I can help him."

With another wince of pain, Menno stood up and again glanced at Joanna. "*Denki*, Verla Ann, but I will manage. I'm going to need to figure it out soon enough. Once I go back to Idaho, potty training will fall to me."

Verla Ann looked positively stricken as she stood up too. "*Ach*, do you have to go back?"

"*Jah*. I've got to plant my sugar beets."

Verla Ann rocked back and forth on her heels, as if anticipating *gute* news. "And then, Lord willing, you'll come back for the wedding in October."

"Uh, *jah*. I suppose so." Menno's face turned a bright shade of greenish pink. Joanna couldn't begin to guess what he was thinking, but it was obvious he was as uncomfortable with this conversation as she was.

Verla Ann must have sensed his hesitation. "Or I suppose a wedding in November would work, even though it would be wonderful chilly."

Joanna had to put a stop to this, even if that meant forcing herself to speak. "Where are you going on your picnic?"

Verla Ann looked at her as if she'd forgotten Joanna was in the room. "It's not a real picnic because it's fifty degrees out there." She picked up the picnic basket and hooked it around her elbow.

"That is an adorable basket," Joanna said. "Where did you get it?"

Verla Ann smiled with her whole face. "I made it. My *dat* helped me cut the wood, then I shaped it and glued it and wove it. It took me two full months."

Menno brushed his fingers down the side of it. "That's amazing."

"It's really darling," Joanna admitted. Was there anything Verla Ann couldn't do?

Esther's smile stuttered. "She also makes those fold-down wooden baskets out of a single cut of wood. They're very clever."

Verla Ann batted her eyes as if trying to deflect the praise. "Oh, that's nothing. They don't take but a few hours to make. I love using Dat's jigsaw."

"Most girls don't know how to use a jigsaw," Menno said. "I'm impressed." He cocked his head to one side. "So where are we going on this picnic?"

Verla Ann seemed simply delighted with anything that came out of Menno's mouth. "I thought we could go to my house and sit on the kitchen floor. Doesn't that sound fun?"

He grimaced so slightly that Joanna might have been the only one to notice it. "It sounds fun, but I might have to sit on a chair. My back is a little sore."

Verla Ann was all concern. "Oh, no, Menno. What happened?"

"I'm just getting old, I suppose."

Verla Ann laughed and tapped him on the arm. "You're not old. You're only twenty-eight, silly."

"If you're old, I'm ancient," Esther said.

Menno's smile was strained. "I'm the only one who's old."

Levi chuckled. "*Nae*, Esther is sort of old."

Esther gasped in mock indignation. "Just because I'm six years older than you doesn't mean I'm old. You're a spring chicken."

"I've always considered myself a spring chicken." They all turned in unison to see Cathy Larsen standing in the doorway. "But I'm not getting any younger sitting out there in the van playing Candy Crush on my phone."

Esther sprang into action. She grabbed the grocery list that had been hanging on her fridge. "*Ach*, Cathy, I'm sorry. It just got very interesting in here, and I didn't want to leave."

Cathy pursed her lips. "It's called FOMO. Fear of missing out. I know the feeling. I've been sitting in the van for fifteen minutes."

Esther gave Joanna a quick hug and whispered in her ear. "I'm sorry and *denki*. Eat whatever you want."

"To drown my sorrows?" Joanna whispered back.

Esther and Levi followed Cathy out the door, leaving Menno, Verla Ann, and Joanna staring awkwardly at each other.

Menno stretched a smile across his face. "I suppose we

should get going." He took the astounding homemade picnic basket from Verla Ann. "*Denki*, Joanna. I really appreciate this."

"*Jah*," Verla Ann chimed in. "We really appreciate it."

Was there a *we* between Verla Ann and Menno? Joanna didn't even want to think about it.

Verla Ann grabbed the kitchen timer from the counter and handed it to Joanna. "Set the timer each hour, and be sure to take Lily to the toilet. No drinks right before bed, and watch her. If she makes a face, she has to go right now."

Joanna didn't know what the *face* looked like, but she wasn't going to ask. She wanted Menno and Verla Ann gone as soon as possible. "Okay, *denki*. Have a *gute* time."

Did she want them to have a *gute* time? What did it matter? It was a nice thing to say. She would worry about her own feelings another day when she wasn't standing in the kitchen trying to keep her gaze off Menno.

She took a couple of small steps backward so she could watch them walk down the hall and out the front door. Surely she could stare when Menno wasn't looking. He was definitely limping. What had he done to hurt himself? Contrary to what he said, he wasn't getting old. He was the very picture of health and masculine vitality.

Joanna sighed. Would she ever be able to get over Menno Eicher?

All *die kinner* had been tucked into bed, and Joanna sat in the living room making a few stitches on one of Esther's quilts. Esther always had a quilt set up so she could work on it when she had a few free minutes during the day. Her quilts sold for hundreds of dollars at the quilt shop, and she was always trying to finish one. Cathy Larsen, Levi's *mamm*, and several other quilters in the area, Amish and

Englisch alike, sold their quilts on consignment in Esther's shop. The few tourists who came through Byler always stopped in Esther's quilt shop and almost always bought something.

Joanna ran her hand along the soft squares of patchwork fabric. It was a beautiful pink and lime green baby quilt in a Log Cabin pattern. Joanna was one of the few people Esther trusted to put stitches in her quilts because Joanna had a small, even stitch, and she was a deliberate and careful quilter. Other people, like Beth and Esther's *schwester*, Ivy, weren't allowed within three feet of the quilt for fear they'd ruin it.

Esther had used Walmart as an excuse to get Joanna to babysit, but it was obviously a real need, because they'd been gone for two hours, and could be gone for two more hours, for all Joanna knew. She heard the clip-clop of horse's hooves on the pavement, and her heart did a flip and a belly flop.

Ach, she was hoping Esther and Levi would be home before Menno, but he had just pulled Levi's buggy into the driveway. She held her breath and listened as Menno drove the buggy behind the house. The sound faded, but her attention was focused on the shed where he was no doubt unhitching the horse and hanging up the tack.

Her heart betrayed her as the minutes ticked by. Menno would come in and feel obligated to visit with her while she waited for Cathy to bring Esther and Levi back and take her home. Or maybe he would sneak into the house, ignore her completely, and go straight to his bed in the quilt shop. She didn't know what she dreaded more. Her fingers shook, and she abandoned her needle. Esther would be unhappy if Joanna made a shaky, uncertain stitch in the quilt. Instead, she laced her fingers together and sat still, breathlessly waiting for him to walk in the back door.

But he didn't come.

And he didn't come.

Or had he come in so quietly she hadn't heard him?

Her curiosity got the better of her embarrassment, and she tiptoed into the kitchen and peeked out the window. She couldn't see him in her field of vision. Growling to herself, she glided down the back hall and slowly opened the back door. Menno sat on the porch steps with his head in his hands, sniffling quietly.

He was crying?

Joanna very nearly closed the door and let him have his privacy, but she couldn't just turn her back on his pain, whatever it was. Had Verla Ann said no to his proposal? Her heart skipped a beat. *Had* he proposed to Verla Ann? Had he cried like that when Joanna refused him? And did it matter?

Surely he hadn't proposed to Verla Ann, because she would have said yes. Maybe she had said yes and Menno was crying because he didn't want to marry her. *Ach.* That was just wishful thinking. She shoved her misgivings aside and marched out onto the porch.

Menno turned, looked up at her, and winced. "Joanna, I'm sorry. You've caught me at a bad moment."

The longing in his voice almost undid her.

"Wait just a minute." She ducked back into the house and grabbed two thick quilts from Esther's linen closet. Back on the porch, she draped one over Menno's shoulders. He had a jacket on, but the breeze was chilly, and the cement couldn't have been anything but cold.

He glanced at her again, his eyes shining with emotion. "*Denki.* That's very nice."

She unfolded the other quilt, wrapped it around her shoulders, and sat next to him on the step. "Not *very* nice.

I wanted a quilt and thought it would look bad if I only got one for myself."

He chuckled. "It definitely would have made you look bad."

"How was your picnic?" she said, pushing the words out of her mouth before she lost her courage.

Menno wiped his eyes and stared into the far pasture. "Verla Ann is a sweet girl. She made fried chicken and coleslaw."

Joanna smiled weakly. "I'm guessing it wasn't the food that brought you to tears."

He gave her a reluctant grin. "The food was *appeditlich*. The fried chicken was nice and spicy, and her biscuits were extra flaky. She even made each of us our own little chocolate cake."

"Sounds nice."

He pulled the quilt tighter around his shoulders. "I should have been more of a help to Suvilla. Right before she got sick, she potty trained Rosie."

"Could you have potty trained Rosie?"

"Absolutely not."

Joanna smiled to herself. She couldn't have potty trained Rosie either.

"I'm not sure how my life got to where it is right now," Menno said, "but I've failed Gotte, and He's punishing me."

Joanna wanted to protest. From what she could see, Menno hadn't failed at anything, but she was smart enough to let him talk himself out of that ridiculous notion. "Why do you think you've failed Gotte?"

"When I left Verla Ann's house, memories of Suvilla unexpectedly knocked me over, and I realized I have disappointed Gotte and failed my family. Suvilla was a *gute mater* and *fraa*. She cooked and cleaned and cared for our children and bottled fruit and raised chickens and loved me. I was busy on the farm with my head down and my shoulders laden, and I took her for granted. I didn't appreciate what she did, and Gotte punished me by taking her away."

Joanna shook her head vigorously. "I don't believe Gotte is like that, Menno. His rain falls on everybody."

He trained his eyes on her face. "Do you mean, 'He maketh his sun to rise on the evil and on the good, and sendeth rain on the just and on the unjust'?"

She wanted to tease him for showing off, but he wasn't showing off, and his mood was low. She wouldn't do anything to make it worse. "That's right. If Gotte punished everybody every time they did something wrong, why would anyone choose anything but good? And then what would happen to free will?"

"But I know better."

"That doesn't make you less susceptible to sin and weakness. It just makes you harder on yourself."

He sighed. "But I should be hard on myself. Gotte and the bishop want me to find a *fraa*, and I can't bring myself to do it. It's my choice. I came out here for one purpose, and I failed. I've failed my *dochters*. I've failed my parents, and I've failed Gotte."

The self-doubt rushed over Joanna like a wave of water. Maybe it was she who had failed by not telling Menno yes when he'd proposed. But as much as she regretted it, she wouldn't change that decision even now. If she'd said yes to Menno, she would have lived the rest of her life wondering if he'd married her because she was the convenient choice or because he loved her.

"I leave in less than a week, and I'm not going to be engaged by then." His eyes searched her face. "To be honest, I'm dragging my feet, and I think Gotte is punishing me for my procrastination. My mind is muddled, and nothing is clear."

What could she say to comfort him? He was mistaken about so many things, she didn't know where to begin. "You have it all wrong, Menno."

"Do I?" he said, with just a hint of exasperation in his voice.

"When I'm frustrated or unhappy, I find that I'm trying to force Gotte to conform to my life instead of molding my life to His will. I'm no Bible scholar, but I know that one of the fruits of the Spirit is peace. Another one is joy. Are you feeling either of those?"

"Not really. But that's what I'm trying to tell you. The Spirit isn't giving me any direction because I don't know if I want to do Gotte's will anymore."

"Maybe what you think is Gotte's will isn't really Gotte's will. The Spirit can't give you peace if you've set your feet on the wrong path."

"It also can't give me peace if I'm running away from the path."

Joanna tried a different tack. "What do you think Gotte's will is?"

"He wants me to find a *fraa*."

Her heart fluttered just a tiny bit. "You don't want to find one?"

"This is terrible to say, but I don't like the choices I've got."

Joanna's heart broke into a trot. "Not terrible." She didn't even want to ask the question because she was afraid of the answer, but she did anyway. "What about Verla Ann?"

He folded his arms across his chest with two ends of the quilt firmly in his fists. "I need more time."

"That doesn't sound like running away to me. It sounds

like you're working hard to understand Gotte's will. You don't have to rush."

"I shouldn't procrastinate either." He closed his eyes and took a deep breath. "Being in Colorado is only causing me more confusion. I'm headed home as soon as I can make the arrangements. I'll go back to Idaho and try to listen to Gotte's voice, if He'll still talk to me."

"Of course He's talking to you. You've only been listening for what you want to hear. Listen for what *He* wants you to hear." Joanna swallowed past the lump in her throat. "If you're going to spend the rest of your life with someone, you should take your time and be sure."

He opened his mouth as if to say something then swiped his hand across his mouth and fell silent.

That was quite enough talk of marriage for one night. "How is your back feeling?"

Menno straightened his spine and winced in pain. "I don't think anything is permanently damaged, but I went ice blocking with Sadie last night, and I think I bruised my tailbone. Do you know what ice blocking is?"

"Oh, *jah*, *die youngie* do it at the park all the time."

He frowned. "I deeply regret letting Sadie talk me into it. I ache from my shoulder blades to my tailbone, and I'm going to have a huge bruise on my thigh where Enos Herschberger's head crashed into my leg."

Joanna caught her breath. "Is he okay?"

"He seemed fine. My leg is softer than his head, and he was wearing a beanie."

"So you had a date with Sadie?" Joanna didn't want to feel hurt, but Sadie had seemed so adamantly on Joanna's side.

He suddenly seemed very interested in the apricot tree. "She's a sweet girl."

Sadie was a sweet girl. Verla Ann was a sweet girl. Just

what did he mean by that? Was he trying to be a Nathanael, or did he really think Sadie and Verla Ann were sweet? More importantly, did he want to marry one of them?

He turned his face toward her and smiled. "Your nose is turning red."

"So is yours."

"We should go in. Esther and Levi will be here soon, and we don't want them to wonder where we are."

They stood and gathered their quilts around them and walked into the house.

"Just so you know," Menno said, "Verla Ann's cakes were *appeditlich*, but nothing can hold a candle to your fry pies. I'll never taste anything better."

Joanna felt her cold face get warm. He always knew the right thing to say, and he'd managed to make her smile once again.

Chapter 13

"Dada!"

Menno jerked his head up and opened his eyes. He sat on Rosie's bed between Rosie and Lily, holding a book in his hand. He'd fallen asleep mid-sentence again. Could he help it that Rosie wanted to read the same book every night, and they'd read it so often he had it memorized? Flicka, Ricka, and Dicka would be searching for wild strawberries until Judgment Day, and he would probably be reading this book to Rosie until she got married.

Lily's little hand rested on his arm, and she gazed at him with those wide eyes that always melted his heart. "Sweepy?" she asked.

Sleepy? Exhausted was more like it. Menno was bone-tired, worn out, all the time. He woke up in the morning looking forward to bedtime. He slogged through his days as if he was walking through cold tar, and he slept like a newborn *buplie*—awake every two hours and fussy through the night.

If he'd been able to find a *fraa* in Colorado, maybe he'd be sleeping better. Maybe he wouldn't. His heart throbbed with a familiar ache, but he shoved the feeling down until it was buried deep in his chest. The trip to Byler had been the worst decision of his life. He'd wasted two weeks on the wrong girl, and then there hadn't been time to find someone else before he was forced to return to Idaho to get his sugar beets planted.

He rubbed his bleary eyes. He was just kidding himself. There had been plenty of time to find someone else. In fact, he had two marriage proposals and three other women who would marry him if he asked. And he didn't want any of them.

Was Gotte mad at him or ignoring him, or had Gotte thrown up His hands and given up? Menno closed the book.

"Daddy, *nae*," Rosie whined.

Lily tapped on the cover. "Read," she said.

Menno kissed each of his angels on the head. "I'm sorry, but I can't stay awake. We'll have to read the rest tomorrow."

"*Nae*," Rosie howled.

Lily eyed Menno and sucked on her index finger.

He slid off the bed and set the book on the chest of drawers. "Get under the covers, and I'll tuck you in."

Rosie must have sensed he was completely spent, because after staring at him for a few seconds, she rested her head on the pillow without another word of protest. Lily jumped into her bed and pulled the sheet up to her chin.

Menno gave each of them another kiss. "See you in the morning."

He tiptoed out of the room and closed the door softly behind him. Mamm stood in the hallway as if she'd been waiting for him. She leaned on her cane and gave him a worried smile. Anxiety was the only expression he had seen on her face for over a year.

"*Cum* and sit with me," she said. "I'll make you a cup of herbal tea."

"It's okay, Mamm. You don't have to do that."

"*Cum* into the kitchen. The teapot is already whistling."

Two weeks after Suvilla died, Menno had rented his house to his cousin Isaac and moved in with his *mamm* and *dat* so Mamm could watch the girls while Menno worked the farm. He also kept an eye on Mamm and Dat. That was another reason he needed a *fraa* so badly. Mamm was sixty-five, and Dat was seventy. They shouldn't be burdened caring for their grandchildren in their old age.

Menno followed Mamm into the kitchen.

She motioned for him to sit at the table and took two mugs from the cupboard and caught him looking at her cane. "I know what you're thinking, but I'm not old. I can still milk the cow and tend to my grandchildren just fine."

Menno cracked a smile. *Mamm* truly could read his thoughts. "I hate being a burden to you. 'A man should leave his *fater* and *mater* and cleave unto his wife.'"

She poured the water into the mugs and plopped a teabag into each mug. "You don't have a *fraa* yet, but it isn't for lack of trying. I know you're doing your best. And you're not a burden. I love the girls. Rosie shrieks, and Lily won't eat her vegetables, but they're nearly perfect, and I love feeling useful." She sat next to him and stirred her teabag with a spoon. "I heard you pacing the floor last night."

Ever since Colorado, Menno had paced the floor every night. He smiled at her. "You use a cane, but there's nothing wrong with your hearing."

She gave him the stink eye. "I know you think I'm ancient, but just wait till you get where I am. You won't be so smug." She leaned closer to him. "I worry that you're not sleeping well. How are your bowels moving?"

He nearly spit out the tea he'd just swallowed. "We are *not* talking about this."

She gave him a stern look. "You have to pay attention to these things. Constipation leads to all kinds of problems."

Menno took the lid off the sugar bowl and plopped four cubes of sugar into his tea just to annoy her. "I've got a lot of things on my mind, Mamm. That's why I can't sleep."

The worry lines around her eyes deepened. "Like which girl to propose to?"

He stared into his mug. "I can't decide which one to choose." The truth was, he didn't want to choose any of them, and that in and of itself was probably a sin. He was dragging his feet, and that was probably a sin too.

"You tried your best with that Joanna person, and I don't see as Gotte will condemn you for something that wasn't your fault. The only thing Gotte expects of you is to keep trying."

Jah, Gotte was surely displeased with him. Even though he'd written dozens of letters to four Colorado Amish girls, Menno had given up trying weeks ago.

Mamm so desperately wanted to fix everything that was wrong in his life. "You don't need to lose sleep over it. Surely at least one of those girls in Colorado would make a *gute*, sturdy, dependable *fraa*. Just make the best choice you can, and Gotte will smile on your efforts. Any two people can be happy together if they love Gotte and obey the Ordnung. 'It's not *gute* for man to be alone.'"

"I know, Mamm." Every time he thought about marrying anyone but Joanna Yoder, a gaping hole opened up in the pit of his stomach. It was ridiculous to feel this way. He needed a *fraa*, and Joanna was just one of several *gute* choices.

A loud and enthusiastic knock sounded on the front door. Dat was sitting in the great room, and they heard him groan, get up, and open the door. Someone on the porch started talking very loudly. Menno and Mamm looked at each other in puzzlement and went into the great room.

To Menno's complete shock, Sadie Sensenig stood on the porch with nearly half a dozen people behind her. Looking a little bewildered, Dat invited her in, along with everyone else. Sadie practically hopped into the house, followed by her parents, her *bruder*, Freeman, Freeman's *fraa*, Mattie, and of all people, Cathy Larsen!

What in the world were they doing in Idaho?

Sadie squealed as if she'd just met a long-lost friend. "Menno Eicher, we found you! Cathy was a grumpy goose and was sure this house didn't exist."

Cathy hobbled to the love seat and sat down. "Don't gloat, young lady. It doesn't exist on Google Maps."

Sadie strode across the room and grabbed Mamm's hand. "I'm Sadie Sensenig from Byler, Colorado. You must be Menno's *mamm*."

"I am. I'm Rebecca," Mamm said, shaking hands as her ears perked up at Sadie's name. "The girl Menno has been writing to?"

Sadie waved her hand in the air. "One of *four* girls. He's not very subtle."

Menno didn't know what *subtle* meant, but it didn't sound like a compliment.

Sadie's smile was as wide as the Snake River. "It's so nice to meet you. Menno talks about you all the time in his letters. How you take care of his *dochters* even though you're sixty-five and don't move as well as you used to."

Mamm looked sideways at Menno, obviously irritated that he thought she was old.

Sadie opened her arms wide and motioned to her family. "Menno, you remember my *mamm* and *dat*, Erda and David? Freeman and Mattie came too."

Freeman stepped forward and shook Menno's hand,

then Dat's. "Nice to see you, Menno. Nice to meet you all. This is Mattie. We got married last year."

Sadie hooked her arm around Mattie's elbow. "My *schwester* Sarah couldn't come because she's in a family way." She peered at Menno as if evaluating his health. "She said to tell you *hallo*."

Erda cleared her throat. "We apologize for intruding. We know you weren't expecting us, but Sadie said it was an emergency. What could we do?"

"We could have written a letter," Freeman said.

Sadie propped her hands on her hips. "Freeman, you know very well a letter wouldn't have made it in time, and some conversations are better in person."

Dat, looking as confused as Menno felt, hooked his fingers around the back of his neck. "You came all this way to have a conversation?"

Everyone looked at Sadie like she was the only person in the room who had any idea what was going on. She smiled as if Dat had told a joke. "We did come all this way to have a conversation, but we also came because we're on our way to Yellowstone."

Cathy tapped her fingers on the arm of the love seat. "Everybody should see Yellowstone at least once in their life."

The wrinkles on Dat's forehead piled on top of each other. "Yellowstone is five hours out of your way."

Freeman glared at Sadie. "You should have just sent a letter."

Sadie made a face at her *bruder*, even though she was twenty-one and too old for that.

Should Menno cross her off his list? She was exuberant and energetic. His girls needed someone who could keep up with them. Okay. She was still on the list, but he'd keep his eyes open for more flaws.

Mamm was just as *ferhoodled* as the rest of them, but she loved visitors. "Isn't this nice? Why don't you sit down, and I'll make you all some herbal tea."

Sadie bounced onto the couch. "I'd love some. That's very kind of you."

The rest of her family hesitantly sat down, as if not quite comfortable with the entire situation. No one looked comfortable except for Sadie, and she seemed oblivious to everyone else's uncertainty.

Mamm headed for the kitchen then turned back. "If you tell me your health problems, I can make a specific kind of tea for each of you."

Cathy closed one eye, thinking very hard about it. "I sometimes have gout, but my main complaint is chronic bladder infections."

Almost everyone in the room ducked their heads in embarrassment. Cathy and Mamm were the only two people Menno knew who said *bladder infection* right out loud.

Mamm's face lit up like a kerosene lamp. "Chamomile tea should do the trick, but another remedy is half a teaspoon of baking soda."

Cathy raised her eyebrows. "I'll try that."

Mamm looked around the room. "Anyone else?"

Menno wanted to say something to divert everyone's attention from the awkward tea conversation, but he was afraid Mamm would launch into a lecture about constipation, and he just couldn't risk it.

Sadie laced her fingers around her knees. "I get pimples sometimes."

Mamm seemed very pleased that Sadie got pimples. "Spearmint tea. Drink it twice a day, and you'll never get acne again."

Did Menno want to marry someone who got pimples? Sadie was getting younger and younger all the time.

Mamm looked around the room. "What else can I make for you?"

Dat stared faithfully at the pattern in their worn linoleum floor.

Erda had a green tinge to her face as if she was in shock. She probably wouldn't be able to speak a word for several days. Sadie's *dat* looked as if his lips had been pressed together with an iron. Mattie's mouth curled upward in amusement, and Freeman was surely wishing they had written a letter instead of coming five hours out of their way.

Menno had to do something to break this horrible silence. "Why don't you just make everyone else a cup of lavender tea, Mamm?"

Mamm tapped her cane on the floor in a cheerful rhythm. "*Gute* idea, Menno. Nice and relaxing just before bed."

Sadie grinned and looked around the room. "This is a big place. Do you hold *gmay* here?"

Dat coughed, trying to recover some of his composure. "*Jah. Jah*, we do, but there are only a few families in the area, so church is very small. We don't even have our own bishop. We borrow the bishop from Rexford and see him four times a year."

And every time the bishop came to Baker, he made sure to remind Menno he needed to get married.

Menno sat down next to Dat on the couch. "Cathy, did you leave Lon in Colorado to fend for himself?"

"No, we dropped him off at the hotel in Salmon with his oxygen tank. The drive up here wore him out. Last night we stayed in Salt Lake City, and tomorrow night we're staying in Yellowstone. We want to see Old Faithful first thing when we get there."

Menno was reluctant to bring up the subject about why Sadie had come all this way to talk to him. For sure and certain the conversation was about marriage. Had she come to propose to him? It seemed the only reasonable explanation for the visit. His throat tightened. He didn't want Sadie to propose to him. He didn't want to marry Sadie, even though he *should have wanted* to marry her, just like he should have wanted to marry Lydia or Naomi. Or even Priscilla. Any of them would be a solution to his problems, and since they were all willing to marry him, was it a sin to reject such an opportunity from Gotte? *Ach!* What should he do?

Menno couldn't speak, couldn't begin to make a decision about Sadie and marriage. Should he hide in the bathroom until she and her family gave up and left? If he did that, he'd surely get a lecture from Mamm about constipation, and she'd have him on a special diet for a month. *Nae*, he needed to muster some courage and do what needed to be done . . . whatever that was. He had no idea.

Dat saved him from having to change the subject. He asked David about farming, and they talked about the hardships and advantages of growing potatoes versus sugar beets for several minutes before Mamm was back with a tray of cups. She handed Cathy her bladder tea and pointed out the tea for Sadie, then served everyone else a steaming cup of lavender tea. Menno took some tea, even though he'd just had some. His heart raced, and he needed all the calming help he could get.

Mamm settled onto the couch next to Menno and sipped her tea as if she'd never been curious a day in her life. She was being sneaky. She was wildly curious about their visitors, Sadie in particular. Menno could tell by the way her eyelid twitched whenever she glanced in Sadie's direction.

Sadie nodded to her *mamm*, took one more sip of tea,

and set her cup on the coffee table. Freeman picked up her cup and slid a coaster under it.

"Now," Sadie said, leaning back into her seat, "there really is an important reason we've come all this way to talk to you."

"There'd better be," Freeman muttered under his breath.

Sadie gave him a sideways glance and kept right on talking. She looked at Mamm. "Did you know that Menno is writing to four different girls in Colorado?"

Mamm nodded. "He told me. He wants to find a *fraa*. It seems the most efficient way to do it."

Sadie shook her head so hard, she fanned up a breeze. "I don't want to contradict you, Rebecca, but it was a terrible idea from the start. Just terrible."

Menno growled under his breath. "Why is it a terrible idea? I want to find a *fraa*, and I'm trying to narrow down my choices."

Sadie looked at Menno through half-closed eyes. "I really don't know why I went along with this in the first place, except to do Esther a favor. Menno, you're treating us girls like items in a grocery store. You can read the whole label, but a can of corn is a can of corn, and it's a lousy way to shop for a *fraa*. No girl wants to feel like she's just one of the crowd."

"What about corn?" Mamm asked.

"I have a corn sensitivity," Cathy said. "My ears turn bright red when I eat it."

"Menno," Sadie scolded, "you're writing to *four* girls. It seems like you don't care if it's me or Verla Ann, Naomi or Lydia. You just need a *fraa*. And to you, any *fraa* will do."

Joanna had told him the same thing, and her rejection had thrust a paring knife right into his heart. "I've been honest with you. You know I'm writing to three others."

"Hmm, *jah*. I feel like a cow in an auction."

Menno swiped his hand across his mouth. "You misunderstand me. Choosing a *fraa* is not like a trip to the grocery store. I don't want just anyone." His voice cracked. "I-I want a woman I can fall in love with. I want a woman who loves me."

Sadie folded her arms and eyed him resentfully. "You could have fooled me."

All eyes were on Menno. No one moved. He didn't think anyone was even breathing. "What's so wrong with going about it in an organized way?"

Sadie heaved a long, I'm-barely-putting-up-with-you sigh. "I am officially withdrawing my offer to marry you."

Dat nearly choked on his tea. "You proposed to Menno?"

Apparently, this was news to Sadie's family. The looks of surprise they gave her could have powered all the electric light bulbs in Baker.

"You want to marry Menno?" Freeman asked, his eyes bulging out of his head.

Sadie looked at her *bruder* as if she was completely out of patience with him. "If you must know, I never wanted to marry Menno. I told him I was willing, but I certainly wasn't going to say yes." Her words were like a punch in the gut.

Menno frowned. "Then why did you tell me you'd marry me?"

"Because I knew you wouldn't ask."

Freeman threw up his hands. "You said you'd say yes but didn't mean it?"

Sadie swatted at the air in front of Freeman's face. "You don't have to be so snippy about it."

"We just drove five hours out of the way, Sadie. I can be as snippy as I want."

Mattie laughed and hooked her arm around Freeman's elbow. "Okay, *heartzley*. Just let Sadie have her say. We've come all this way, and you'll have five hours in the car to give her a piece of your mind."

Freeman glared at Sadie but didn't say another word. Instead, he tenderly put his hand over Mattie's and settled into the couch. No doubt his affection for Mattie overshadowed his irritation at Sadie.

It was *gute* Sadie didn't want to marry Menno. She'd been very kind to come all this way, but he decided to take her off the list. He'd have a constant headache if he married her.

Sadie took a sip of her acne tea. "Lydia also proposed to Menno."

Seized with enthusiasm, Mamm slapped Menno in the leg and nearly made him lose his tea. "Lydia! She's the one."

Lydia wasn't the one, but how could he break that news to Mamm?

Sadie set down her cup and eyed Freeman as if she expected him to say something sarcastic, but he kept his mouth shut. "Lydia didn't really propose to Menno. It was her *mamm*, so I can't be sure if Lydia wants to marry Menno or not. But we can be sure of one thing." Sadie leaned forward. "You don't want to marry Lydia."

The lines around Mamm's mouth etched themselves into her face. "You don't want to marry Lydia?"

Sadie wasn't done. "Then there's Naomi, who is on my side. She told Menno she would marry him, but she only said that for Joanna's sake."

Menno's heart crashed against his ribcage. "What about Joanna?"

Sadie's gaze turned into a full-on glare. "For sure and

certain, Verla Ann wants to marry you, but there's nothing I can do about that."

Mamm's mood again rocketed to the ceiling. "Verla Ann wants to marry you?" She slapped his leg a second time. "She's the one. I had a great aunt named Verla. Such a sweet woman."

Dat looked as if he was ready to succumb to a panic attack. "It's all so confusing."

Sadie clicked her tongue. "If Menno marries Verla Ann simply because she's the only girl who says yes, then it's no better than settling for a can of corn."

Mamm set her teacup on the coffee table. "A can of corn is better than nothing, especially if corn was what he was shopping for in the first place. There's nothing wrong with corn."

Dat was trying to follow the conversation. Menno could barely follow it himself. "Are we still talking about Menno finding a *fraa*?"

Sadie took another sip of tea as if to cool her temper. "I can see why Verla Ann is interested. You are wonderful handsome, and you own a farm and a house, even though they're in Idaho."

"I'm glad to know I have some slice of your approval," Menno said.

Sadie ignored him. "Verla Ann is a *gute* girl. She knits baby booties for orphans in Romania and has *Das Lobleid* memorized. But she doesn't know you, Menno. She doesn't know that you read to your *dochters* every night or that you can't carry a tune in a bucket. She doesn't know you can make a bed with hospital corners or cook a package of ramen without a recipe. She doesn't know that you washed all of Esther's windows inside and out before you left Byler."

Menno stared at Sadie, slack jawed. "How do you know all of this?"

"Joanna."

Menno's pulse raced. "Joanna told you?"

Sadie laced her fingers together, looking a tiny bit sheepish. "*Ach, vell,* I got it from Beth who got it from Joanna. We can't help ourselves. We love to gossip."

"It feels like the *gute* kind of gossip," Mattie said.

Sadie nodded smugly. "I think so."

"I don't," Freeman interjected, before glancing at Mattie and clamping his mouth shut.

Menno's heart thawed just a little. Joanna had said all that about him? Was it possible she'd forgiven him?

Mamm's frown sank deep into her face. "Why don't you just propose to that Verla Ann girl. Sadie says she'll marry you."

The thought of proposing to Verla Ann made Menno's teeth hurt. He just couldn't do it. Not today. Not tomorrow. But how much time would Gotte give him?

"It's not Verla Ann," Sadie blurted out, making Dat flinch again. She eyed Menno. "The letter writing has got to stop. It only gets Verla Ann's hopes up and hurts Joanna's feelings."

Menno's heart had been doing acrobats for several minutes. Now it did a complete nosedive. He hated the thought of hurting Joanna's feelings, but of course that was exactly what he'd done. He'd made her feel like a can of corn, then he'd paraded four other girls in front of her after she'd rejected him.

He tried to hide behind his ignorance. "What does Joanna have to do with this?"

Sadie snorted loudly. "Don't tell me you haven't thought about her."

Dat flinched. Mamm widened her eyes in surprise. Erda did her best to disappear into the couch cushion.

Hadn't thought about her? Menno thought about Joanna day and night, but Gotte didn't want him wasting time, did He? That was why Menno was unenthusiastically writing letters to four other girls.

"Joanna already refused me," he said, his heart aching like a fresh bruise.

Sadie blew a puff of air from between her lips. "Of course she did. She wasn't about to humiliate herself by saying *jah*."

That was going a little too far. "Are you saying it would be a humiliation to marry me?"

"Now you're willfully misunderstanding me, Menno."

His irritation was growing by the minute. How hard would it be for Sadie to get to the point, if she even had one? Sadie took her time drinking another sip of tea, and Menno almost lost his patience. She was treating her own *emergency* too casually by half.

"You made Joanna feel like she was a cow waiting to be auctioned off. She wanted to feel special."

"She is special. She is *gute* with *die kinner*, she can bake fry pies that melt in your mouth, she makes goat cheese. I wanted to marry her."

"Not for the right reasons, and that's why she said *nae*." Sadie cradled her cup in her lap. "'By their fruits ye shall know them.'"

Why was she quoting scripture? Quoting scripture was Menno's inclination, not Sadie's. He stifled a growl and kept his temper locked up. "What are you trying to say?"

"I'm trying to get you to think. I know you mean well, Menno. You're organized and have a plan and a list." She said *list* as if it were a bad word. "You're also clumsy and insensitive. Joanna knew you were looking for a *fraa*, but you didn't convince her that you wanted to marry *her* and *only her*. Then when she rejected you, you moved on to four other girls. Five, if you count Priscilla, which I don't."

Menno couldn't have felt any worse if Sadie had stomped on his big toe. He had been in such a hurry to do what he thought Gotte wanted him to do that he'd ignored his own heart and Joanna's feelings as if she were a dirty pair of socks to be thrown in the wash. Changing girl-friends shouldn't be like changing socks . . . or bidding on a cow at auction. What he'd done was indefensible, but he tried to defend himself anyway. "I needed to do my duty."

Sadie stretched her lips over her teeth in disgust. "You went on dates with me, Naomi, Lydia, and Verla Ann the week after you proposed to Joanna."

Freeman broke his determined silence. "Are you kidding, Sadie? Menno would never do that."

It was Cathy's turn to glare at Menno. "No, I saw it. Menno went on four dates with four girls the week after he proposed to Joanna. That's why I refused to give him a sucker."

Sadie lifted her chin in Freeman's direction. "Is it any wonder Joanna thought she was just one of many choices?"

Cathy narrowed her eyes at Menno. "Was she just one of many choices?"

Menno didn't have much to say for himself. "Um . . . I don't know. I met Joanna by chance at the bakery that first morning. I saw it as a message from Gotte that He had chosen her to be my *fraa* and I didn't need to look any further."

Sadie scoffed. "Gotte wants us to use our brains, not wait for Him to hand us everything. You're acting like the slothful servant in the parable of the talents, Menno. Haven't you read it?"

Read it? He'd memorized it. How annoying that Sadie,

with her acne tea and cell phone, was quoting scripture to him. He was the one who knew the Bible. He was the one who lived strictly by every word of Gotte.

And, oh, wasn't he so proud of that!

The truth kicked him in the teeth. He knew the Bible backward and forward, yet he was as miserable as he had ever been. Sadie was cheerful and determined and earnest. Here she was, five hours out of her way to deliver a message while he was floundering in an ocean of uncertainty, unable to get his bearings, frustrated by what he thought Gotte wanted him to do.

Menno slowly rubbed his hand down the side of his face then turned his eyes to Sadie. "Do you think I've used Gotte as an excuse to be slothful?" he said quietly.

She must have noticed the change in his countenance. Her expression softened, and she gave him a warm smile. "I think it's pride disguised as obedience."

Freeman's jaw dropped. "That is the first intelligent thing I've ever heard you say all day, Sadie."

She kept her eyes glued to Menno and poked Freeman with her elbow. "'Then he which had received the one talent came and said, Lord, I knew thee that thou art an hard man.'"

Menno finished the verse. "'And I was afraid and went and hid thy talent in the earth.'"

Sadie handed her teacup to Freeman, who took it resentfully. "You're afraid of making mistakes, so you use Gotte as your shield and blame it on Him when things go wrong."

Menno shook his head. "I don't blame Gotte for my troubles."

Sadie looked around the room, as if giving someone older and wiser the chance to answer, but everyone seemed content to let her take things where she had obviously planned them to go. "I guess it's better said that you use Gotte to blame yourself, as if Gotte is looking down on you like He would a naughty child, shaking His finger at you and withholding his love until you get it right."

Menno felt as if he was on the cusp of something life changing. How was he like the slothful servant? "I've worked hard to avoid making mistakes because I don't want Gotte to be mad at me."

"That's right," Cathy said, brushing some lint from the sleeve of her bright yellow pantsuit. "You're what we Englischers call a perfectionist."

Sadie's eyes were full of compassion. "You forgot that we 'all have sinned and fall short of the glory of Gotte.'"

"When you first came to Colorado, it was plain you needed a large dose of humility," Cathy said, her voice oozing with irritation. "Lucky for all of us, Joanna handed it to you on a platter."

It didn't feel so lucky to Menno, but maybe he'd needed it. "I-I was proud of my obedience, proud that I always did what Gotte wanted me to do."

Sadie smiled. "But when Joanna refused you, she derailed your perfect plan and you thought you'd failed. You told yourself Gotte would be mad unless you found someone else immediately. You used the threat of Gotte's wrath to bury your heartbreak."

Menno was just starting to wrap his head around the consequences of his behavior. "I was deeply hurt, but I thought it was wrong to be disappointed. I shouldn't be sad if I have faith in Gotte's plan, right?"

"Wrong," Cathy said. "Being sad is sometimes part of the plan. How will we learn anything by experience if we never have experiences? Sad and happy ones."

Mattie nodded. "Life can be hard, and it doesn't matter

how many lists we make, some things can't be fixed except by Gotte and in his timing."

Menno sighed, more confused and disheartened than ever. "But what does Gotte want from me and how can I know?"

Sadie didn't seem sorry for him. "Don't be so thick, Menno. You already know the answer."

Freeman tried to hand Sadie's cup back to her. She wouldn't take it. "You're acting so smart about it, Sadie. Do you know the answer?"

She made a face at Freeman that Rosie had used on Menno a time or two. "I'm not going to speak for Gotte, but if He wants Menno to find a *fraa*, He wants Menno to find the *right* fraa, not just *any fraa*." She pinned Menno with a stern look. "You should quit hiding behind your stubborn obedience and ask Gotte to give you the courage to do what you should have done all along."

"And what is that?"

Sadie rolled her eyes. "Joanna is wildly in love with you. And you are crazy in love with Joanna, though you're too proud to admit it. Do you have the courage to fight for her? Or is it easier to use Gotte as an excuse to settle for someone else?"

Freeman smirked. "Are you saying he'd be settling if he chose you, Sadie?"

"*Jah*." Sadie dug her elbow into Freeman's ribs again. "Because he doesn't love me. Settling for anything less than love and using Gotte as an excuse is cowardly."

A warm sensation trickled down Menno's spine and through his whole body. Sadie said that Joanna loved him. Nothing else mattered. Sadie had insulted him up one side and down the other, and he'd never been so grateful. She'd said exactly what he needed to hear.

His longing for Joanna grew like a pleasant ache in his

gut. He loved everything about her. He adored the pies and cakes and rolls she baked, but even more, he loved the graceful, skillful movement of her hands as she kneaded dough or sprinkled powdered sugar over a batch of doughnuts. He loved how she tilted her head just so when she worked out a problem and how she caressed Rosie's cheek whenever she got close to her. He loved Joanna's irrepressible smile and her genuine delight when Lily learned a new word. Joanna was his other half and only Joanna. He'd rather live alone the rest of his life than marry anyone else.

Menno felt as if he were standing on the edge of a sheer cliff, but he didn't know if he would fall off or take flight. He needed to see her. He needed to apologize to her. He needed to marry her. He knew it deep down to the very marrow of his bones.

"You could have put all this in a letter, sis," Freeman said, his lips twitching with a tease.

Sadie practically hissed. "You don't know very much, do you, Freeman?" She turned back to Menno. "We've got an emergency in Byler, and you need to get down there before it's too late."

Menno furrowed his brow. "What kind of emergency?"

"You've been gone for three months, and Jakob Glick has been to dinner at the Yoder house three times in the last three weeks. He's courting Joanna, and Beth's afraid Joanna might agree to marry him."

Menno was shocked and shaken at the thought that Joanna would choose Jakob Glick over him. Had he come to his senses too late? "He's an old man in his sixties."

Mamm shot lightning out of her eyes in his direction. He should probably stop talking about old people.

"He's fifty-five, and he has three hundred acres," Sadie said.

Menno frowned. He only had twenty-five acres, and he was living with his parents. Then again, Jakob Glick had a wide girth, and Menno had always prided himself on staying fit and trim. But maybe Joanna liked men with wide girths.

"Joanna might marry him. She is, after all, a desperate old *maedel*." Sadie was being sarcastic, but her words cut Menno to the core.

That was how he had treated Joanna, and if she believed it, he had no one but himself to blame.

"I'm not telling you what to do," Sadie said, "but you must go back to Colorado immediately."

Freeman laughed but was silenced by the look on Sadie's face and a poke from his *fraa*.

Menno glanced at Dat. "What about my farm?"

Dat pursed his lips. "If you feel you have to go, we can take care of your farm for you. I know how to grow sugar beets."

Menno thought his chest might explode. He loved Joanna. She was his perfect match. He could have floated up to the ceiling if the thought of losing Joanna hadn't weighed him down. It would have been a disaster if he'd asked one of the other four to marry him. Joanna was the only woman he loved. His heart bolted like a skittish horse. "I've got to go down there and get her."

Sadie grunted her disapproval. "Whatever you do, don't charge in there like a bull and ask her to marry you. Joanna needs time, romance, and affection. Don't ask anything of her. She'll think you're just looking for a convenient *fraa*. *Do not* make any sort of a list, and for goodness' sake, don't give yourself a time limit. That got you in trouble last time."

Menno loved Joanna with his whole soul. He would go anywhere, make any sacrifice to be with her. He knew what he had to do. He took both of Mamm's hands tenderly in his and looked into her eyes. "'Who so findeth a wife findeth a good thing, and obtaineth favor of the Lord.' I'm moving to Colorado."

Sadie grimaced. "Don't quote that scripture to Joanna."

Menno's gaze flicked in Sadie's direction. "Why not?"

"'Who so findeth a wife findeth a good *thing*?' A *fraa* is not a *thing*."

"You shouldn't criticize the scriptures," Menno said.

Sadie looked at him with round, innocent eyes. "And you shouldn't criticize my advice." She stood up as if too agitated to sit any longer. "Whatever you do, don't disappoint me." Sadie gave Freeman a smug smile. "I like to think five hours out of our way was worth it."

Freeman wouldn't give an inch. "I like to think you could have written a letter."

"Freeman, you don't know anything."

Chapter 14

Joanna was just pulling the last of the rolls from the oven when Ada came in the back door carrying a grocery bag.

"Guess who's back in town," Ada grumbled as she slipped off her shoes and left them on the mat.

Joanna's heart leaped into her throat. She didn't want to know who was back in town because it meant he'd found someone to marry, and it wasn't Joanna. She brushed bits of glaze from her fingers. "How was the store? Did they have any baker's sugar? I need to make four dozen fry pies tomorrow."

Ada set the bag on the counter. "You're not curious? I guess that is wise."

"*Denki*. Wisdom comes from hard experience."

Ada grunted. "I'm going to tell you anyway, because you want me to, even if you don't think you do. Menno Eicher is back with his two *dochters*."

Joanna's heart felt as if it had been hollowed out with a spoon. She thought about Menno every day, and every memory left her sadder and sadder, with a deep longing that sat right in the middle of her chest. The ache was like an annoying houseguest who refused to leave.

"He's staying with Esther again."

How nice that Menno had just given Joanna a *gute* reason to be annoyed with him. She'd rather be mad than sad or curious or hurt. "Poor Esther. Doesn't he know what an imposition he is? The baby is only two months away, and Menno is making a pest of himself again." The righteous indignation made Joanna feel better, but she still choked on her next question. "Is he engaged?"

"I don't know," Ada said. "He and his *dochters* were coming out of the Bent and Dent grocery store when I was walking in. Unfortunately, I couldn't avoid him. He recognized me immediately."

Joanna laughed. "Of course he recognized you. He came to our house several times when he was here the first time."

"I know, but I was hoping he'd forgotten me since I wasn't on his list."

Joanna didn't want to be curious, but she was. "What did he say?"

"He asked about you."

Joanna snorted. "I don't know why. I haven't heard a peep from him for three months. Surely I'm not on his list anymore. What did you tell him?"

Ada got a sly look on her face. "I told him a lot has happened since he's been gone. I said you're making goat's milk soap and selling it at the variety store. I also might have mentioned that Jakob Glick has had dinner at our house five times in the last month."

Laughter burst from Joanna's lips. "What does Jakob Glick have to do with me?"

Ada batted her eyes innocently. "It doesn't hurt to make Menno a little jealous."

"Menno doesn't get jealous. He just crosses ornery girls off his list. Besides, I can't believe for one minute he would think I'm interested in Jakob or Jakob is interested in me."

Ada's eyes sparkled with mischief. "He believes it."

Joanna rolled her eyes. "He does not."

"*Jah*, he does. I mentioned Jakob's name, and Menno frowned like a large-mouth bass. Then sweat started trickling down the side of his face."

Joanna couldn't bring herself to hope anything so *wunderbarr*. "It's a hot day."

Ada's lips curled upward. "I guess it is. Anyway, he says he's staying at Esther's until he can move into his new house."

"His new house?"

"He just bought the old Miller place. Moving in next week."

Joanna's heart tumbled off a cliff. "Then . . . then he's found a *fraa*. Probably Verla Ann."

The light faded from Ada's eyes. "It would seem so."

"But it doesn't make sense. Why would he buy a house? He can't be here that long. He's got to harvest his sugar beets." Joanna kept a tally in her head. Idaho was one more reason she would never marry Menno Eicher. It made her feel better about refusing him.

"You'll have to ask Menno all those questions. I don't know, and I wasn't curious enough to ask. I wanted to finish my shopping."

Joanna scolded herself for caring. She didn't intend to ask Menno anything because she never planned to talk to him again. Lord willing, he'd finalize his engagement and go away, but if that was his plan, why was he buying a house?

Ada picked up the pastry brush and brushed the tops of the rolls with a generous amount of butter. "Rosie and Lily are cuter than ever."

"I'm sure they are." For sure and certain Menno was more handsome than ever. Joanna leaned against the counter. "I've missed them." Losing Menno was bad enough, but she missed Rosie and Lily like winter missed sunshine. "Rosie is so determined. She wants to make her own decisions and doesn't like being told what to do."

Ada smiled. "It's always better if she thinks something was her idea. But there's no one more loyal. She adores her *dat*."

"They both do. Lily loves the goats, but she hates getting her hands dirty."

"She's as tidy I am," Ada said. "But much cuter."

Joanna finished brushing the rolls. "I'd say you're pretty cute, Ada. Though I'm sure you don't want anyone to know it."

"Keep it to yourself."

Chapter 15

Joanna slid the boxes from the buggy seat and left the buggy door open. She was only going to be in the bakery for two minutes to deliver her fry pies, and she didn't have enough hands to close the door. She also didn't have enough hands to open the bakery door. Hopefully, Myra would see her coming and open the door for her.

The emotion was bittersweet, remembering the first time she'd met Menno. It was right here at the bakery. He'd opened the door for her because her arms were full. No matter how things had turned out, it was a happy memory, and Joanna was grateful for it. She remembered the pleasant shock at seeing him for the first time, his brilliant green eyes shining with excitement, his handsome face, his strong jaw.

His kind heart.

She hadn't actually seen his kind heart that first day, but it had been apparent almost every day after that. She saw it in the way he cared for his girls, the way he treated other people, the way he looked to Gotte in every thought.

Joanna peered through the bakery door. Myra was standing at the counter ringing up someone's purchase. Joanna kicked lightly at the door to get her attention, but

just as Myra looked up, Menno was there opening the door
for her. Joanna was so startled, she nearly dropped her
boxes. Smiling like a saint, he reached out and took them
from her arms before they tumbled to the ground.

"JoJo!" Rosie jumped off her chair, ran at Joanna, and
threw her arms around Joanna's waist.

Joanna lifted Rosie into her arms and hugged her tightly.

It took Lily a little more time to slide off her chair, but
she also ran to Joanna and wrapped her arms around
Joanna's legs. "I miss you," she squealed.

Joanna blinked back tears as she bent and picked up
Lily with her other arm. She gave each girl a kiss on the
cheek. "I missed you too. The goats and Pepper asked
when you are coming to see them."

Rosie let out a high-pitched giggle. "Goats can't talk."

"They can't talk like people, but they said, '*Maa, maa*.'
That means 'Where are Rosie and Lily? We want to play
with them.'"

Both girls laughed in delight.

Rosie turned to look at her *dat*. "Can we go see them,
Daddy?"

"Not today." His gaze pierced through Joanna's de-
fenses. "Maybe tomorrow?"

"I would like that," she said breathlessly. *I* meaning
Pepper and the goats.

Menno slid the boxes onto the counter, and Joanna set
Lily and Rosie on their feet. They ran back to their table
and climbed into their chairs. Joanna handed Myra the in-
voice, and Myra handed her a receipt.

Menno didn't take his eyes from Joanna's face. "You
don't know how hard I prayed I would see you today."

His vulnerable honesty always disarmed her. She
couldn't help but smile. What was it about him that made

her either want to laugh with pure joy or cry her eyes out? There didn't seem to be any middle ground.

She tried to make his words into a joke, but she sounded shaky and unsteady. "I don't know that I've ever been an answer to someone's prayer before."

"I can't speak for anyone else, but you've been an answer to several of my prayers."

A warm sensation spread through her chest. *Ach*, she'd missed him, even though he'd broken her heart and made a mess of her life.

He motioned to the table where his two girls sat. "I bought four fry pies, hoping that maybe you would want to eat one with us." He widened his eyes then grimaced with his whole face. "*Ach*, why would you want to eat one of your own fry pies?"

Joanna smiled. "I love fry pies. I'm glad they still have some."

"I bought the last four. You came just in time." He glanced at Rosie and Lily. "Would you . . . could you spare a few minutes?"

Joanna nodded hesitantly, unsure if the urge to stay or run was stronger. Menno's eyes lit up, and she decided she was glad to stay. He pulled an empty chair from another table, and Joanna sat across from him between Lily and Rosie. Rosie was already a third of the way through her fry pie, and Lily hadn't touched hers, even though her *dat* had cut it into several small pieces.

"I like the cherry ones," he said.

"One of my favorites." The way he looked at her made her self-conscious. She distracted herself by taking a bite of her fry pie.

Menno handed Lily a piece, and she took a small bite, pinching it between her thumb and middle finger. "We've been here since six hoping to see you."

Joanna raised her eyebrows. "You've . . . you've been here since six o'clock?"

"I was afraid I'd miss you."

Ach, du lieva. He'd been waiting over an hour already. Would he do that for just anybody? Joanna suddenly didn't feel so much like a can of corn. She took a huge bite of her fry pie so she wouldn't have to speak.

Menno kept staring. "I've done so many things wrong, and I want to apologize."

She quickly chewed and swallowed. "Um, water under the bridge." She didn't want to talk about his feelings or her feelings. The emotions were just too raw, and she couldn't revisit them today.

"Can you ever forgive me?"

"Of course I forgive you, Menno, but I don't want to talk about it. Is that okay?"

He must have sensed her pain because he leaned back as if he couldn't leave the subject fast enough. "*Jah, jah.* We don't have to talk about it."

"We were always friends. Can't we just be friends?" Joanna didn't know why she asked that question. She didn't want to be Menno's *friend.*

"I have three friends," Rosie said.

Joanna smiled. "That is a lot of friends. What are their names?"

"Liza, Katie, and Cathy."

"Cathy Larsen?"

"*Jah.* She gives me candy." Rosie thought about it for a minute. "I have four friends. Liza, Katie, Cathy, and Joanna."

"It's nice to have friends," Joanna said, glancing at Menno. "I hear you are moving into the old Miller place."

"In a couple of weeks. I didn't want to be a burden on Esther."

"Will you be working with Levi again?"

"He says he has plenty of work to go around."

Joanna looked down at her hands. "Is . . . uh . . . Verla Ann going to be babysitting *die kinner*?"

A shadow passed over Menno's features. "I was thinking —" He cleared his throat and started over. "I haven't made babysitting arrangements yet. I don't want to be a burden to Esther, but I won't be asking Verla Ann."

Joanna's heart did a little jig, though she didn't know why. Maybe it was because Verla Ann was so exacting, and Rosie and Lily needed sunshine and happiness and laughter more than they needed *gute* manners and strict discipline. What would Menno think if she volunteered to babysit? Would he think she was trying to worm another proposal out of him? Would he think she just wanted to earn some extra money? What did she care what Menno thought? She missed the girls something wonderful, even if their *dat* wasn't a suitable husband.

But no, even in this, she refused to be the readily available, convenient choice. If Menno wanted her to babysit, he would have to ask, and then he'd have to offer to pay her, even though she'd never dream of taking his money. But what would it hurt to sneak over to Esther's occasionally and help her with *die kinner*? Menno would never have to know.

"Esther says she's happy to watch them until I can find a more permanent arrangement."

By that, he surely meant until he could find a *fraa*.

His lips curled slightly. "But Esther doesn't have goats."

"You're welcome to bring the girls over anytime to see the goats. If Esther needs a day off, I'm happy to watch them."

His smile could have lit up the whole valley. "Really? *Denki*. That's wonderful nice of you."

"I miss my sweet girls."

Lily slid off her chair and held out her arms to Joanna. "Hold me."

Joanna lifted Lily onto her lap. Rosie wasn't about to be left out. She patted Joanna's knee, and Joanna let her slide onto her lap as well. She put her arms around the girls and grinned teasingly at Menno. "I'm the favorite."

"I don't doubt it," he said, chuckling softly.

Lily held her hands away from her body because there was a little glaze on her thumb. Menno reached over the table with a wet wipe and cleaned Lily's fingers. "Sadie tells me Jakob Glick has been spending a lot of time at your house. I hope you're finding him *gute* company."

Joanna's gaze flew to his face in surprise. "Do you?"

He pulled his lips across his teeth. "Not really."

Joanna wanted to laugh at the look on his face. Ada had been right. For some reason, he was concerned about Jakob Glick. Joanna felt smug for about three seconds, but the emotion didn't last. She hated the thought of Menno being upset, no matter the reason.

"Jakob is on *Dat's* sheepshearing crew. They are planning a trip to the Grand Canyon, just the two of them. *Dat* thinks he can hike from rim to rim. I think he'll get stuck at the bottom, and they'll have to call a helicopter to get him out."

Menno smiled doubtfully and stared into his *kaffee* cup. "Oh. Okay. So you're not thinking of marrying him?"

Joanna grinned, ecstatic that Menno cared enough to embarrass himself by asking. Laughter burst from her lips like a geyser.

Lily covered her ears.

"He's older than my *dat*."

Relief overspread Menno's features. "Don't let my

mamm hear you say that. She gets touchy when people think she's old."

"My *dat* does too."

Lily pointed to the pieces of fry pie Menno had cut for her. "More, please."

Since Joanna's hands were occupied securing Lily and Rosie on her lap, he reached across the table again and handed Lily another piece. "Here you go, *heartzley*."

Joanna hated to put a damper on things, but they needed to talk about the elephant in the room—or more to the point—the can of corn. "How long do you think you'll be in Colorado?"

His *kaffee* must have been very interesting this morning. He stared at it faithfully. "I'm planning on being here permanently."

He could have knocked her over with a puff of air. "Permanently? Why?"

"Everything most important to me is here in this room."

Joanna's face felt as if it was on fire. He wasn't including her in that group, was he? "You didn't find a *fraa* last time you were here. Are you back to try again?" The question made her feel a little ill.

He traced circles on the table with his cup. "Maybe I came back to see you."

Her whole body tensed. "You came back to see your favorite can of corn?"

He winced.

Joanna immediately regretted it. She'd already forgiven him. At least that was what she'd told him. The pain was still raw, but she didn't need to flog him with her resentment. "I'm sorry. That was rude."

He gave her a kind smile. "I came back to talk you out of marrying Jakob Glick."

His expression, the tone of his voice, the light in his

eyes felt like a warm blanket. Joanna had made things uncomfortable, and he'd managed to set them on familiar, friendly ground again. She was ashamed of herself and proud of Menno. He truly was without guile, even if he was clumsy about finding a *fraa*.

She gave him a teasing smile. "You've been here three days, and you've already accomplished what you set out to do. You've talked me out of marrying Jakob Glick."

"I'm *froh* I could be successful at something."

She didn't miss the sadness in his tone. Menno needed help, and she took pity on him. "Show me your list."

"What?"

"You came back to Colorado to find a *fraa*. I don't wonder but you have a list."

His eyes darted back and forth between her and the door. Was he thinking of making an escape? "Sadie told me not to make a list."

Joanna laughed. "But you did anyway."

He crossed his arms over his chest. "I'm not showing you my list."

She knew it! "Oh, *cum*. Let me see it."

His frown was angular and deep, and he seemed to retreat into himself. "I'm sorry, Joanna. I'm taking this one to my grave."

Joanna didn't know what to think. Did his resistance mean she was on the list or not on the list? The bigger question was, did she want to be on the list? She didn't have the guts to ask, mostly because she didn't know which answer she'd like better. *Ach*! Only Menno could make her feel so unsure of herself.

She decided to change the subject. "I bet shoes aren't on your list anymore. I see you bought Rosie a new pair."

He stiffened like cement, and Joanna realized her mistake. Three months ago, almost the last words she'd said to him were, "Did you buy Rosie a new pair of shoes yet?" Joanna would have kicked herself if Lily and Rosie hadn't been sitting on her lap.

Menno went back to staring into his *kaffee*. Maybe Joanna was on his list now, but for sure and certain he would go home and cross her off. How could she be so insensitive? What was wrong with her?

Rosie held up her foot so Joanna could see. "I got new shoes."

"Your *dat* is so nice," Joanna said, hoping Menno would sense she meant it. She kept her eyes fixed on Rosie. "He takes *gute* care of you and Lily. He wipes your hands when you get dirty and buys you doughnuts and washes your clothes. He cuts your food and cleans windows."

"And reads us stories."

"And reads you stories and kisses you good night."

Lily nodded. "He kisses good night."

"You have just about the best *dat* in the whole world," Joanna said, daring a glance at Menno.

He hadn't moved, but he relaxed and his eyes shone with their own light. "If you're trying to make me forget all my horrible mistakes, you're doing a *gute* job."

She gave him a weak smile. "I'm trying to make you forget how rude I can be."

He raised his eyebrows. "I don't know what you're talking about."

Joanna laughed. "There you go again, being all nice and guileless when I don't deserve it."

He grew more serious. "You deserve every *gute* thing, Joanna."

She felt herself blush and decided that was quite enough of that. She kissed the girls and nudged them off her lap. "I have to go. I still need to make cheese."

Lily clamped her arms around Joanna's elbow. "Stay, JoJo."

She stood and patted Lily on the head. "I have to go, sweetie." She glanced at Menno, who looked at least as disappointed as Lily did."Do you want to come tomorrow to visit the goats?"

"Can we, Daddy?" Rosie whined.

"It will have to be in the afternoon," he said.

Joanna nodded. "It's a date." She almost choked on her own words. Could she say nothing right?

He smiled that mysterious, noncommittal smile that she loved . . . and hated. Then he stood and took Lily's hand. "What time do you come to the bakery on Fridays? I don't want to miss you, but I'd rather not drag the girls here at six."

He didn't seem eager to avoid her, in spite of all the rude things she'd said. She could have floated off the ground. "I'll be here next Friday at 7:15, if you want to see me."

He laughed softly. "*If* I want to see you? I would rather see you than breathe."

She'd never heard a nicer thing in her entire life.

Chapter 16

"Joanna, chewing your fingernails is a very bad habit," Ada said, wiping her hands on a dish towel and pinning Joanna with a stern gaze.

Joanna pulled her fingernail from between her teeth and clasped her hands together behind her back so she wouldn't be tempted. "I can't believe I'm nervous. Menno has been over here plenty of times."

"But not since you rejected his perfectly *gute* marriage proposal."

Joanna scrunched her lips together and eyed Ada. "Don't remind me. I've rethought that decision about a million times."

Mary wiped off the table. "Don't let Ada make you doubt yourself. You did the right thing."

Beth swept up a pile of dirt and tapped her broom on the floor. "*Jah*, don't listen to Ada. She's never read a romance novel."

Ada blew a puff of air between her lips. "I'm not trying to make Joanna doubt herself. I'm just being realistic. Menno has plenty of girls to choose from, and Joanna has already said *nae*."

Mary sighed and gave Ada a look. Ada shrugged and

closed her mouth. Even she knew when she'd gone too far. They were cleaning up after lunch.

Dat had gone right out to the alfalfa fields after eating. Clay, Mary's husband, had eaten with them, and he had also left, apologizing for not helping clean up.

"I've got to get that baseball field groomed for the players coming in on Monday," he'd said.

This was the first summer of Clay's clinics for aspiring high school baseball players. He'd run four weeks of clinics already, and they seemed to be very popular, with seven or eight boys coming each week. Clay did the instruction, and Mary cooked a midday meal for the attendees every weekday. The clinic ended on Fridays, and they got a new batch of boys at the farm every Monday. It was a lot of work, but Clay and Mary seemed happier than two people had a right to be.

Ada swiped her towel across the counter. "What time is Menno coming?"

Joanna glanced at the clock for about the hundredth time in the last hour. "He said he'd bring the girls over this afternoon. I wish we'd set a definite time. I've been a nervous wreck since eleven."

Mary also checked the clock. "It's 12:02. Just barely after noon."

Joanna's heart sank. "And he's still not here. Do you think he's decided not to come?"

Mary flicked some crumbs off the table. "I don't think a team of Percherons could keep him away."

Joanna wanted to run upstairs, throw herself across her bed, and pout until bedtime. "And yet, he's still not here." She pressed her lips together. "I was rude to him at the bakery yesterday. For sure and certain he changed his mind about coming."

Beth giggled. "For sure and certain, he should be here already."

Joanna was wound so tight, she nearly jumped out of her own skin when someone knocked on the door. "It's him!" she whispered breathlessly.

She bolted for the front room, but Beth shot out her arm and pulled her back. "Let me get it. You don't want to seem too eager, or he'll think you're a flirt. Believe me, I've read plenty of books."

Beth had some strange notions, but Joanna backed away and took over the sweeping job. Wait a minute! Maybe that was the real reason Beth wanted to answer the door. She'd do anything to get out of doing chores.

The house exploded with sound as Lily and Rosie bounded into the kitchen, squealing and skipping and jumping up and down with excitement. Rosie made a bee-line for Ada, and Lily jumped into Joanna's arms as the broom crashed to the floor.

Lily didn't waste any time. "JoJo, goats!"

Joanna cooed and bounced Lily on her hip, but she was more interested in Lily's *fater* who strolled into the kitchen as if he'd just stepped out of one of her happiest dreams. His smile was tentative, as if he wasn't sure he was welcome, and he held two small terracotta pots, one in each hand. Joanna kissed Lily on the cheek, hiding her face so Menno wouldn't see her blush.

Ada gave Rosie's hand a squeeze. "Menno, it's about time you paid us a visit. You haven't been here since the birthday party."

Joanna wanted to crawl into a hole. It had been the worst birthday of her life. From the look on Menno's face, he felt the same way. At times like this, she wished Ada wasn't quite so plainspoken.

Menno coughed as if choking on Ada's words. "It's been too long, and I've sure missed the four Yoder *schwesteren*." He stared at Joanna as if she were the only *schwester* in the room. "*Denki* for letting me come over." He flinched as if he just remembered the pots he carried. "I brought you a present, Joanna."

Joanna couldn't repress a grin. "Really? You didn't have to."

"But I wanted to, very much."

If he didn't quit looking at her like that, she'd have to go to the sink and splash her face with cold water. Steam must be rising from her head already.

He held the pots out to her. "They're herbs you can grow inside. Just put them on your windowsill and water them occasionally, and you can use the leaves in cooking. This one is rosemary. The lady at the store says it's *gute* in spaghetti and soups. These are chives. They taste sort of like onions."

"How *wunderbarr*," Mary said. "What a thoughtful gift."

His eagerness faltered. "I should have brought something for everyone, but I was just thinking of Joanna"—he coughed into his fist—"and how she likes to cook."

Ada swatted away his concern. "We don't want gifts. Spend your money on Joanna and leave the rest of us out of it."

Beth nodded. "Joanna is the important one." She laced her fingers together. "Joanna and you. You and Joanna."

"Okay, Beth," Ada scolded. "You've said enough."

Beth stuck out her bottom lip. "I've read a lot more romances than you have, Ada Yoder. I know what I'm doing." Since Joanna's arms were full of Lily, Beth took the pots from Menno and set them on the table.

Joanna couldn't help but be touched. Amish men weren't known for their gift-giving skills.

"This is so nice of you, Menno," she said. "I've never cooked with fresh herbs. Everything will taste that much better now."

"I don't know how anything you make could taste any better," he said, and then he just stood there, staring at her as if she were a sunset or a newly planted field.

Lily squished Joanna's face between her palms. "JoJo, goats. Peppa."

"Can we see Blue?" Rosie asked.

Menno seemed to awake from whatever stupor he was under. "*Jah*. I'm pretending we came to see the goats and Pepper." He pulled a dog biscuit from his pocket. "I brought a treat for Pepper."

"He'll love you forever," Joanna said.

From behind, Beth took Joanna by the shoulders and nudged her in Menno's direction. "You go with them, Joanna. We'll finish the dishes."

Joanna gave Beth a grateful smile. It wasn't like her to volunteer for anything. "I'd love to." She winced at the eagerness in her tone. Beth had warned her not to be a flirt, but she couldn't help it if her voice betrayed her. She was just so happy to be near Menno again, even if it was only for one afternoon. She wanted to make the most of it.

She set Lily on her feet, and Menno opened the door and ushered them outside. Lily and Rosie skipped down the stairs and ran toward the chicken coop where the chickens were pecking at the dirt or staring glassy eyed into the alfalfa fields. Pepper appeared from behind the barn, barking and wagging his tail as if Lily and Rosie were his favorite people. In his enthusiasm, he nearly knocked Lily on her *hinnerdale*, but she grabbed onto his neck and kept her balance. Rosie squealed and tried to pet him as he ran around and around her. He finally came to rest and let Rosie press her cheek to his face. He was still for a few seconds, then leaped away from Rosie and licked her face with his pink, wet tongue.

Menno whistled to get Pepper's attention then threw him the dog biscuit. He yipped happily and gobbled it up.

All four goats trotted from the barn to greet the girls. Lily giggled and tried to catch each goat in turn before giving up and letting the goats chase each other. Menno and Joanna laughed when Lily shook her finger and scolded Smiley for nibbling on her dress. It was the most adorable thing Joanna had seen for weeks.

"When do you move into your new house?" she asked, as they strolled toward the chicken coop, not in any hurry to get anywhere.

"In about two weeks. I'm just waiting for all the paperwork to go through."

"Do you need help moving in?"

He smiled sheepishly. "*Ach, vell*, I don't really have anything to move. I sold my farm, my house, and all my furniture before I came. Everything I own fit in two suitcases, a large plastic storage container, and a safe-deposit box in Baker."

Joanna's heart lurched and galloped away from her like a runaway horse. Why would he sell everything and upend his life and family to move to Byler, Colorado? Why would he do something so rash, so impetuous. So romantic? It was incomprehensible to think he'd done it for her, but she couldn't shove the idea from her mind. "That seems so drastic. Why . . . why . . . ?"

She shouldn't have assumed it was a romantic gesture instead of a practical one, but if he married Naomi, he wouldn't need to buy new furniture. For that matter, he wouldn't need to buy a house. If he married Lydia, they could furnish their house with stuffed animals. If he married Verla Ann, she could probably build them a bed with a jigsaw, some scrap wood, and her own two hands. Anybody who knew how to potty train a toddler and make a picnic basket could probably build furniture with her eyes closed.

Menno hadn't answered her yet, so she dared a glance at him.

His gaze was glued to hers, and he had that serene, *all-is-right-with-the-world* expression on his face Joanna found so comforting. He was strong and capable and steady, and if she believed for one second that he truly loved her, she'd tell him yes in less time than it took for her heart to skip a beat.

He propped his hand on top of one of the corner posts of the chicken coop. "You get prettier every time I see you."

She remembered to take a breath. "But . . . what about a kitchen table. What are you going to do about a kitchen table?"

His lips curled upward. "Cathy has a friend with a pickup truck who can take me to the thrift store in Alamosa. I'm hoping to find everything I need there." He looked into her eyes, and his gaze made fireworks go off in her head. "Well, not everything."

Oh, *sis yuscht*! What was he up to? If he'd set out this morning to make her feel completely discombobulated, he had achieved his goal.

He drew in a deep breath. "I've missed this. Strolling around your yard, watching the girls play, sharing our opinions about goats and child rearing and birthday cakes."

Ach, she had missed it too. "All very exciting subjects, for sure and certain."

Menno had been her anchor and her wall, someone to keep her grounded and bounce ideas off of at the same time. He folded his arms across his chest and looked at her as if trying to see into her skull. She tried not to let his good looks unsettle her. Those muscles were as big as anything she had ever read about in *Rapturous Regency Romance*.

"Joanna, I have been needing to apologize to you for months. I badly botched my proposal, and I've regretted it every day since. I'm very sorry."

She tried to laugh it off, cuffing him casually on the shoulder. "I'm sure you'll do better next time."

Hope flickered in his eyes. "Will there be a next time?"

Her heart tried to claw its way out of her chest. "For sure and certain there will be a next time for you." She didn't know who the girl would be, but surely Menno would do a better job of proposing. That thought made her feel worse.

The warmth and life in his expression died a quick death. "Oh. I see what you mean." He pulled his foot out of the way as Lily raced between them chasing down a chicken. "I don't want to make you uncomfortable, but you deserve my complete honesty. You might not believe this, but I was devastated when you said no . . . though I certainly didn't act like it." He winced. "I spent two days nursing my wounds, then I went right back to looking for a *fraa*, as if the person I truly wanted to marry hadn't just broken my heart."

Joanna swallowed hard. He was right. This topic was making her very uncomfortable. She hated, *hated*, the thought that she had hurt him, but she also hated how deeply he had hurt her.

She didn't want to talk about it. "Rosie, Lily," she called. "Let's go get some carrot peels from Ada and feed them to the chickens."

Rosie was halfway to the house before Joanna even finished her sentence.

Joanna tried to follow, but Menno grabbed her hand and pulled her back. "Please don't turn away from me." His voice cracked in a thousand different places.

Joanna pressed her lips together and closed her eyes momentarily. "I'm sorry." She squeezed his hand and tried for a smile. "The easy thing to do is to run away from this. I'll stand my ground and hear what you have to say."

"I want to hear what you have to say." He didn't let go of her hand.

She didn't necessarily want to pull away. She was a hopeless case.

Lily and Rosie didn't even look back. They tromped up the porch steps and knocked on the back door. Ada answered and shepherded them into the house.

Joanna watched them go, then screwed up her courage and laid her heart bare to him. "Three days after I refused your proposal, you asked four girls on dates." She felt the sting as if it had happened yesterday, and she tugged her hand from his grasp. "How do you think that made me feel?"

The pain in his eyes was raw and intense. "I can't even imagine. I proved true everything you'd accused me of."

"It proved that crossing a task off your list was more important than my feelings. It proved that your sense of duty was stronger than any love you might have felt for me." There. She'd said it. All of her heartbreak wrapped up in two sentences.

He curled his fingers around the back of his neck. "*Jah*."

She looked past the chain link fence that surrounded the yard. "To be fair, I had refused you. I had no right to judge your choices after that. Still, three days is an indecently short amount of time."

His lips twitched with a hint of irony. "You don't have to defend your feelings to me. I was a hundred percent in the wrong."

"*Jah*, you were." It felt *gute* to say it, even though she could tell she was making him feel worse and worse.

"I don't want you to think I'm justifying myself, but I want you to understand." He passed his hand across his eyes. "I always try to be honest with everyone and faithful to Gotte. My *mamm* says I wear my heart on my sleeve."

"It sounds painful and kind of disgusting."

He gave her a reluctant smile. "I guess it's easier to crush someone's heart if it's on their sleeve."

"Very disgusting."

"When I'm faced with a problem or a challenge, all I know how to do is put one foot in front of the other. When Suvilla died, the bishop told me the acceptable mourning period was one year and no longer. I always try to do the next thing I'm supposed to do. It was the same when I got married. Suvilla came to Baker from Pennsylvania for the summer, and she was the only girl in Baker who was even close to my age. I felt it was my duty to marry her. I didn't want to hurt her feelings by looking elsewhere for a *fraa*."

"Did you love her?"

"*Jah*, of course I did. It was hard to separate my desire

to obey the commandments from my love for her, but I think she was happy. I was happy. We had a *gute* life together. When I asked you to marry me"—he grimaced in embarrassment—"I didn't know if I was in love with you or in love with the thought that I'd found someone so perfect in two weeks' time. Between grieving for Suvilla, looking for a *fraa*, caring for my girls, and trying to do my duty, I didn't even know what I wanted anymore." He reached out as if to take her hand but must have thought better of it and let his arm drop to his side. "I'm so sorry about how I hurt you."

"You're forgiven, as I've already told you."

"My blindness got in the way of something you and I could have had together. But now, I'm determined to be selfish. I want to marry for love, not because my girls need a *mater* or I need a *fraa*. Not because it's my duty. Not because Gotte wants me to. Not because the bishop is persistent."

She winced as a sharp ache cut at the base of her throat. "Menno, I . . . I know what you're trying to say, but I can't help but believe this is all a waste of time. I can't bear the thought of moving away from my family. My home is here."

He didn't seem the least bit upset. "Of course not. Why do you think I bought a house? I'm in Colorado for as long as it takes. I'm here forever, really, because you don't want to move to Idaho, and I won't ask you to. Why should I ask you to upend your life to fit into mine?"

Something heavy lifted off Joanna's shoulders. She hadn't even known she'd been carrying it.

He reached out again, and this time their hands met. He twined his fingers around hers. "Please tell me I haven't ruined things beyond repair."

Joanna's breathing was shallow, and a bead of sweat trickled down her neck. "I believe in Jesus. Nothing is beyond repair."

His whole face lit up, and he took a step closer.

Joanna caught her breath. Their lips were mere inches apart.

"Do you really mean that?"

She knew she shouldn't be so easily persuaded, but he was so close and so handsome, and he smelled like summer rain. "Do you know how badly I want to believe you right now?"

"Do you know how badly I want to kiss you right now?"

Joanna's pulse raced. Did he know how badly she wanted to be kissed?

Pepper must have sensed the danger. He trotted to Joanna's side and barked a warning.

Alarm bells went off in her head, and reason grabbed her by the throat. She took a step back, and the disappointment on his face hurt to her very bones.

"It's too soon, Menno. I need to protect my heart." She shouldn't have said that. It sounded like she loved him, which she did, but she refused to let him use it against her. It wasn't enough for her to love him. He had to love her too, and he couldn't just love the idea of a *fraa*. She wanted to be sure he loved the idea of marrying Joanna Yoder. "I want you to be sure of your heart."

"I'm sure," he blurted out, before pulling back into himself and patting Pepper on the head. "You have every reason to feel that way. I haven't done anything to make you believe my sincerity yet. Can you be patient with me?"

He looked so earnest and so miserable, she couldn't stand it.

She scrunched her lips to one side of her face and

cocked an eyebrow. "Patience has never been a strength of mine, but what kind of a Christian would I be if I didn't give you another chance?"

His gaze warmed her heart like a steaming cup of hot chocolate. "Take all the time you need. I'm not going to rush you, but I'm not going to give up. Ever."

"*Denki*," Joanna said breathlessly, though she wasn't quite sure why she felt so grateful. Maybe she looked forward to his efforts to prove his love. Maybe she liked the thought that he refused to give up on her. They'd given up on each other once already, and once was enough.

He still had hold of her hand. "I've already set my sneaky plan in motion."

"Sneaky, huh? What are you planning that's sneaky?"

"If I told you, it wouldn't be sneaky. My first step was to buy a house in Byler. My second step was to hang out at the bakery on the chance I might see you. Are there any other places I need to be aware of?"

She laughed. "*Nae.* I go from home to the bakery to the grocery store and back home again."

"Can I make an order for a dozen of your potato rolls? When can I come and pick them up?"

His boyish enthusiasm made her heart swell bigger than the sky. "I bake rolls on Wednesdays."

He slumped his shoulders. "Once a week is not enough."

Rosie and Lily came out the back door. Rosie carried a red plastic bucket, and the two of them carefully stepped down the stairs. Once they were on solid ground, both girls skipped to the chicken coop.

"Look, Dada," Lily said. "Peels."

Rosie showed Menno her bucket. "Carrot peelings from Ada for the chickens."

"They'll love those," Menno said. "Do you want help?"

"We do it."

He cupped his hand over Lily's head. "Don't get your fingers pecked."

"They no peck us," Lily said. "They our friends."

Rosie gazed up at her *dat* with a sly look on her face. "Ada said we have to stay for dinner because she made too much food."

Menno glanced at Joanna and chuckled. "Has she even started making dinner yet?"

Joanna rolled her eyes. "*Nae*. Ada is also a little sneaky."

His gaze intensified. "Would that be okay?"

Joanna couldn't think of a nicer way to spend the evening meal than with Menno and his girls. "Was this part of your plan?"

He grinned. "For sure and certain."

"I'm impressed at how you managed to get Ada to work herself into your plan without even asking her."

"I told you, I'm sneaky." He shrugged. "And Ada likes me."

"It's true. She's already told me I shouldn't have refused your proposal."

His eyes flashed with surprise. "I'm glad to have her on my side. Now I just need to work on getting the most important person on my side, and I'll be the happiest man who ever lived."

His fervent expression sent a shiver of anticipation down Joanna's spine. She bit down on her tongue and willed herself back to reality. It was very possible and very likely she was going to get her heart broken all over again. Menno was too attached to his list and his duty, and Verla Ann was quite persistent and quite impressive. But for now, Joanna would take him at his word and try to enjoy the things she'd grown to love about him—his common sense, his kindness, his faithfulness to Gotte.

If tomorrow didn't work out between them, at least she had today.

That was all anybody had because life gave no guarantees.

Chapter 17

Joanna and Esther stood in Menno's empty kitchen unpacking dishes and pots and pans from boxes.

Menno had been to two thrift stores and Walmart in the last week and had found enough cookware to supply his whole kitchen and all the bedding and towels he and the girls would need to be comfortable. Joanna had donated some knives and forks, and Esther had given him half her collection of plastic cups.

"I'm not sure where he wants us to put all this," Joanna said, pulling out a stack of second-hand plates and setting it on the counter.

The whole house echoed with noisy activity as people tromped in and out, bringing in furniture, washing windows, sweeping floors, and setting up beds. Rosie, Lily, Winnie, and Junior were "helping" Ada and Levi's *bruder* Ben in the girls' bedroom, putting together the two twin beds Menno had bought just yesterday. Levi's *bruder* Caleb and Joanna's *dat*, Try, were working on the bed in Menno's room. Beth and Sadie were sweeping the old wood floors and wiping the dust off everything from top to bottom.

Cathy Larsen and her husband Lon were also there, but

they were "on call" as Cathy described it, which meant they were sitting in Cathy's van listening to Britney Spears. It was the perfect job for them. Neither Cathy nor Lon could lift much, and Lon didn't like to do anything unless he could sit. They had already made a trip into town for some cleaning supplies, and everyone agreed that having someone on call was very helpful.

Esther turned on the water and filled the sink. "We should wash these plates. Everything has a layer of dust."

Joanna pulled a towel from one of Menno's boxes. "I'll dry."

Esther cocked her head to one side. "You don't seem your cheerful self today. Is everything all right?"

Joanna huffed out a breath and lowered her voice. "Menno asked Ada to babysit *die kinner* since your baby is coming soon."

Esther set the entire stack of plates in the water. "I know. I can't say that I'm disappointed. I'm the size of a whale, and chasing around two children is hard enough."

"But . . . why didn't he ask me?" Joanna felt silly for even saying it.

Esther gave Joanna a wry smile. "Why do you think?"

Esther acted as if Joanna should know, but she was too uncertain to have any concrete answers. "When I was their sitter, Lily had seven or eight injuries and an impressive collection of Band-Aids and bruises. Rosie's hands got so filthy she had permanent dirt under her fingernails for days."

Esther looked too amused for such a serious topic. "Verla Ann did an excellent job clipping the girls' fingernails, and she used one of those little fingernail brushes on their hands twice a day. Did you know she keeps a tube of hand sanitizer in her apron pocket?"

Joanna's heart dropped. Should she keep a tube of hand

sanitizer in her pocket? And where did someone purchase
a little fingernail brush? "The night you went to Walmart,
I let the three girls stay up an hour past their bedtime and
eat ice cream. We finished the entire carton. Was Menno
annoyed about that?"

Esther handed Joanna a dripping-wet plate. "I can't
speak for Menno. You should ask him yourself."

"He offered to pay Ada to babysit, but she of course
said *nae*. We're all trying to help him along until he can
find a *fraa*."

Esther's lips twitched as if she was trying not to laugh.
"*Ach, vell*, he could have asked Verla Ann to babysit."

Joanna mulled that over for a few seconds. Why hadn't
he asked Verla Ann? Wasn't she the best babysitter in
Byler?

Joanna clamped her mouth shut when Levi and Menno
carried the table into the kitchen. They set it down, and she
felt the bittersweet tug of being in Menno's company. He
and the girls had been to her house nearly every day in the
last two weeks. They came after work and always stayed
for dinner. It was a load off Esther's plate, and it never felt
like Joanna's day was complete unless she saw Menno.
She was growing more and more in love with him every
day, and she didn't know how she would bear it if he
decided he didn't love her and chose someone better . . .
like Verla Ann, who could teach his *dochters* how to read
and could knit a pair of baby booties with one arm tied
behind her back.

Levi took a bandana out of his pocket and wiped his
forehead. "You just had to choose the end of July to move,
didn't you, Menno. I don't wonder but we'll all die of heat
exhaustion."

Menno smiled. "The *gute* news is, I'm moving out of

your house. While you're dripping with sweat, think of how nice it will be to get your privacy back. Think about how much extra room you'll have."

Esther fingered the crochet hook tucked behind her ear. "Just in time for the baby."

Levi gave Esther a quick kiss on the cheek. "I don't want to be rude, Menno, but I'm happy you're finally moving out. We love you, but fish and house guests stink after three days."

Menno scooted the table closer to the window. "*Ach, du lieva.* I hope I don't smell that bad. I've been staying at your house two weeks already."

"We'll air out all the rooms when you're gone," Levi teased.

Joanna held up the plate she'd just dried. "Menno, where do you want us to put everything once it's clean?"

He brushed off his hands and gave her a tender look. "Arrange the kitchen the way you would want it."

She turned away from him so he wouldn't see her blush. She knew exactly what he meant, but certainly didn't want him to know that she knew exactly what he meant. She opened the nearest cupboard and set a stack of plates on the lowest shelf for easy access. That's where she would put them if this were her kitchen. She imagined living here, baking cakes and pies and rolls for Menno and the girls. The whole scene was too easy to picture. This was going to hurt wonderful bad if it ended.

Ben came into the kitchen holding a socket wrench, and Ada and all *die kinner* followed after him. He was huffing and puffing as if he'd just run a 5K. Ada held on to Rosie and Winnie's hands while lecturing Ben at the same time. "You know, if you hadn't taken up smoking, you wouldn't be trying to cough up a lung every day."

Ben leaned against the counter. "There's no call to chastise me, Ada. I regret ever starting, and I haven't smoked for more than two years. Sometimes I just feel the aftereffects of it."

Ada cupped her hand over her mouth and loudly whispered to Ben. "I know. I'm scolding you for *die kinner*'s benefit. They need to see the consequences of smoking. This is a teaching moment."

Rosie grabbed Menno's hand. "I'm hungry, Daddy."

Menno glanced at the clock Joanna had just hung on the wall. "Should we see if Cathy and Lon can go and get us some pizza?"

"Pizza, pizza!" Winnie and Junior cheered.

Ada took Junior's hand. "Come on. Let's give Cathy our pizza order."

She and all four children ran out the front door like a stampede of cattle. *Ach*, *vell*, Ada didn't stampede, but she was definitely caught up in the mayhem.

Ben watched as she shut the door behind her. "Is she always this bossy?"

Joanna giggled. "Ada can't help herself. She's trying to fix the entire population of Byler by herself."

"First she got mad at me because I used to smoke, then she gave me a talking-to about the way I was setting up the beds. It wasn't the easiest job since Lily and Junior wanted to bounce on the mattresses while I was trying to secure the safety rails."

Ada was particular, and she liked to be in charge. Ben had just been her latest victim.

"You'll get used to her."

He folded his arms. "I'll work in a different room from now on."

Levi looked down and tapped his toe on the worn

wood floor. "This could be a pretty floor with a little elbow grease."

Menno squatted and looked up at Joanna. "What do you think? Do you like it? It has an old-fashioned look to it. We could strip it and apply a lighter stain. It would be a lot of work, but it would be pretty."

Every eye was on Joanna, and she wasn't unaware as to why. Menno had said *we*, unconsciously including her in the decision about the floor. She pretended not to notice, as if all of them were in on the decision together. "A lighter stain would brighten up the whole room, don't you think, Esther?"

Esther wasn't fooled. "It will be nicer to bake in a bright kitchen. You should paint the cabinets too. They're so dark."

Menno nodded. "The kitchen is the heart of the home. It's worth the extra work."

Joanna wanted to tell him not to go to all that work on her account, but it would make everyone in the room feel awkward, especially Menno, and maybe she *did* want him to go to all that work on her account. *Ach*! Couldn't they all just leave her alone to unpack dishes in solitude?

Esther pulled another plate from the sink. "Menno, you should show Joanna what you've planned for the laundry room."

Menno gave Joanna a handsome smile. "Do you want to see?"

"For sure and certain."

He motioned for her to follow him and strode down the long hall with single-minded purpose. She had to skip and hop to keep up with him. He stopped at the small room just inside the back door and pointed to a two-tub wringer washer inside. "This is the only thing the Millers left in the house."

Joanna ran her hand along the wringer between the two water tubs. "The best thing they could have left, ain't not?"

Menno's enthusiasm was contagious. "*Jah.*" He bent over and picked up the power cord. "I can plug this into the wall and power it with a generator or a solar panel. I'm going to have Levi and Ben help me put solar panels on the roof. It's a lot of money, but it will be easier for you . . ." He cleared his throat. "I can power the washing machine, heat my water, and light the whole house with solar power."

Joanna smiled at how excited he was. "Byler is a sunny place. We've learned to take advantage of it."

"I'm going to build a row of shelves along this wall for extra storage. It might be a *gute* place for canned goods." He took her hand, as if it was the most natural thing in the whole world.

Her heart skipped like cold water on a hot skillet.

"*Cum*, let me show you what I've got planned for the backyard." He pulled her out the door and down the steps.

She should have protested that holding hands wasn't proper for unmarried couples, but his calloused hand felt too *wunderbarr* in hers to even think of objecting.

He pointed to the pasture. "I've only got thirty acres, but that might be enough to try my hand at planting potatoes or alfalfa. Levi says I can keep working with him and his *dat*, so I won't need to farm full-time. There's a third of an acre on the side of the house that would be a nice garden, but you wouldn't have to plant the whole thing." He pressed his lips together as his eyes went wide.

She felt the excitement all the way to her toes. "*Ach*, Menno," she said, laughing at the sheepish look on his face. "I don't mind that you talk about me as if I already lived here."

"You don't?"

"You're a man who likes to make lists. The more specific the better. If you want to use me to fill in your blanks, I am willing to endure it."

He squeezed her hand tenderly. "You fill in all my blanks, Joanna. Every single one."

She held up her hands and laughed. "Okay, too much pressure for one day. I'm helping you move in. How much more can you ask of one woman?"

He pressed his palm to his chest. "Nothing less than I'm willing to give. I'll give you my whole world."

She rolled her eyes. "Now you're starting to sound like *Rapturous Regency Love.*"

He chuckled. "Rapturous what?"

"Never mind."

They got to the fence on the far side of the backyard, and he propped his elbow on the post. "I was trying to be romantic."

She snorted. "Well, you're not the romantic type. You make lists and plans and memorize scriptures. I like the real Menno better."

"That's the nicest thing I've heard all day."

She gave him a playful smile. "I didn't say I liked the real Menno a *lot* better."

His face lit up. "But you do, don't you?"

"Today is not the day to talk about that. We're moving furniture and sweeping floors."

"There's never a bad time to talk about love."

Laughter burst from Joanna's lips. "Yep, I like the real Menno better."

"I sold my horse and buggy in Baker. Levi's *dat* is going to help me buy another horse at auction, and Eli Gingerich's *mamm* isn't using her buggy anymore. He said I could use it until I can get my own." Menno pointed to the dilapidated shed on the other side of the fence. "I don't have money for it yet, but I'd like to put up a steel building and tear down that shed. What do you think? The steel buildings around here aren't bad looking."

"*Ach*, everybody has a steel building, it seems like. The Herschbergers have four, and I like their yellow siding. Light blue siding would be pretty too."

"Light blue it is," he said.

Joanna bit her tongue. Menno was deep into his planning, and she didn't have the heart to dampen his mood by pointing out that maybe he'd end up marrying Verla Ann and maybe she liked yellow better . . . or white or green. "Can I ask you a question?"

"Anything."

"Anything? Can I see your list?"

He chuckled. "Anything but that."

She nibbled on her bottom lip. "Why did you ask Ada to watch the girls?"

He shrugged. "I can't expect Esther to do it anymore. The baby is coming soon, and I've already imposed on her kindness far too long."

"But why d-didn't you ask *me* to babysit?" she stuttered.

A spark ignited in his eyes. "Why do you think?"

He and Esther must have been comparing notes. "I don't know what to think. Verla Ann is so much more skilled than I am. She uses a fingernail brush, she feeds the girls healthy meals, she makes sure they're obedient, and she potty trained Lily. I can't measure up to that."

He donned the exact same amused expression Esther wore not fifteen minutes earlier. "*Nae*, you can't measure up to that."

Her heart plummeted to the ground. "Do you see why I'm confused?"

He heaved a sigh. "Joanna, I'm shocked that you have

been worried about your babysitting skills compared to Verla Ann's. Do you even know yourself? Do you even know me? I loved it when you babysat my girls and not because it was convenient."

Joanna dared a glance at his face. He was earnest and a little irritated. The man without guile got irritated? She found the expression endearing.

"I love that my girls get disgustingly dirty at your house. That means they're having fun just being children. I don't want them to grow up too soon, worrying about adult things like keeping the house clean or making too much noise. They love your goats. They love Pepper. They love your *schwesteren*. They love your fry pies." He snaked his arm around her shoulders. "All things that I love about you, by the way."

Joanna couldn't help but lean into him, nor could she seem to catch her breath.

"Lily doesn't care who potty trained her. She loves you because you give her kisses and hugs and never scold her about finishing her vegetables. Rosie loves you because you don't get mad when she screams right in your ear, and you aren't impatient when she gives you her grumpy face. If I wanted to marry just anyone, those things might matter to me. Sadie told me I wasn't supposed to mention marriage, but I have to be honest with you, Joanna. With my whole heart, I want to marry you."

She curled her lips upward. "I kind of figured that out."

"*Gute*, because I'm not very *gute* at tiptoeing around things."

"But why did you ask Ada and not me?"

He sighed louder. "Why do you think?"

"Stop saying that."

"I asked Ada because I didn't want you to start believing you are just the convenient choice. I want my girls to have a loving *mater*, but everything is secondary to me being in love with my *fraa* and my *fraa* knowing how much I love her."

Joanna lowered her head so he wouldn't see her face glow with embarrassment. It was the loveliest answer she could have hoped for. "That . . . that makes sense."

"Ada was kind enough to say yes, but she also gave me a very stern lecture about not being a *dummkopf* and not making you cry again." He smoothed his hand up and down her arm. "I'm sorry I made you cry the first time."

"It's . . . it's okay," she said, hoping he didn't hear the trembling in her voice. He would wonder what was wrong if she burst into tears.

He tightened his arm around her. "Enough of this rapturous romantic talk."

Joanna laughed. He was catching on right quick.

He pointed toward the front of the house. "I think we should plant two or three cherry trees in the front yard, so eventually you'll have plenty of cherries for your fry pies."

"You can't plant cherries in the San Luis Valley. It's illegal."

He looked at her as if she'd grown cat whiskers. "Illegal? What do you mean it's illegal?"

"I don't know. All I know is that three years ago Dat wanted to plant an apricot tree, and they didn't sell any at the local nursery. They told him it was illegal to plant certain trees here. I think they attract bugs that like to eat potatoes or something like that."

"So no fruit trees?"

Joanna nestled her head on his shoulder. "I think we can plant apple trees. That might be fun in the front yard if there's water enough."

He took her hand as if all was right with the world again. "Let's go look."

They strolled around to the front, and Joanna tensed and pulled her hand away.

Verla Anna stood in the front yard holding a monstrous picnic basket, and she was vehemently lecturing all four of *die kinner*. She eyed them sternly, as if she'd completely forgotten how to smile. Lily wrung her hands, too concerned for a two-year-old. Rosie's lips were puckered into a you're-not-the-boss-of-me frown with her arms folded around her waist. Winnie had hold of Junior's hand, as if ready to jump in and protect him at any sign of danger.

Verla Ann's expression changed from stern to concerned when she caught sight of Menno and Joanna. "Menno," she called. "Somebody let *die kinner* play in the front yard unsupervised." She glared at Joanna when she said *somebody*, as if Joanna had personally put Menno's children in danger.

How did Verla Ann manage to teach school without losing her mind? Did recess, with kids running every which way, drive her crazy?

Menno looked puzzled and a little uneasy. "I thought Ada was out here with them."

Rosie tugged on Menno's hand. "Look what I can do." She did an awkward and childish somersault in the dirt, covering the back of her dress and her arms and hands in a layer of dust.

Verla Ann gasped.

"Very nice, Rosie," Menno said, brushing a little stick off her sleeve.

"It kind of hurts," Rosie said, scratching her nose. "We need grass."

Menno glanced at Joanna, his eyes dancing. "I think

we need grass so Rosie can do gymnastics without hurting herself."

Verla Ann eyed Joanna curiously even while she talked to Menno. "Hardly anybody around here has grass. It uses too much water. You don't need grass. Rosie can learn to behave herself. Little girls shouldn't be doing somersaults or cartwheels. It shows their underwear."

Joanna nearly laughed. Then she realized Verla Ann wasn't joking and started doubting herself. Should little girls be allowed to do somersaults? Joanna had always thought little girls shouldn't be kept from activities simply because they wore dresses. Was she wrong? What did Menno think? Would her opinion make him doubt his desire to marry her?

Ach, *vell*, if it did, she wouldn't want to marry him anyway.

"I don't mind if my *dochters* do somersaults," Menno said, with the slightest hint of coldness in his tone. "They're children, not china dolls." He bent down and gave Lily a hug and kiss on the cheek. "Go play for a few more minutes before the pizza gets here."

Verla Ann's expression drooped like a wildflower in July. "Pizza?" She tapped on the picnic basket hooked over her elbow. "I brought Black Forest ham and gruyere sandwiches and chips for everybody."

"Um . . . that's very nice of you. You didn't need to do that."

"I heard just this morning that you were moving in today, and I knew you'd be hungry." Her bottom lip trembled. "I must admit that I'm surprised and a little hurt that you didn't tell me sooner. I would have been happy to help you today. I'm a *gute* cleaner. I know how to wax a wood floor until it shines like new."

Of course she did.

Menno didn't seem regretful. "Moving is a big job. I didn't want to impose on your time."

Verla Ann nodded in Joanna's direction. "But you didn't care about imposing on her time?"

Oh, *sis yuscht.* Joanna wasn't the type to cower to anybody, but she refused to try to justify herself to Verla Ann. Menno had made his own choices and had led Verla Ann to believe he might ask her to marry him. He would have to be the one to either deflate her hopes or tiptoe around her feelings.

"Well," Menno said, his expression gentle and subdued. "I know you're getting ready for school to start. I didn't want to make your burdens any heavier than they already are."

Verla Ann smiled with her whole face. "You're never a burden." She set the picnic basket on the ground and lifted the lid. "This morning after I made sandwiches, I edged half a dozen cleaning rags so you'd have plenty if you needed them today." She handed six bright white terry cleaning cloths to Menno.

He took them as if she was giving him the pearl of great price. "That is wonderful nice of you, Verla Ann. You're very thoughtful."

So. He had chosen to tiptoe around Verla Ann's feelings. If he was dead set against Verla Ann, why wasn't he plain and direct with her? Why didn't he send her away? Was Joanna Menno's *only* choice, or was Verla Ann his backup plan? And what about Naomi and Lydia?

Those doubts were what held Joanna back from giving Menno her whole heart. She didn't believe in him, didn't know if she could count on him even now. Didn't know if he was still just looking for a can-of-corn *fraa* or if he truly wanted *her*. Maybe she was holding back her forgiveness or holding fast to her resentment, but maybe she was being wise and cautious, guarding her tender feelings the only way she knew how.

Despite his many flaws, Menno was the most *wunderbarr* man she knew, and he had the very real power to stomp on her heart and grind her self-assurance to dust.

Joanna had heard enough. She didn't need to stand there policing Verla Ann and Menno's conversation. The sooner she could finish unpacking things, the sooner she could leave. Maybe some time alone with Verla Ann would give Menno more clarity and help him make a better decision.

Joanna's heart ached. There was no doubt that Verla Ann was the better decision. She made picnic baskets and fancy, unpronounceable sandwiches. Her cleaning rags were edged and immaculate white. She knew how to potty train a toddler. She had everything a man could want in a *fraa*.

Joanna smoothed her hands down the front of her apron as if brushing Menno from her thoughts. "It was *gute* to see you, Verla Ann, but I've got pots and pans in boxes yet."

A shadow darkened Menno's expression. "They'll still be there in an hour. Just relax for a bit. You've been working so hard."

Joanna didn't even pause. She took three steps toward the house then turned back and snatched the bright cleaning rags from his hand. They'd be useful in the kitchen. "Let me know when the pizza gets here. I'm starving."

Chapter 18

"*Aendi* Joanna," Winnie whined. "Can we please go outside now."

Joanna rolled her pie crust dough into a ball and stuffed it into a plastic bag. The girls had been cooped up inside all day while Ada had cleaned and Joanna had made rolls and pie crust and fry pie filling. "Okay but stay close to the house where I can see you."

Winnie cheered, and Rosie jumped up and down. Lily clapped her hands, always willing to join in the celebration.

Joanna slipped her bowl into the sink. "I just have to wash my hands and this bowl, and then I'll come out and play with you."

Winnie helped Lily on with her shoes then put on her own. Going barefoot in the dirt on a hot day like this would burn their feet. Not even Rosie was that stubborn. With shoes and smiles in place, the girls ran out the door as happy as a whole sea full of clams. Joanna kept one eye out the window as the girls skipped down the porch steps and were greeted by Pepper and the goats, who apparently had been waiting the whole day for *die kinner* to come out and play with them. She smiled as Winnie grabbed Smiley around the neck and gave her a big kiss on the head. Lily squealed when Pepper licked her face, and Rosie opened her hand and fed Blue a piece of cookie she'd been saving. Joanna sighed and wiped the sweat off her forehead with the back of her arm.

Ada glanced at her as she swiped a towel across the plate she'd just washed. "Now they're gone, we can talk about Menno."

Joanna plunged her hands into the dishwater. "We can talk about Menno anytime. The girls are too young to understand anything."

"You never say anything around a child that you don't want repeated ten years later."

Joanna laughed. "You're funny, Ada."

Ada grunted. "Nobody has ever called me funny before. You're trying to divert my attention." She handed Joanna a towel. "You're unhappy about something. I can always tell because you clean things when you're upset."

"I clean things all the time."

"Not well," Ada said. "I always have to go back and redo your floors and your counters when you're happy. But when you're troubled, you use a toothpick on all the crevices and a Magic Eraser on the counters."

Joanna frowned. "That's not very nice to say. I'm a *gute* cleaner. Mamm taught me how to clean."

"I couldn't have loved Mamm any more than I did, but she was as bad a cleaner as you are. You do most of the baking. I don't mind doing the cleaning up afterwards." Ada swiped at a crumb on the counter. "But that is really beside the point. Ever since we moved Menno into his house, you've been unhappy and very annoying."

"Annoying! What a thing to say."

"That's three whole days of you being annoying and me having to put up with you."

Joanna glanced out the window. "I need to go outside with *die kinner*. We can talk about it later. Maybe after Menno leaves tonight."

Ada rolled her eyes. "That's the problem. Menno never leaves until way past everybody's bedtime. We spent the whole day Saturday at his house doing more cleaning, then he came over on Sunday after *gmay* and stayed until after dark."

Joanna stared absentmindedly into the far pasture. "Did you notice that he hung around after fellowship supper and talked to Verla Ann?"

"Is that what you think he was doing? Because it looked to me like he was doing his best to dodge her and she was doing her best to corner him. He is too nice to tell her he's not interested."

"She was at his house all day Saturday with the rest of us."

"Well, she wanted to make sure those rags she edged didn't unravel." Now Ada was teasing her. Joanna could see it in her eyes.

Joanna chucked the towel on the counter. "She wanted to make sure her *relationship* with Menno didn't unravel."

Laughter exploded from Ada's mouth. "That was very clever how you turned that around on me." She grabbed the towel, folded it neatly, and set it by the sink. "Do you still think Menno is interested in Verla Ann?"

Joanna didn't want to believe it, felt sick about believing it. "I don't know."

"You know me. I'm a realist. Beth says I'm a pessimist, but I'm too charitable to argue with her about it. But even I can see he is serious about his love for you and only you. Verla Ann is wonderful pretty, very talented, and especially persistent. She sees her chances for a husband fading away because she's twenty-five and she lives in Byler,

Colorado, where Amish boys are as scarce as water rights. She's choosing to ignore the way Menno looks at you, and she's going to pursue him until he tells her "*nae*."

"Menno has a hard time telling his *dochters nae*," Joanna said. "He has a hard time telling me *nae*. He has a hard time telling Pepper *nae*. It's just the way he is. But if he loves me that much, shouldn't he be willing to fight for me?"

Ada shook her head. "I didn't say he was perfect. Menno has made enough mistakes to fill a flatbed wagon."

Joanna's lips twitched with a smile she couldn't contain. "You're wrong, Ada. He's perfect just the way he is."

Ada gave her an *I'm-barely-putting-up-with-you* face. "Then don't be so hard on him. He's doing his best."

Joanna sighed. "I'm going outside. After you've fixed my cleaning mistakes, come out and play with us."

"You didn't make any mistakes today."

Joanna pulled off her apron and looked out the window again. Lily had run clear out to the edge of the yard, where the chain-link fence separated the house and barn from their alfalfa fields. She must have been following one of the chickens. "*Ach*, Lily knows she shouldn't wander so far from the house."

Ada shrugged. "She's only two. She doesn't even know what a rule is yet."

Joanna opened the back door and stepped out onto the porch.

Their *dat* would be there soon, and he didn't like it when she let *die kinner* outside by themselves, even though the back was completely fenced in and Pepper was the best guard dog in Colorado. She squinted into the field and realized what Lily was chasing. Bitty the chicken had somehow managed to scale the five-feet-high chain link fence and was standing on the other side, pecking at the dirt as if she hadn't a care in the world.

Joanna's heart lurched when Lily reached up and somehow lifted the latch on the gate that opened up into the fields. "Lily," she called, though Lily was far enough away that she might not have heard her. "Don't go out there."

It all happened so fast Joanna was momentarily paralyzed with shock. Lily strolled out of the gate when a tan, furry figure jumped out from behind a clump of sagebrush, clamped its teeth around Bitty's neck, and took off like a shot across the field with the chicken dangling from its mouth. Joanna's heart stopped as Lily screamed and started running after the coyote. Bless her, she was trying to save the chicken. Pepper barked like a mad dog and tore off in Lily's direction.

In her panic, Joanna tripped down the porch steps and fell hard on her knees. A lightning-hot pain shot up her leg. Gasping, she did her best to ignore the pain, leaped to her feet, and bolted for Lily. "Ada, get the rifle!" she yelled.

Joanna went crazy with fear when Rosie, Winnie, and the goats chased after Pepper and Lily, screaming and wailing as if the world had come to an end. Joanna ran past *die kinner* and out the gate. She shoved the girls back into the yard, knocking Rosie onto her *hinnerdale* and making her scream louder. Joanna slammed the gate shut behind her.

Pointing a shaky finger at Winnie, she yelled, "Stay here. You all stay here." She turned and half hobbled, half ran. The pain in her bruised knees was excruciating, but nothing mattered except Lily's safety.

She groaned when she heard the gate open behind her and at least one of the goats and one little girl following. *Ach, du lieva!* Couldn't Rosie choose to be obedient just this once?

Up ahead in an amazing show of speed, Pepper ran past Lily, caught up with the coyote, and nipped at its hindquarters. The coyote turned and dropped Bitty as it yelped and bared its teeth. Incredibly, the chicken fluttered to her feet, flapped her wings wildly, and ran around and around like her head had been cut off. The coyote sprang at Pepper, and Pepper barked and jumped back.

Joanna's lungs were on fire and the pain in her knees traveled all the way to the tips of her fingers.

The coyote lunged at Lily, clamping its teeth onto the hem of her dress. Joanna cried out as Lily went down, her feet yanked out from under her. Lily's scream rent the air as the coyote dragged her backward. Pepper catapulted himself onto the coyote's back and sank his teeth into its neck just as Joanna reached Lily. She scooped Lily into her arms and heard Lily's dress rip away from the coyote's sharp teeth. She kicked the coyote in the face, and it snapped at her leg even with Pepper on its back. Joanna's knees shrieked in pain as she raced back toward the fence.

Rosie and Winnie scurried toward her, their faces smeared with dirt and tears. Smiley was the only goat brave enough to follow them. Ada was right behind them, with the rifle in one hand and a kitchen knife in the other.

"Go back, Rosie, Winnie," Joanna screamed, angrier and more frightened than she had ever been. "Get back behind the fence."

Lily moaned in her arms, and she felt Lily's hot tears against her neck. Ada passed her without a word, running toward the melee in the other direction.

Joanna hooked an arm around Lily's waist to free her other hand and grabbed Rosie's wrist. "Rosie, take Winnie's hand *right now* and hold tight."

Thank Derr Herr, Rosie did as she was told, and Joanna pulled the screaming little girls back to safety behind the fence. Smiley did not need to be coaxed. She had trotted ahead of all of them and had reached the gate before Joanna had.

Joanna sank to the scorching earth, gathered all three girls onto her lap, and tightened her arms around them. "You naughty, naughty girls," she said, panting in pain and exhaustion. "Next time, do as you're told." She looked into the alfalfa field.

The coyote was gone. Ada stood next to Pepper gazing to the south, holding her knife at the ready and the rifle at her side. She slipped the knife into her apron pocket, bent over, and picked up Bitty with one hand. The chicken didn't even squirm. Was she dead or just shocked? Pepper, with tongue lolling from his mouth, led the way back to the yard.

As soon as Ada and Pepper and Bitty were safely inside the fence with the gate closed, Rosie and Winnie rushed to Pepper's side and hugged him, crying and carrying on as if their hearts were broken.

"Is everybody okay?" Ada asked, setting Bitty, who was indeed alive, on the ground.

Joanna cradled Lily in her arms. "Are you hurt?"

Lily nodded, tears streaming from her eyes and nose dripping with snot. She pointed to her arms. "Owie."

Joanna gently turned Lily's hands palms up. Both elbows were bleeding, and the backs of her forearms were lined with angry welts from being dragged across the hard ground. Her knees and legs were also scraped and dotted with specks of blood.

"Oh, you poor thing." It was going to hurt something awful when they were cleaned off.

Ada knelt down, wrapped her arms all the way around Pepper's neck, and gave him the biggest kiss she'd probably ever given anyone. "Pepper, you beautiful, brave dog.

You get all the doggie treats you can eat for the rest of your life."

The coyote had taken a slice right out of Pepper's nose, and his blood dripped into the dirt, although he didn't seem to mind his injury. He wagged his tail and jumped up and down and licked all nearby faces, almost knocking Rosie and Winnie over several times. The goats were much less enthusiastic. Except for Smiley, they huddled against the barn wall, shivering as if they were cold.

Joanna felt sorry for them, but at the moment, she couldn't give them any comfort. Closer to Pepper, she reached out a shaky hand to pull him in for another hug. "*Denki*, you silly dog. I love you forever," she whispered. Her voice trembled, and no matter how hard she tried, she couldn't catch her breath. Her heart raced, and the pain in her legs was excruciating.

Rosie and Winnie were shaken up, half laughing at Pepper and half whimpering with fear.

Ada propped the rifle against the barn wall and took their hands. "Let's get everyone in the house."

Joanna motioned toward the rifle with her head. "We can't just leave that there."

"I'll come back for it as soon as we take care of the girls."

Joanna took a deep, shuddering breath. "I'm *froh* you didn't have to use it."

"Me too, especially since it's not loaded."

Joanna thought her eyes might pop out of her head. "It's not loaded?"

"Of course not. I'd never keep a loaded gun in the house, and there wasn't time."

Joanna growled. "Ada, what good did it do to bring it outside?"

"I thought I could use it as a stick. Besides, if I'd tried to scare the coyote off with a bullet, I might have accidentally shot Pepper."

"I guess you did the right thing." Joanna groaned as she shifted her weight. "*Ach*, Ada, you're going to have to carry Lily. I can't even stand up."

Ada drew her brows together in concern. "What happened?" Letting go of the girls' hands, she knelt next to Joanna, reached out her arms, and pulled Lily from Joanna's lap.

Lily whined and sniffled, her arms and legs obviously hurting worse with the movement.

Joanna's legs were tucked underneath her, but even getting Lily's weight off her lap didn't help. When she tried to straighten her legs, a searing pain shot up her side. "I-I can't move," she said breathlessly.

"Oh, Joanna, look." Ada pointed to Joanna's right knee.

Joanna pulled back her dress. Her black tights were ripped to shreds, and a huge gash in her knee looked as if it went right to the bone. Blood soaked the dirt. Pepper whined. Rosie, Winnie, and Lily started screaming again.

Ada patted Lily's head. "Hush. Hush. Joanna is going to be okay."

"She's bleeding," Winnie wailed.

"It's okay," Ada insisted, her voice thick with reassurance and just a hint of a scold. "Joanna is going to be just fine. Crying won't help her one little bit. Winnie, can you think of a song we can sing to make us feel better?"

Winnie gulped down her tears, nodded, and started singing. "God, make my life a little light, within the world to glow, a little flame that burns so bright, wherever I may go."

"*Gute, gute*, Winnie. Do you know the second verse?" While Winnie sang verses two and three, Ada glanced at Joanna. "Do you want me to carry you?"

Joanna clenched her teeth and willed herself not to pass out. "Just get the girls inside, and I'll crawl."

"Daddy! Dada! Dada!" Rosie and Lily squealed at the same time.

As Menno came around the corner of the house, Rosie burst into tears and ran to him, throwing herself into his arms as if he could save her from all future prowling coyotes.

His wide grin died on his lips when he lifted her up and saw the tears. "What's the matter, *heartzley*?"

"A dog bit Bitty and then Lily," Rosie sobbed. "There's blood."

Lily had also started crying at the sight of her *dat*. She reached her arms out to him.

In four long strides, Menno was next to them. He balanced Rosie in one arm and took Lily from Ada with his other arm. Lily cried out and showed Menno one of her elbows.

"Oh, *heartzley*, your arms!" He turned on Ada as if ready to attack. "Did Pepper bite her?"

"*Nae*, Menno. Nothing like that. They were playing with the goats and—"

"Where were you?" Fire burned behind his eyes.

"Joanna and I were in the house. Joanna walked out the door just as—"

Menno was barely keeping his temper. "We need to clean this off and get her something for the pain." He kissed Rosie's cheek. "Are you hurt?"

Rosie rubbed her hand up and down her backside. "Joanna pushed me."

Joanna could almost see the steam coming out of his ears.

"You pushed her?"

"*Jah*," Joanna said, "but she—"

His face was a black thunderstorm. "Joanna, you never push a child unless it's to push them out of the way of a speeding car. You never raise your voice unless the house is on fire."

Really? He wanted to lecture her on child rearing at this very moment?

His voice rose. "Why is there a gun sitting not ten feet from my *dochters*? What is going on here? Don't you know anything about safety? Or maybe you just don't care."

"We care," Joanna said weakly.

Menno was beside himself. There would be no reasoning with him until he calmed down.

"My girls are never coming back here ever again if I can't trust they'll be safe." Before she could utter another word, he made a beeline for the back door with both girls in his arms. "Ada, where are the Band-Aids?" he called over his shoulder. "Do you have some antibacterial soap? Will someone, anyone, come and help me?"

Joanna was struck dumb. Could Menno not spare two minutes to listen? She looked at Ada. "Go. Go. I'll get to the house somehow."

"Maybe not before you bleed to death," Ada said through gritted teeth. She glanced toward the house. "I'll go take over for Menno and send him out to get you."

Joanna pressed her lips into a hard line. "I'm sure he'll be very happy about that."

"Happy or not, he's coming out."

Winnie stared transfixed at Joanna's blood in the dirt.

"Take Winnie," Joanna said.

Ada nodded and grabbed Winnie's hand. "*Cum*. Let's go see how Lily is doing. For sure and certain she would like you to sing to her. Joanna will be okay. Pepper is with her."

Winnie glanced back at Joanna before letting Ada lead her into the house. Pepper whined and licked Joanna's face.

"I'm okay, boy."

Pepper sat down next to her and kept his eyes trained on her face. There really wasn't anything he could do. Joanna leaned to one side and braced herself on her arm, then slowly slid her stiff legs out from under her, grunting in pain. She'd never experienced such agony. Finally managing to straighten her legs in front of her, she pulled her dress over the wound so she wouldn't have to look at it, then cradled her head in one hand, closed her eyes, and concentrated on not fainting.

Pepper nudged her cheek with his head. How long would she have to sit there? Menno was furious. Maybe he'd refuse to help her. Then again, Ada was very determined and very pushy when she thought herself to be right.

Joanna heard the back door open and Menno's heavy steps come toward her. How did he manage to make his footfalls sound angry? She lifted her head and peered up at him.

He was a six-foot-and-three-inch pillar of resentment and frustration. "Ada says you're hurt." He couldn't see the blood or the ripped tights or the Colorado-size gash in her knee.

If he could, maybe he'd feel a little guilty about being so snippy.

"I just need help getting into the house, then you can tend to Lily."

"Because you and Ada didn't."

Joanna wasn't going to argue. She *had* let the girls go outside by themselves. She *had* been sidetracked by her conversation with Ada. This whole thing was her fault, but maybe she didn't deserve to be left in the dirt as punishment. If she had been three years old, she would have burst into tears.

Menno pressed his hand over his eyes. "I'm sure Ada sent me out here just to distract me from Lily's injuries, but it's not working. Let's get you into the house so I can go back to my *dochter*. She needs me right now."

And then suddenly, Gotte took pity on her. Dat must have just returned from the Bent and Dent. He came running out of the house, his expression saturated with concern. Joanna would take his sympathy over Menno's hostility any day. "Dat!"

"Joanna, are you okay?" He was Pepper's favorite person, but Pepper didn't leave Joanna's side, not even to say hello to him.

Joanna waved her hand in Menno's direction. "Go be with Lily. Dat can help me."

Menno didn't even pause a full second to consider before he turned and jogged back to the house. Joanna barely had the energy to feel upset about his lack of concern. The pain was blinding. Dat fell onto his knees next to her and patted Pepper on the head. "Ada says there was a coyote. That was about all I got out of her."

"Pepper chased him off. He truly is the best dog in the world."

"For sure and certain," Dat said, cupping his hand under Pepper's muzzle. "Oh, *sis yuscht*, Pepper. He got your nose but good." Dat turned his attention to Joanna. "And what about you?"

Joanna pulled her dress above her knee. The wound was deep but had mostly stopped bleeding.

Dat's eyebrows nearly flew off his forehead and took wing. "That is a very impressive gash," he said, as if getting injured was some sort of accomplishment. He was sympathetic, but he was also fascinated by blood and non-life-threatening injuries.

He'd once given Ada stitches—with her full agreement, of course—when she cut her finger. She never wanted to spend money if there was a cheaper way to do something.

"It must hurt bad if you can't even walk."

Joanna concentrated on her breathing. "I would say I broke something, but after I fell, I ran a hundred yards into the field chasing after Lily. I couldn't do that if it was broken, could I?"

"You can get pretty far on adrenaline."

"Moving is agony."

The lines deepened around his eyes. "Both legs?"

"The right one hurts worse than the left, but they're both bad."

Dat nodded thoughtfully. "You and Ada both have a high tolerance for pain, so if you say it hurts, I know it *really* hurts. I can try lifting you up and carrying you into the house, but it will be very unpleasant, and I don't know if I'm strong enough to lift you all the way off the ground. I should get Menno back out here. Or I could go to the Seamons' house and call an ambulance."

"No ambulance and no Menno. I'd rather spend the night out here on the ground. You should call Cathy and see if she can drive me to the hospital."

He fingered his beard. "But we need to get you to the house first."

"I think I could put some weight on my left leg—

enough to stand up if you help me. Then you wouldn't have to lift me all the way off the ground."

"Are you sure I shouldn't just fetch Menno?"

"I can't face him, Dat."

Dat must have understood how distressed Joanna was because he didn't argue and didn't ask why. "What about . . . what if I jog over to Clay and Mary's and bring Clay back with me?"

"That's a *wunderbarr* idea."

He patted her on the shoulder. "Okay. Don't go anywhere, and don't die while I'm gone."

"I won't promise anything."

"Stay with Joanna, Pepper." Dat went through the back gate and took off across the fields.

Joanna should have warned him about the coyote, but Lord willing, it was long gone. She started shivering, even though it had to be eighty degrees outside. Her head spun, and she decided she should lie down before she fell over. Pepper sidled next to her and lent her some of his heat. She closed her eyes and heard an occasional car pass on the highway. After a few minutes, she heard the sound of a buggy pulling away from the house.

Menno was leaving. He'd obviously decided not to stay for dinner, not caring about her at all. His abandonment hurt worse than her knees.

Ada came out the back door and was immediately at Joanna's side. "He's gone, and good riddance. Are you alive?"

Joanna opened one eye and squinted up. "How is Lily?"

"It was rough trying to wash out all her cuts and scratches. She screamed like we were killing her. It just about tore Menno apart. We covered her with ointment and wrapped her up, and I don't wonder but she'll be running around the house good as new by tomorrow morning."

"*Ach*, poor thing. For sure and certain she's *froh* to be with her *fater* again."

Ada laid a hand on Joanna's arm. "Your skin is clammy."

"It really, really hurts. Could you get me a blanket?"

"Where's Dat?"

"He ran to Clay's for some help. Could you get me a blanket?"

Ada shot to her feet. "Sorry. I'll be right back."

She came back just as Dat opened the gate and led Clay and seven teenage boys—the baseball players from Clay's weekly pitching clinic—into the yard. Mary wasn't far behind. Clay and the boys surrounded Joanna on every side, and she felt like an odd clump of roadkill.

"That looks bad," one boy said.

Mary nudged everybody out of the way, knelt next to Joanna, who couldn't stop trembling, and placed her hand on Joanna's forehead. "She's going into shock. We need to get her into the house." She took the blanket from Ada and spread it over Joanna. "On second thought, we need to call an ambulance."

"No ambulance," Joanna mumbled.

One of the boys pulled a cell phone from his pocket. "Should I call 911?"

"Yes," Clay said. "Thanks, Brody."

Joanna couldn't make out what Brody was saying into the phone, but he looked upset. Everybody looked upset. Of course they were upset. Menno was gone, and her whole world had gone dark. She closed her eyes and opened them again. The boys and the sky and the barn looked fuzzy, as if she was gazing at them from a long distance. She felt like taking a very long nap. Or maybe this was what it felt like to die.

Would Menno be sad when she was gone?

Chapter 19

Lily woke up earlier than usual the next morning, whimpering that her legs hurt. Menno gave her some children's pain reliever and checked her bandages. Ada had done a *gute* job of wrapping Lily's elbows and forearms, plus her knees and lower legs all the way down to her ankles. Her left arm was barely injured at all compared to the right arm. There were three superficial scratches on her left forearm and a tiny scrape on her left elbow. Her right elbow had the deepest cut, but even it wasn't too bad.

It had stopped bleeding before he had even gotten her into the house. Her knees and legs had taken the brunt of the fall with scrapes and cuts covering her shins, but there was nothing exceptionally deep, and she would heal right as rain within a couple of weeks. The scrapes still looked sore, but the angry red welts that covered Lily's arms and legs yesterday had calmed down considerably. In another week or two, her fall would be nothing but a bad memory.

Menno let Lily lie in bed next to him while he tickled her face and hummed her a song. She loved it when he tickled her face. Once the pain medication kicked in, she drifted off into a peaceful sleep. He wasn't so lucky.

He couldn't be completely comfortable with how he'd behaved yesterday. He had always considered himself a patient, tender-hearted person, but he'd lost his temper and said some things he regretted. His mother-bear instincts had kicked in when he saw Rosie's tears, and unfortunately, Ada and Joanna had gotten the brunt of his righteous indignation. Joanna had admitted to pushing Rosie—probably out of anger—and he had lashed out at her.

How was his reaction to Joanna any better than what her reaction had been to Rosie?

Ach, vell, he hadn't physically assaulted anyone, and he hadn't taken his temper out on one of his children, but that fact didn't make him feel any better about how he'd talked to Joanna. He'd been distraught and hadn't stopped to consider her reasons. Had he really threatened never to bring his girls around again? Surely she recognized it was said in the heat of the moment. He planned on marrying her. His girls would be at the Yoders often.

Ada had tried to distract him by sending him outside to help Joanna into the house, but it hadn't worked, and he'd gotten impatient when he should have been kind.

Joanna knew him well enough. If there was anything that kept him up at night, it was the safety of his *dochters*. Lord willing, Ada and Joanna understood how upset he had been and would forgive him for being an overprotective *fater*. Still, he shouldn't have scolded them in the heat of his anger.

As so often happened with Menno, a Bible verse came to mind. *"Whoever is angry with his* bruder *without a cause shall be in danger of the judgment."* Of course, he had just cause to be angry, but his anger hadn't stopped Lily from getting hurt or made her feel better after it happened. And he certainly hadn't helped his suit with Joanna.

He'd just been so angry because it had seemed as if Joanna didn't care about Lily's tears. While Lily was bawling her eyes out, Joanna had sat in the dirt, with a rifle not ten feet away. What was wrong with her?

His stomach tightened. He'd been so upset about Lily that he'd completely disregarded Joanna—the woman he loved with his whole heart. Had she really been so hurt she couldn't have walked into the house on her own power? Was it a tactic to distract him? At the time, he'd thought maybe she was embarrassed about pushing Rosie and about letting the girls play outside by themselves, but maybe she truly hadn't been able to walk into the house. He'd seen a little spot of blood on her dress when he went back outside to help her into the house. He'd assumed it was Lily's blood, But surely Joanna hadn't been hurt as badly as Lily. Maybe she was just being overly dramatic.

He'd been harsh. Would she hold it against him?

Menno frowned. *Would* she hold it against him? He'd been making progress, of that he was confident. Hadn't she let him hold her hand on Friday when they were strolling around the backyard together? Hadn't she sounded just as enthusiastic as he was when they talked about the garden and the washing machine and the apple trees? Surely she understood how distraught he had been over Lily. Surely he hadn't hurt her feelings.

Surely.

He pressed his lips together. When he took Rosie and Lily there this morning, he would apologize and then kindly and calmly ask that they never go outside without an adult to supervise. That was all he needed to say, and he would never bring up the subject again. Ada was doing him a huge favor. He should be grateful for that. Joanna had a few minor flaws, and though everyone could improve, no one was perfect.

He loved her no matter what.

He still hadn't figured out exactly what had happened yesterday. From what he'd gathered from Rosie, a stray dog had come into the yard and chased Lily, and Pepper had run it off. The thought of it still made him shudder. How had a stray dog gotten over the fence?

Since Menno couldn't go back to sleep, he got up and read his Bible until the girls woke up. Then he helped them dress, combed and put up their hair, fixed them breakfast, and loaded them into the buggy for Joanna's house.

The closer he got to the house, the heavier a sickening sense of dread became. Was *Gotte* trying to tell him something?

The girls hopped out of the buggy before he had even set the brake. Lily and Rosie skipped up the porch steps just as Menno got out of the buggy. Lily acted as if she'd never been hurt a day in her life, even though she was bandaged up to her knees and elbows.

Rosie didn't even knock. She opened the door, and she and Lily disappeared into the house showing no signs that they remembered the horrible experience they'd had yesterday. Lily shut the door behind them, leaving Menno in the awkward position of having to knock. It took a full minute for someone to answer the door, which gave him a chance to doubt every decision he'd ever made in his entire life. Were they keeping him waiting on purpose? Were they punishing him for how he'd acted yesterday?

To his surprise, Esther answered, very pregnant and very puffy. She looked more uncomfortable every time he saw her. She was barefoot, and her feet were swollen to twice their size. Her face was speckled red, and a thermometer sat behind her ear.

"Esther, what are you doing here?"

She gazed at him through half-lidded eyes. "You know, Menno, just looking at you makes me grumpy. You seem determined to destroy your own happiness. It's better if you just turn around and go to work. Levi says you two are working on a bathroom in Monte Vista. That floor isn't going to tile itself."

Oh, *sis yuscht.* "Are you mad about what happened yesterday?"

"*Jah.* What else?"

He squared his shoulders. Ada and Joanna deserved half the blame, and he wasn't going to apologize for being concerned for his *dochters'* safety. "I don't know what you've heard or what I did, but maybe you don't have the full story."

"Maybe *you* don't have the full story. Maybe you need to give Joanna some grace."

"Maybe you need to give me some grace. Maybe you can forgive me for being a *fater* who constantly worries about my *dochters* getting hurt."

Esther tilted her head to one side and studied his face. "Hmm, how inconvenient that you're right. I wanted to stay mad at you until Christmas."

"Can I please talk to Joanna and Ada? Then I'll be out of your hair."

Esther folded her arms. "Are you going to apologize?"

"Of course." He cleared his throat. "And set some guidelines going forward."

Her eyebrows traveled up her forehead. "Like a list?"

"I know Ada is doing me a favor babysitting my girls, but they are my girls and I just need to be clear about my expectations. I don't want them going outside unsupervised. I don't want them to eat lunch without washing their hands. I don't want them anywhere near Try's rifle. Doesn't that seem reasonable?"

Esther nodded as if she was thinking about it really hard. "Very reasonable. Would you rather be reasonable or married to Joanna?"

Now she was just talking nonsense. "I'd rather be both," he blurted out.

Winnie and Rosie came up behind Esther and grabbed each of her hands.

"Mamm," Winnie said. "Can we go visit Joanna in the hospital?"

Menno stumbled backward as if he'd been smacked across the face with a garden hoe. "Joanna's in the hospital?"

Esther gave him a rather smug look and peered at Winnie. "Let's just wait until she gets home. She'll be here before lunch."

Menno wanted to pound on his chest in frustration. "Why didn't you tell me first thing that Joanna is in the hospital?"

Esther stretched a fake smile across her face. "Just looking at you makes me grumpy. Talking about it makes me even grumpier."

He resisted the urge to force his way into the house and get some answers from someone who wasn't mad at him, but his temper was what had gotten him into trouble yesterday. He was determined not to make the same mistake this morning, no matter how aggravated and stunned he was. He swallowed whatever indignation and pride he had left and took a deep breath. "Please, Esther, and I'm sorry. Is she okay?"

Esther sighed. "I've been hard on you, Menno, but you can be so blind sometimes. *Cum reu*, and I'll get Ada, because she was there and saw everything."

She headed toward the kitchen with Winnie holding one hand and Rosie holding the other. Menno followed her. She turned around. "Make yourself comfortable. I'll be back soon."

"I'm not about to wait in suspense in the living room while Ada finishes cleaning a toilet or wiping down the counters."

"Suit yourself." Esther led him out the back door and pointed to the barn. "In there."

As Rosie and Winnie skipped down the steps, Esther closed the door behind them. Menno and the two girls strolled to the barn where Ada was milking one of the goats and Lily was chattering about the bandages on her legs.

She had one arm draped around Pepper's neck. "Look, Dada. Peppa hurt nose."

Menno had seen Pepper's injury yesterday, but it had barely registered. He'd been so upset about Lily. "That's too bad. Be sure to give him some extra love."

Ada didn't look at Menno.

He was smart enough to try for a little humility and squatted next to her stool, his heart pounding in his ears. "Ada, I'm wonderful sorry about yesterday. Can you please tell me why Joanna is in the hospital? What happened, and is she going to be okay?"

Ada finally made eye contact. "There are just some days you wish you could have back again, aren't there?"

"I guess we have to learn from every decision and move on. 'Sufficient unto the day is the evil thereof.'"

Ada slipped the rope from Smiley's neck and sent her on her way. "The first thing I need to know is, what are you going to do now?"

Menno nearly growled, but he shoved the sound down

his throat. "What do you mean? I'm going to go to the hospital to see her."

Ada stood and Menno rose with her. "Verla Ann is the most conscientious babysitter I know. She always made sure the girls' hands and feet were clean. She rarely let them eat sugar. She made them try two bites of everything at lunchtime, and she potty trained Lily. She had strict rules that she insisted the girls follow, and they obeyed her faithfully."

"I guess," Menno said, mostly because he wanted to hear how Joanna was doing and Ada seemed to want to lecture him first. What could he do to hurry this along?

"If Verla Ann had been babysitting your girls yesterday, this wouldn't have happened. Verla Ann would have done a much better job."

"That's not true." A different kind of anger bubbled up inside Menno's chest. Was Ada deliberately provoking him, or did she really believe what she was saying?

"Joanna thinks it's true. She feels terrible for what happened to Lily, terrible about pushing Rosie, even though it was out of the way of danger. Terrible that you wouldn't even stoop to help her off the ground. Your girls never would have disobeyed Verla Ann. They wouldn't have been outside by themselves, and Lily never would have opened that gate."

"What gate?"

Ada picked up her bucket of goat's milk and strolled toward the house. "Joanna thinks she's lost you. She never believed you wanted only her. She always thought you'd pick just about anybody for a *fraa* as long as she was Amish and single, and now she thinks you're going to choose Verla Ann. She's truly the perfect *fraa* for a man like you—fussy, anxious, and overprotective."

Every cell in Menno's body rebelled against that

statement. "That is the most ridiculous thing I've heard in my whole life." He took off his hat and scrubbed his fingers through his hair so he wouldn't put a hole through the barn wall.

Ada stopped walking and looked him in the eye. "Verla Ann is a very *gute* choice, but if you choose her over Joanna, I want you to take your girls, go away, and never come back here, because you are about the sorriest excuse for a man I've ever seen."

Were those tears in Ada's eyes? He'd never seen her so upset.

He'd never seen himself so upset.

In desperation, he grabbed her by the shoulders. Goats' milk sloshed into the dirt. "Ada, you are wrong and judgmental and so wrong."

"I'm not judgmental," she protested.

"You're all those things. Verla Ann is a fine babysitter, and I don't want to speak ill of anyone, but Joanna is superior in every way. I love Joanna too much to let you say those things."

"You sure have a funny way of showing it."

"I was distraught about Lily. I was mad at Joanna. That doesn't mean I don't love her. She is everything to me, and I made a mistake."

Ada took an abrupt step back, and more milk dripped to the ground. But a smile tugged at the corners of her mouth. "Okay. I guess I like you again."

"Will you please quit torturing me and tell me what happened to Joanna?"

"I wish you would have been this curious yesterday. Maybe then she wouldn't be sitting in a hospital bed mourning your loss."

His heart lurched. "She's given up on me?"

"She thinks you've given up on her."

"What happened?" Menno said, as forcefully as he could without being rude.

"Joanna let *die kinner* go outside, and she was just about to follow them out when we got into a discussion about you and how much you like Verla Ann."

"I don't like Verla Ann," Menno snapped, beyond caring how rude he sounded.

"*Vell*, Joanna doesn't know that." Ada glared at him. "Bitty somehow got over the back fence, and Lily went after her. I don't know how she opened the latch on the back gate, but before we knew it, she was on the other side of the fence."

"*Jah*. She knows how to do that now."

"Joanna ran outside as soon as she saw Lily wandering close to the fence. A coyote was lurking and snapped his teeth around Bitty's neck and ran away."

"A coyote?"

"Lily is a brave girl. She ran after the coyote to try to save Bitty. Pepper tore out of the yard after her. Joanna tried to follow, but she fell down the back porch steps and broke her kneecap."

"Her kneecap?"

"*Jah* and made a huge gash in her knee right to the bone. Twenty-seven stitches and a tetanus shot. She was not happy. *Dat* says she was working off pure adrenalin because she got up and ran after Lily. Pepper tore out there barking and carrying on. Rosie and Winnie wanted to chase the coyote too, but Joanna screamed at them and shoved them back behind the fence. Rosie fell back on her *hinnerdale*. I don't know about you, but I think that's *gute* enough reason for pushing a child."

It was, but Menno had given Joanna a lecture about it. He felt like a snake. "I should have listened before reacting like I did."

Ada nodded as if he was the stupidest person she'd ever met. "Pepper fought off the coyote, but it got hold of Lily's hem. Joanna snatched Lily away and kicked the coyote right in the face, without caring if she got bit. She took Lily back to the yard and grabbed Rosie and Winnie on the way because they had disobeyed again and wouldn't stay behind the fence. I went out with the rifle but by the time I got there, the coyote had run away. Pepper did his job, but Joanna is the real hero. She risked herself to save Lily. And without a second thought. After everyone was safely back in the yard, Joanna sat down in the dirt and couldn't get back up."

"I'm so *sorry*." That word didn't even begin to express his regret. He was sorry for all the assumptions he'd made about Joanna, sorry for accusing her of pushing Rosie out of anger. Sorry he had been so wrapped up in his own distress he couldn't see Joanna was in real pain, and sorry he hadn't helped her into the house. He was sorry he'd abandoned her when she needed him the most, and he was sorry that when his character had been tested, he had failed miserably and Joanna had borne the brunt of his failure.

He didn't want to hear anymore. "I need to get to the hospital."

"No hurry."

"There's a great hurry."

"They said they would release her this morning. If you go to the hospital, you could very well miss her."

Menno hated the thought of missing her at the hospital, but he also hated the thought of waiting, doing nothing. He was a man of action, a man of lists, a man who did whatever was necessary. Idleness was not in his nature. "Did she have to get surgery on her knee? Is that why she stayed overnight?"

"After you left, *Dat* fetched Clay to help Joanna to the

house, but she went into shock so we called an ambulance. The doctors were a little worried, so once X-rays were taken and her knee was stitched, it was decided to keep her overnight for observation. I'm not sure what observation is, but I know it means an extra two thousand dollars. She didn't have to have surgery on her knee, but she has to wear a cast for a few weeks."

This story was getting worse and worse. "I'm *froh* she's okay," he mumbled.

Ada trudged up the porch steps, and Menno followed her into the kitchen. She pulled a strainer and a stainless-steel bucket from the cupboard. "Our yard is fenced in and safe, despite what happened yesterday. We try to be careful and vigilant, but you can't live your life worrying about what horrible thing might happen next. Do you remember the story about Jesus's disciples when they were in a boat in the storm?"

"Of course I remember." He had it memorized.

"They thought they were going to sink, and Jesus was asleep in the back of the boat. They woke him up and said, 'Lord, don't you care that we're going to die?'"

"'Carest thou not that we perish?'" Menno said.

"Whatever. Jesus calmed the storm and asked why they were so afraid? I can imagine him sitting there in the boat on the smooth water, reassuring them that they would be okay. Whenever I worry about something, I remember that I'm going to be okay because Jesus is in my boat. He's in your boat too, Menno. You need to quit worrying and be still."

He scoffed. "Easier said than done."

"It always is." Ada set the strainer on top of the stainless-steel bucket. "The worst part about having Joanna gone is that I have to make the cheese, and I'm very bad at it." She smiled at him when he grabbed the bucket and poured the milk through the strainer for her. "I trust that Gotte gives His angels charge over His little ones. We can't do Gotte's job, but you've been trying to do Gotte's job . . . and it's quite exhausting. You were concerned about Lily, so you abandoned Joanna. I can forgive you for that, but I don't know that Joanna will ever believe you mean what you say. You couldn't spare five minutes to help her into the house. After you've fretted and fussed over your girls, will there be anything left for her in the end?"

"There is everything left. The more love you give away, the more you have."

Ada gave him a wry smile. "So wise and long overdue. And you're saying it to the wrong person."

"I know that, but she isn't here. I'm aching to see her."

Ada peered at him. "That's a start. You should probably have a wonderful *gute* apology ready—for Joanna and my *dat*."

"Your *dat*?"

"He is forgiving but not very forgetful. You know how it feels when someone hurts your *dochter*."

Menno knew exactly how that felt, and he wouldn't be surprised if Try greeted him with a rifle instead of a handshake the next time they met. "I should probably apologize to your *dat*."

"That would be wise. You are in the doghouse, and you're going to have to do a lot of talking to get yourself out."

Chapter 20

A dull ache at the base of her skull woke Joanna from a very deep sleep. She rolled over in bed and grimaced in pain. It was time for another pain pill, but they made her groggy and loopy and dizzy, and she wondered if maybe a double dose of ibuprofen would be sufficient. She draped her arm over her forehead and looked up at the ceiling. What time was it? The sun patterns on her wall suggested it was early afternoon, but she had no way of knowing how long she'd slept.

After Dat and Cathy Larsen had brought her home from the hospital this morning, she vaguely remembered Clay carrying her up the stairs and Mary tucking her into bed. Even fuzzier was the memory of several voices in the house, asking questions she couldn't begin to answer, expressing concern, giving her sympathy. She was fairly sure she had heard Rosie and Lily's voices, but she must have been delirious, because Menno's voice had also intruded into her thick head, and surely he was already at Verla Ann's house making plans for an October wedding, no doubt with homemade picnic baskets as a gift for every guest. Joanna remembered Dat telling everyone to go home and let her rest right before Clay had carried her up the stairs and she'd fallen into welcome unconsciousness.

She slid her hand between the sheets and fingered the knee brace that would be her companion for the next four to six weeks. The doctor had said the fracture was minor, and she didn't need a cast, which was a huge blessing. She'd have a nasty scar, but at least she still had her legs and arms and all her fingers and toes.

Her heart, however, seemed to be damaged beyond repair.

She sat up, and the room spun slightly to the right. "*Ach*," she moaned. Lord willing, that would go away soon.

Mary must have been standing right outside the door listening. Looking positively stricken, she blew into the room. "How are you feeling?" she asked, as if Joanna were on the verge of death.

Did she know something Joanna didn't?

"I won't be chasing goats for a while."

"You won't be doing much of anything for a while. Cathy Larsen is going to help Clay with his baseball clinic, and I am spending the rest of the week here taking care of you."

"*Ach*, Mary, I hurt my knee. My hands and arms are working just fine, and I intend to be up and around tonight helping Ada with dinner."

Mary shook her head so hard, she fanned up a breeze. "*Nae*. You should stay in bed for at least two days. You've been through quite an ordeal, and you need to heal."

"I can heal while I make fry pies for the bakery."

"I've already talked to Myra. I told her there would be no fry pies this week. She was very disappointed."

Joanna pinned Mary with a scolding look. "I'm very

disappointed too. I was going to make some chocolate ones."

"Just give it a little time, Joanna. I know you're in a lot of pain." Mary snatched Joanna's prescription from the chest of drawers. "Do you need more pills?"

"I thought I'd try something not quite as strong. That stuff makes me loopy."

Mary sighed. "Maybe I should tell you the news first and then you can decide if you want the strong ones."

Joanna's chest tightened. "Okay. Go ahead."

"Verla Ann met with the school board this morning and quit her teaching job. She told them she's planning on getting married."

Instead of needing stronger pain pills, Joanna felt numb, like her heart wasn't even part of her body anymore. "Where did you hear this?"

"Sadie's *dat* is on the school board, and she told Beth."

"Menno didn't waste any time, did he?"

Mary sat next to Joanna on the bed and traced her finger around one of the Nine Patch quilt blocks. "Menno was here this morning when we brought you home from the hospital."

"Was he?"

"He was beyond upset and said he'd die if he couldn't talk to you."

Joanna grunted her disapproval. "Probably wanted to tell me that he's decided to marry Verla Ann. He wants to let me down easy, to explain that she would be a much better *fraa*, and better *mater* to the girls." Joanna's anger turned to despair in a heartbeat. She blinked back tears. "He's wise. If Verla Ann had been babysitting, Lily never would have gotten hurt or been in danger. I understand why he would choose Verla Ann over me. I don't like it, but I understand."

Mary slumped her shoulders. "We joked that he was treating everybody like cans of corn, but I sincerely thought he would never settle for anyone but you. I can't believe he would change his mind so easily."

"I don't think it was an easy decision, but his *dochters* are more important than anything, and he just couldn't take the risk of marrying me."

Mary put her arm around Joanna. "It's ridiculous, that's what it is."

Joanna wiped away a few tears and stiffened her spine. Life would go on without Menno— just barely—but it would go on. She needed to do something now, or she'd sink into despair. She tested her brace by lifting her leg slightly and bending her knee up and down. "I know you want me to stay in bed until Christmas, but I'll go crazy sitting here even a minute longer. I need to feel useful, like my life means something to somebody."

"Your life means a great deal to me. To all of us."

To everyone but Menno. "*Gute.* Then help me down the stairs so I can make cheese or rolls or cookies. I need to be doing something with my hands which, by the way, are perfectly healthy." Joanna saw the moment Mary gave in.

"Okay, *schwester*, but don't overdo it, or I'll have Clay come over and carry you back to your room."

Joanna couldn't contain a smile, even though her heart was broken. "*Denki*, Mary. I promise I'll be careful. It's *gute* I don't have to bake with my feet."

Mary retrieved Joanna's *kapp* from the hook on the wall. "Dat told him to go away and come back when he was good and sorry."

"Who?" Joanna said, knowing full well Mary was talking about Menno.

Mary studied Joanna's face. "He said he was already good and sorry and asked Dat to forgive him. Dat told Menno to go home, think on his sins, and say his prayers. Menno asked permission to come back this afternoon and see you."

Joanna's heart stopped. "I don't want him to come."

Mary nodded curtly. "That's what I suspected you'd say, especially after hearing about Verla Ann."

"So did Dat give him permission to come?"

"He told Menno it was up to you, and Menno looked as if he had just received very bad news. For sure and certain he'll come over. It seems like he really wants to talk to you."

"Well, I don't want to talk to him. I'd prefer to hear the bad news through the Amish gossip mill."

Mary giggled while she twisted Joanna's hair into a bun. "Why not make Menno deliver the bad news himself? A little discomfort would do him a world of *gute*."

Joanna caught her bottom lip between her teeth. That made too much sense to disregard. "Conflict makes him uncomfortable. He wants to be without guile, so he tries to spare people's feelings, but if he's going to marry Verla Ann, then he should tell me to my face, no matter how unpleasant that conversation will be for him. Why should I make it easy?"

Mary's lips twitched in amusement. "He deserves to squirm a little."

Joanna braced her hand on Mary's shoulder and pushed herself to her feet. "He does. No matter what Dat says, I'm going to let Menno in when he comes today."

"And then make him squirm."

"Like a fish on a hook." Maybe it was uncharitable of her, but Joanna savored the perverse sense of satisfaction she felt when she thought about Menno trying to wriggle his way out of marrying her.

The pain of his rejection would overtake her soon enough.

Mary helped Joanna down the stairs. It would take some time to get used to the brace and the crutches. Both knees hurt something wonderful, but the pain was bearable, and Joanna would rather be up and about than lying in bed staring at the ceiling.

Ada stood in the kitchen slicing carrots then she turned and frowned as Mary helped Joanna into the kitchen. "You should be in bed."

"I tried to tell her, Ada," Mary said, "but she doesn't want to be cooped up in her room all day."

"I'm feeling much better, and I have two *gute* hands to chop vegetables. Just hand me a knife and cutting board, and I'll sit at the table and help you."

Ada heaved a sigh. "*Ach*, you're so stubborn. But I'm stubborn too, so I can appreciate how you feel." She pulled a cutting board from the long cupboard above the fridge and set it on the table. "Don't cut any fingers. You already have enough scars."

Joanna sat at the table, and Ada handed her a knife and an onion. "I'm making stew, and *jah*, I know it's almost eighty degrees out there, but you need a *gute*, hearty meal for your bones."

"I'll make you some turmeric tea for the pain," Mary said, rummaging through the cupboards for a mug and Ada's stash of herbs.

Ada turned back to her cutting board. "Menno's coming over later."

Joanna's heart drooped. "Mary told me."

"He deeply regrets how he treated you. I feel wonderful sorry for him."

Joanna eyed the back of Ada's head. It wasn't like her to feel sorry for anyone. "I'm sure he is. He always feels very guilty when he loses his temper."

Ada put down her knife and turned around. "Can you find it in your heart to forgive him?"

Joanna swallowed past the lump in her throat. "I can forgive him for losing his temper. I can't forgive him for moving on to Verla Ann."

Ada grunted as if there was something stuck in her throat. "What is that supposed to mean? He hasn't moved on to Verla Ann. He still wants to marry you."

Mary filled the teapot with water. "Verla Ann quit her teaching job this morning. She told the school board she's getting married."

"Who else would she be marrying but Menno, especially after yesterday? No doubt he realized what a horrible *fraa* I would be, biked over to Verla Ann's house last night, and asked her to marry him. Then she went to the school board this morning and resigned."

Ada looked at Joanna as if she'd taken a bite of the raw onion on her cutting board. "Joanna Yoder, that is the biggest load of nonsense I've ever heard. I visited with Menno not seven hours ago. I gave him a very stern talking-to about how he treated you. I told him if he chose Verla Ann over you, that he could go away and never come back. He's not interested in Verla Ann. He wants to marry you. You've always been the one."

It was Joanna's turn to question Ada's sanity. "You never believed that. Didn't you tell me that for sure and certain he'd be marrying some other girl this fall?"

"I'm telling you what I know *now*. He loves you, not Verla Ann."

Joanna wanted to cry. "It doesn't matter who he loves. It matters who would be the best *mater* for his *dochters*, and that's not me."

Ada slammed her knife on the counter. Both Mary and Joanna flinched.

Ada was forceful, but not prone to fits of passion. "*Ach*, you are so stubborn. I used to think that was a *gute* quality, but now it just makes me mad."

Joanna didn't back down. "You know what makes me mad? False hope. You're not going to convince me otherwise, Ada, so don't even try."

Ada stared at Joanna for a full minute. Then she ripped off her apron, yanked on her shoes, and donned her black bonnet. "There's nothing to be done. I'm going to fetch Sadie."

Joanna sat at the kitchen table stirring the batter for lemon poppy-seed muffins that would pair beautifully with beef stew. Ada had stormed out of the kitchen an hour ago, and Mary and Joanna had finished getting the ingredients ready for the stew.

Joanna looked at the clock. "It's time to turn on the stew."

Mary stepped to the LP gas stove, lit a match, and turned the knob. The ingredients were already in the pot sitting on one of the burners. "Lord willing, Ada will be back before dinner. She was wonderful mad."

Their usually-steady *schwester* was behaving like a March hare, and Joanna was in too much pain to try to sort it out. She didn't want to talk about Ada. "Will you hand me the muffin tin and a dozen muffin cups? And preheat the oven to 350 degrees."

They heard the front door open and what sounded like a gaggle of geese sweep into the house.

"Joanna," someone called. "Where are you?"

Before Joanna could answer, Sadie Sensenig blew into the kitchen followed by Ada, Esther Kiem, Joanna's *schwester* Beth, Naomi King, Lydia Herschberger, Cathy Larsen, and Priscilla Weaver. Six of them were beaming like a sunny day. Cathy never smiled, but she had a pleasant look on her face, as if her gout wasn't bothering her today.

Only Priscilla looked unhappy to be there, but she held a bouquet of flowers in her hand, which she awkwardly handed to Joanna. "I hope you feel better."

Joanna's lips twitched upward. She never would have expected such a gesture from Priscilla. "*Denki*," she said, putting the flowers up to her nose and breathing in their sweet scent. "That's very kind of you."

Mary held out her hands. "I can put them in some water."

"*Ach, du lieva*, Joanna," Sadie squealed. "Look at your legs! A brace and bandages and crutches. Ada says it was a freak accident. She says you caught your knee on a really hard rock and broke it. Does it hurt?"

Joanna didn't know if she had the energy to converse with Sadie or this vast group of people, but Sadie seemed eager, and it was very kind of them to pay a visit. The flowers were certainly a nice surprise. "It hurts something wonderful, but I'm sure it will slowly get better every day."

"The day after is the worst," Naomi said. "I only know because I broke my wrist five years ago moving hose."

"Esther says you fought off a coyote," Lydia gushed,

as if Joanna were a true hero or something ridiculous like that.

Joanna smiled. "*Ach*, *vell*, I kicked it in the face, and it backed away. But if it hadn't been for Pepper, things could have turned out much differently."

"It wonders me if you're being too modest," Sadie said. "For sure and certain, Menno is grateful."

Joanna did *not* want to talk about Menno. "He was *froh* his girls were safe." But mad as a wet hen that Lily had gotten hurt. So mad that he'd abandoned Joanna in the dirt without a second thought.

Cathy pointed to Ada, who had already started filling muffin cups with batter. "Ada says you're being stubborn, so she asked me to round everybody up and come over."

Ada was the one who was being stubborn, but Joanna wasn't going to mention anything with eight pairs of eyes trained on her. She sat up straighter. "I'm allowed to be stubborn. I broke my kneecap and had to get stitches."

"Twenty-seven," Mary muttered.

"And a tetanus shot," Joanna said, trying to justify her stubborn streak.

Mary motioned toward the living room. "Why don't we all go sit down in there? It's more comfortable, and there's room for everyone."

Cathy always appreciated comfort. "Yes, please. A soft chair is much better for my sciatica."

Mary handed Joanna her crutches, and they all waited for Joanna to stand and hobble into the living room before following her. She planted herself on the loveseat, mildly curious yet reluctant to hear what they had to say. For sure and certain Sadie wanted to talk about Menno, and Joanna just couldn't bear the thought of him today.

Sadie raced to the loveseat and nudged Mary aside

before she could sit down, then sat next to Joanna as if they were best friends. "Now, Joanna, Ada says you're confused about Menno and marriage and Verla Ann Miller."

"Don't you want to hear what happened with the coyote?" Joanna asked. The only thing she'd rather talk less about than the coyote was Menno. Surely she could divert their attention.

Sadie completely ignored the question. "Joanna, I'm sorry about all this, but the confusion is your own fault. You should have been patient. Don't you remember I told you I had a plan?"

Joanna hadn't taken Sadie seriously then, and she didn't now. She blew a puff of air from between her lips. "I remember."

Sadie exploded into a grin and giggled. "I'm going to tell you all about it."

Joanna didn't want to be rude, but whatever Sadie had planned seemed like a waste of time. "Are you sure you don't want to hear about the coyote?"

Sadie swatted the question away. "Ada told us everything. You were very brave and all that, but I need to tell you how I made my plan. I know you thought Menno saw you as a can of corn, so I decided that if we could prove to you that you're the only girl he wants to marry, you'd give him a chance and open your heart to him. That's what Fiona McDaniels did in *Scottish Love Affair.*"

Oh, dear. Sadie had used a plan she'd gotten out of a steamy romance book?

Sadie gazed around the room. "We put our heads together and decided that we would each tell Menno we were willing to marry him. That way he would know he had plenty of choices and you would know you're not just another can of corn." Sadie gave Joanna a smug expression.

"I knew he wouldn't want to marry any of us because he's madly in love with you."

Joanna opened her mouth to say something about how Sadie shouldn't manipulate people's feelings like that, but Sadie shushed her and pointed to Naomi. "Tell her, Naomi."

"I liked Sadie's plan," Naomi said, "and I wanted to help. It was obvious from that first Sunday that Menno was only interested in you. I was pleasantly surprised when he asked to come visit me. I got some *gute* work out of him, though he's not very quick at building shelves. I told him that night that if he wanted to marry me, I would say yes." Naomi slapped her knee and hooted with laughter. "You should have seen his face. You would have thought I'd asked him to bathe in a tub of manure."

Sadie took a small notepad out of her pocket. She'd written six names on the page. She made a checkmark by Naomi's name. "I told Menno the same thing, because there was no danger he'd actually ask." She showed Joanna the list and put a checkmark by her name.

Lydia wrung her hands in her lap. "To tell the truth, I wanted to marry Menno. My *mamm* was trying to hurry things along so she proposed to him, but he sort of hemmed and hawed and tried to escape from the house before he finished his pie. I wish my *mamm* hadn't done that. She scared him off." Lydia quickly shed her obvious disappointment and gave Joanna a kind smile. "But Sadie is right. Menno doesn't want to marry anyone but you. It wouldn't have worked out between us. I don't want his girls touching my stuffed animals, and I don't think he would have liked me keeping them to myself."

Joanna waited for Lydia to laugh, as if that comment about stuffed animals had been a joke, but she seemed serious. Lydia was more attached to her toys than Joanna had realized.

Lydia shrugged. "I would have said yes if he'd asked. Does that make me a bad person?"

Sadie scrunched her lips together. "I guess not, but you didn't follow the plan, and I was a little irritated. Then again, it proves once and for all that Menno only wants to marry Joanna."

Joanna wasn't going to argue, but it was obvious that none of them knew how mad he had been yesterday. Most of them didn't know Verla Ann had just quit her teaching job. Still, Joanna's heart beat a little faster thinking that maybe he had been more sincere than she'd given him credit for.

Sadie eyed Priscilla. "You were not part of the plan, but it all worked out, so I'm not necessarily mad at you."

Priscilla pursed her full lips. Was she wearing lipstick? Priscilla had golden hair and deep blue eyes that boys found irresistible when they first met her. "You don't have to be snippy."

"I'm not being snippy." Sadie shut her mouth and nodded as if deep in thought. "It's wrong for me to blame you. You didn't even know about the plan."

An unhappy emotion flitted across Priscilla's face. "You never told me about the plan. Did you ever stop to think that maybe I want to be included in your little group?"

Joanna looked around the room. Did Priscilla think this diverse bunch of women was Sadie's group? Was it possible she felt left out? Joanna studied Priscilla's face. Of course she felt left out. She acted as if everyone was beneath her, so no one enjoyed being with her . . . but

Priscilla had feelings too. Maybe they ran deeper than anyone suspected.

Sadie squirmed in her seat. "I didn't know you wanted to be included. You seem to hate all of us."

"Hate you!" Priscilla's face got red, and she blinked rapidly. "I pretend not to care about any of you because you don't care about me."

"We care," Cathy said, as if she was part of Sadie's imaginary group. "But you're snobby and kind of mean." She was sitting next to Priscilla on the couch and patted her on the leg. "Why don't you try being yourself instead of putting on airs and acting like you're better than everyone else?"

Priscilla sniffed quietly. "What are *airs*?"

The entire conversation had just taken a whole new direction. Joanna felt bad for Priscilla, but at least they weren't talking about Menno anymore.

Cathy put her arm around Priscilla. Joanna had never seen her do that to anyone before.

"If you want to be part of our group, you need to be nicer. You need to care less about what other people think and more about other people. You have it in you to be a wonderful person. You brought Joanna flowers. That was very thoughtful." Cathy pulled a tissue from her giant handbag and handed it to Priscilla.

Priscilla blew her nose. "I really was concerned about Joanna. She almost got killed."

"See," Cathy said. "There's nothing wrong with you. Deep down you're a very good girl. You're just wrapped up in yourself, and a girl wrapped up in herself makes a very small package."

Priscilla sniffled into her tissue. "I felt terrible when Menno refused my proposal. He was desperate for a wife but not desperate enough to marry me. That's when I realized there must be something wrong with me."

Priscilla's tears had subdued Sadie's enthusiasm. "There's nothing wrong with you, Priscilla. Menno loves Joanna. He wouldn't have said yes to you, no matter what."

Unfortunately, they'd circled back to the topic Joanna least wanted to talk about.

Cathy zipped her purse shut. "What do you say? Should we let Priscilla into the group? We girls have to stick together."

Everyone nodded or murmured their agreement quietly. They were probably all wondering how they'd gotten themselves into a group they didn't even know about.

"*Denki*," Priscilla said, her voice cracking.

Sadie put a checkmark by Priscilla's name in her notepad. "So you see, Joanna, Menno has had a chance to marry all of us, and he hasn't done it. I hope that makes you feel less like a can of corn and more like the beloved of his soul."

"Beloved of his soul?" The laughter burst from Joanna's mouth even as the pain of rejection knifed through her heart.

Sadie giggled nervously. "It's in Jeremiah. I looked it up. When you're with Menno, you have to have a lot of scriptures ready to quote if you want to win an argument."

"That's the truth," Cathy said. "He can quote a scripture before I can even look it up on my phone."

Joanna didn't know what to think. Sadie and a half a dozen other women in the room were certain that Menno loved her, and until yesterday, Joanna was starting to believe. But for Menno, love wasn't enough. He was looking for the perfect *fraa*, and he'd found out yesterday that she wasn't the one. It was telling that Sadie had said nothing about Verla Ann. She obviously hadn't gone along with Sadie's plan. Surely unhappy about it, perhaps Sadie wasn't as sure of Menno's heart as she claimed.

Peering expectantly at Joanna, Sadie looked as if she wanted some sort of assurance that Joanna was convinced, and everything was fine.

Joanna couldn't give her the assurance, but she could pretend everything was fine. She smiled as convincingly as she was capable of. "*Ach*, Sadie, you have made me feel so much better. *Denki*."

It wasn't a lie, exactly. The flowers had made her feel better, she'd almost completely forgotten about the pain in her knees for a few minutes, and Ada wasn't scowling at her anymore. All in all, Joanna was feeling much better off.

Sadie's face relaxed in relief. "I'm *froh* we could bring a little sunshine into your life. You've been moping for long enough."

Moping? Was that what Joanna had been doing? *Ach, vell*, all that was over now. Somehow she would put Menno behind her and go back to her regular life, where she had been perfectly happy before he had come along. Surely she could have that again. The goats and Pepper would miss Rosie and Lily something wonderful, but she could invite Winnie and Junior over anytime she wanted, and that would be enough. All she'd have left of Menno would be the cave-size cavern in her chest. "I'm sorry I've been moping. From now on, I'll be the most cheerful person you know."

Ada narrowed her eyes but didn't say anything. No doubt Joanna would hear her lecture later.

Someone knocked on the door, and Joanna didn't know whether to rejoice that their uncomfortable conversation had been interrupted or panic that Menno might be standing on the other side of that door, ready to deliver the final blow to her heart. Ada jumped from her chair and opened the door, and there was a collective gasp from the room.

Menno, looking as handsome as ever, stood on the porch with Rosie and Lily on either side of him. He was holding a black plastic pot with some sort of green leafy plant growing out of it. Maybe it was his idea of a *gute* parting gift.

He took off his hat. "Can I talk to Joanna?"

Rosie and Lily rushed into the house and straight into Ada's arms. Ada gave them an abundance of affection. Both girls drew back slightly when they saw how many people sat in the living room, but then Lily sidled over to the loveseat and nibbled on her fingernail.

With tears in her eyes, she gently patted the bandage on Joanna's right knee. "Ouchie, Jojo."

Joanna was no match for Lily's sympathy. She tugged Lily close and hugged her, being careful not to touch the bandages on her arms that went from her wrists to above her elbows. "Does it hurt?" Joanna said, pointing to Lily's legs, which were also thickly wrapped.

Lily nodded. "I was bleeding." She moved around the room, showing her bandages and getting sympathy from everybody. Then she scrambled onto Cathy's lap.

Cathy opened her purse, pulled out two suckers, and gave one to each girl. "Here," she said. "This will ruin your dinner."

Joanna's gaze flicked in Menno's direction. He didn't seem to mind that his *dochters* would ruin their dinner or their teeth. He stood just inside the door, holding his pot and looking uncertain and miserable, like an uninvited guest at a birthday party. Priscilla was part of their group now, but Menno definitely wasn't.

Sadie cleared her throat so loudly, for a split second, Joanna thought she was choking. "*Ach*, look at how late it is. I told *Mamm* I'd make dinner tonight. Isn't that what you told your *mamm* too, Lydia?"

Esther nudged Lydia with her elbow, and Lydia jumped. "Oh, *jah*. I have to go home and feed the chickens."

Esther stood and lifted Lily off Cathy's lap and set the little girl on her feet. "Cathy, you need to take all of us home. I left Levi with *die kinner* and told him to cook something."

Cathy didn't hesitate. With effort, she pushed herself off the couch and grabbed her handbag. "Come on, everybody. The van leaves in one minute. I've got to get you all home before I have to pick up the baseball players."

Joanna doubted that Cathy could make it to the front door in one minute, but she was a lot faster than anticipated. Everyone but Mary, Ada, and Beth passed by Menno and were out the door faster than Joanna could say *stable patellar fracture*.

Beth jumped up and took Rosie's hand. "I bet you want to see the goats."

"*Jah*," Rosie said, her eyes lighting up.

"Me too," Lily squeaked.

Mary and Ada took Lily's hands and followed Beth and Rosie out of the room.

"We're going outside," Ada called. "You have the whole house to yourselves."

Joanna's chest tightened. They wouldn't need the whole house. One room and ten minutes would be sufficient.

Joanna, you're a terrible babysitter. I'm marrying Verla Ann instead.

Okay, Menno. I'm sorry about the coyote. I'll never stop loving you, but I'm not going to mope.

Menno didn't waste any time. With his free hand, he pulled the coffee table in front of the loveseat and sat down on it facing Joanna, setting his hat on the table and clutching the plastic pot against his chest. His gaze pierced her skull. "How are you feeling? Is there anything I can do for you?"

You can go away and have a gute *life.* "I was just about to take another pain pill," she said. Would a pain pill take care of this ache in her heart?

The tenderness in his expression made her want to cry. "Can I get you one? Where are they? The pain must be unbearable."

"It's okay. Mary is in charge of my medication. She can get it for me when she comes in." A fleeting thought crossed Joanna's mind that no one was watching the stew. *Ach, vell,* they all had bigger fish to fry, and Lord willing, Menno wouldn't be there much longer.

His brows inched together. "Are you sure? I'm sorry you're in so much pain."

"I'm sure."

Menno seemed to remember he had a pot in his hand, held it out, and showed it to her. "It's an apple tree."

"Oh," Joanna said. "That's nice."

His eyes pleaded with her. She had no idea what that meant.

"It's for you."

"That's nice."

He set it on the floor. "To plant in front of the house."

"That's nice."

Her heart banged against her chest when he reached out

and took her hand. For the life of her, she couldn't pull away. "Joanna, can you ever forgive me?"

What did he want her to forgive him for? For breaking her heart again and again? For getting mad at her and leaving her in the dirt? For choosing Verla Ann?

"I was completely irrational yesterday. I saw the welts and scratches on Lily's arms and legs, and I got angry. I have no excuse except I can't bear it when my babies get hurt. I blamed you, and I couldn't see past my own outrage." He pressed his palm to his forehead. "I left you sitting in the dirt, and that decision makes me ill. I didn't know you were hurt. I didn't believe you were hurt. I thought Ada was trying to distract me. I never would have left had I known."

"Of course I forgive you, Menno," she said, forcing the words out of her mouth. What did forgiveness matter if he couldn't accept her love?

"Your *dat* ordered me out of the house for *gute* reason. I hurt his *dochter*." His hand trembled in hers. "I know a little of what that feels like."

"I hope you'll forgive me too. I shouldn't have let Lily and Rosie go outside by themselves."

He squeezed her hand. "You don't need to apologize. Ada says I've been trying to do Gotte's job instead of trusting Him. I forgot that Jesus is in my boat. I don't need to be afraid. You didn't put Lily in danger. Gotte used you to protect her."

A jumble of emotions caught in Joanna's throat, and she could barely speak. "*Ach, vell*, I didn't do much. Pepper was Lily's guardian angel yesterday." She wanted to cry in relief. Menno didn't blame her for the attack. She could be happy on that knowledge for many weeks. But not completely. "This never would have happened if Verla Ann had been babysitting."

"Who can say what would have happened?"

As if waiting to hear her name, Verla Ann walked in the front door as if she lived there.

Joanna flinched in surprise. Menno stiffened like a block of cement.

"Verla Ann, what are you doing?" Joanna didn't mean to sound hostile, but Verla Ann had surprised her almost beyond speech. She tried to pull her hand from Menno's grasp, but he tightened his grip. She couldn't understand it. His fiancée wouldn't like that he was holding hands with another girl, even if he was just trying to get the other girl to forgive him.

Breathing heavily, Verla Ann pressed her lips together as if she were momentarily embarrassed. She was smart enough to know she shouldn't have just walked into someone else's house. "I was sick with worry about Rosie and Lily, and I had to barge in and make sure they were okay."

The lines around Menno's eyes deepened in confusion. "Why are you here?"

Verla Ann's gaze locked on their still-clasped hands, and her face turned red. "I went to your house to see how you were holding up. I heard about the coyote attack. Someone said Lily was badly injured while *Joanna* was babysitting." There was no doubt whom Verla Ann blamed for the attack.

Menno claimed he didn't blame Joanna, but that didn't mean he thought she was a fit *mater* for his children.

Verla Ann marched to the coffee table and sat down next to Menno. He was distracted enough that Joanna had no trouble pulling her hand away.

"I wanted to see if there was anything you needed me

to do," Verla Ann said, her voice saturated with concern and indignation. "Everybody was so concerned about Joanna that they ignored you. Lily could get an infection if she's not properly treated."

Menno frowned in concern. "Lord willing, she won't get an infection."

Verla Ann seemed encouraged by his reaction. "I know first aid, and I've got three kinds of antibiotic ointment in my first aid kit. I took it to your house, but when I pulled up on my bike, you were driving away in your buggy. I followed you here."

Menno's eyebrows slid up his forehead. "You followed me?"

"I was a little ways behind you, and I saw you pull up to Joanna's house. That old *Englisch* lady and about a dozen other women left after you went in. I felt like I needed to hurry in here before something bad happened again. The girls tend to get injured here, and I had to make sure they were safe, no matter how rude it is to walk in uninvited."

Her words stabbed at Joanna's heart because they were true and Menno knew it.

"That's very nice of you to be concerned, but my girls are fine. They're out playing with the goats."

Verla Ann caught her breath. "Alone?"

"*Nae*," Menno said. "Ada, Beth, and Mary are with them."

"I'm *froh* to hear *die kinner* aren't alone outside. You can't be too careful, especially after what happened yesterday."

Menno leaned back as if to get a better look at Verla Ann's face. "All is well. *Denki* for caring about my *dochters*."

"Of course I care," she said. "Next to my own family,

you and the girls mean more to me than anyone." She gave Menno a soft and meaningful look. "That's why I am more than happy to babysit Rosie and Lily from now on."

Joanna frowned in confusion. She would have thought Menno and Verla Ann would have had this conversation last night after the coyote attack. Wasn't that why Verla Ann had talked to the school board this morning?

Menno stood up and moved away from the coffee table. "Ada's their babysitter."

Verla Ann also rose to her feet and sidled closer to Menno. "I can't believe you'd let any of the Yoder *schwesteren* near your children after what happened. You don't have to bring them over here anymore and risk their lives."

That was a gross exaggeration, but maybe Menno didn't see it that way.

He glanced at Joanna with an apology in his eyes. "What happened yesterday wasn't their fault, and I trust them completely with my children."

Worry lines etched themselves deeply into Verla Ann's face. "But why take the risk? I can come to your house and watch them there while you go to work. You won't even have to get them dressed or feed them breakfast in the morning. I can take care of all of that for you."

Joanna hated being looked down on, but she wouldn't have stood up, even if it had been easy for her. Her attention was riveted to what Menno would say next, and she chastised herself for caring so much.

"I couldn't ask you to do that. You have to go back to school in a couple of weeks anyway."

Joanna felt a little dizzy. Menno didn't know that Verla Ann had quit her job?

Verla Ann hesitated, then seemed to gather her confidence around her like a shawl. "I quit my job this morning."

Menno's jaw dropped. "You . . . you quit your job?"

"So I could help you."

He scrubbed his hands through his hair. "I told you not to quit your job for me."

"This is an emergency. You need a babysitter. I am the perfect one."

She was also the perfect *fraa*, but Menno's reaction wasn't what Joanna had expected.

"I don't need a babysitter," he said through gritted teeth. He calmed down as quickly as he had gotten worked up. He fell silent, turned his back on both of them, and rested his hand on the mantel. "I've made a horrible mistake," he said softly. "Joanna, I'm so sorry."

Every muscle in Joanna's body tensed. Even though she knew what was coming, she didn't want to hear what he had to say. She reeled like a boat in a storm when he knelt and took her hand.

"Joanna, I'm sorry for what I've put you through. I was trying to be nice. I was trying not to hurt anyone's feelings."

"I know," she said, the words escaping her mouth in a sob.

"I should have told Verla Ann from the very beginning, but I don't want to marry her."

Verla Ann made a soft noise of distress. Joanna leaned closer, and her heart did a little jig. Had she heard him right?

Menno glanced back at Verla Ann. He stood, took her hand as if he was going to shake it, and pulled her from the table. "Verla Ann, I respect and appreciate all you've done for my family."

Verla Ann gave him a tight smile. "I potty trained Lily."

"You potty trained Lily and took care of the girls for a few days while I was at work."

"Almost a whole week," Verla Anna said, as if it had been a very big chore. "I took you on a picnic and made sure the girls' hands were always clean. Dirty hands spread disease. I never let them outside to play by themselves. I kept them safe."

"*Denki* for everything," he said, with a profound sadness in his eyes. "I apologize that I led you to hope for marriage. It was a horrible thing to do to you and the others. I thought I was doing Gotte's will, but I tried to control things I shouldn't have tried to control. I was trying to do Gotte's job. I hurt Joanna's feelings and your feelings and Priscilla's feelings and Sadie's feelings. Everybody's feelings."

Ach, vell, he hadn't hurt Sadie's feelings, but he was right to feel regret for how he'd treated all of them.

Menno pulled Verla Ann to the front door. "I've done so many things wrong, and I am very, very sorry."

"It's not too late, Menno. I forgive you. That's what marriage is. We forgive and support each other."

"*Denki*," Menno said.

Verla Ann didn't take the hint that he wanted her to leave, even as he opened the front door to let her out.

"You've got to think this through very carefully, Menno. Next time it might be a bobcat or a hill of red harvester ants. Who would you rather have watching out for your girls when a pack of wolves attacks?"

A pack of wolves? Verla Ann wanted to marry Menno very badly.

Joanna knew the feeling. She wanted to marry Menno very badly too. Now that she knew Menno chose her, it was easy to give Verla Ann all of her sympathy.

Menno stood his ground. "I hope you will find it in your heart to forgive me someday, but right now, I want to propose to Joanna, and I don't want you standing here while I do it."

Verla Ann's mouth fell open, but there were no words. She marched out the door and slammed it behind her.

Joanna had never been so proud of Menno and had never been this happy in her entire life.

Once again, he knelt in front of her. He cradled her hand in his and kissed her palm. "I don't love Verla Ann, and I don't care if she's the best babysitter in the whole world. Please tell me I haven't ruined my chances with you."

Joanna trembled with emotion. An overwhelming feeling of lightness and joy filled her body. "Please tell me I haven't ruined my chances with you."

He shook his head as a smile tugged at the corners of his mouth. "Don't believe a word Verla Ann says. My girls adore you, and there is no one else I'd want to be their *mater*. There's no one else I want to be my *fraa*. I've made such a mess of things, but I am telling the honest truth when I say I adore you and no one else. Will you marry me? You are the beloved of my soul."

Joanna couldn't help herself. "That's in Jeremiah," she said, smiling with her whole body.

"How did you know?"

"Sadie says I need to have a lot of scriptures ready to quote if I want to win an argument with you."

He got off his knees and slid onto the loveseat next to Joanna, keeping hold of her hand and putting his other hand around her shoulders. "I'll let you win every argument if you say yes."

"How can I refuse an offer like that?" Joanna tapped her finger to her lips and looked up at the ceiling. "I do have one request before I say yes."

His eyes lit up. He knew she was teasing. "Anything."

"I want to see your list."

Menno groaned in mock reluctance and stuffed his hand into his back pocket. "Sadie warned me not to make a list. She said you'd never marry me if I made a list. But when I made plans to come back to Colorado, I felt unfocused without one." Grinning, he unfolded the yellow notebook paper and handed it to her.

Written across the top, in big, bold letters was MARRY JOANNA YODER. The rest of the paper was blank.

Joanna examined his neat handwriting, her heart beating double time as she rejoiced in winning the love of such a *gute* man. "This is a very short list."

He chuckled. "It felt almost impossible at times." He squeezed her hand. "It's the only thing I want. After this, every other list will just be full of trivial goals."

She folded the paper and slid it into her apron pocket. "Well, I don't want to be the reason you fail at one of your goals. I guess I'd better say yes."

He whooped so loud, he rattled the front window. Joanna had never heard the reserved Menno Eicher whoop before. It was her new favorite sound. The warmth in his eyes made her giddy.

"I love you, Joanna Yoder. With all my heart." He drew her close and kissed her gently, and all the pain of past mistakes, bitter rejection, and broken knees disappeared. She would be perfectly happy in his arms for the rest of her life.

"It's about time."

Joanna and Menno turned toward the sound of Ada's voice.

"Ada," Joanna growled. "This is a very inappropriate time to eavesdrop."

Ada leaned against the wall between the kitchen and

living room, looking not the least bit contrite. "For goodness' sake, Menno, how long does it take to propose? The stew has been simmering unattended, and I was forced to come in and make sure it didn't burn." Her eyes twinkled merrily. "I just happened to hear all the *gute* parts."

Joanna laughed with pure joy. "There were a lot of *gute* parts."

"*Ach*, *vell*, I heard where Menno asked you to marry him and you said yes. That was the best part." Ada strode farther into the room. "Help her up, Menno. I want to give you both a hug."

Menno grabbed Joanna's hand. She put weight on her unbroken leg and stood, then Ada hugged them both.

"I told you so," she whispered into Joanna's ear.

Joanna squeezed Ada tight. "I've never been so glad to be wrong."

Menno took Joanna's hand. "Ada, will you go out and get the girls? We want to tell them the *gute* news."

"They're your *dochters*," Ada said. "You go get them."

Menno raised Joanna's hand to his lips. "I've spent too much time apart from Joanna. I'm not leaving her side for the rest of the day."

Ada cocked an eyebrow. "That will make going to the bathroom difficult." She shuffled out of the living room, and they heard the back door open and shut.

Although of a sober disposition, it looked as if Menno's smile was going to be a permanent part of his face. "The girls are going to be so happy to have a new *mater*."

Joanna couldn't stop smiling herself. "They'll be more excited to be related to the goats."

He helped Joanna sit down again. There was only so much excitement her knees could take in one day.

"Maybe the bishop will let the goats come to the wedding," she said.

"As long as you're there, I don't care who else comes. But I have a request of my own for the wedding dinner."

"What is it?"

His lips twitched. "We can have cake and chicken and chow-chow and noodles and whatever else you want. I don't mind green Jell-O or chicken livers or cow's tongue."

"Who serves cow's tongue at a wedding?"

He leaned close and whispered in her ear. "There's only one food I won't allow anywhere near our wedding."

Joanna smiled and savored the feel of his rough cheek against hers. She didn't even have to guess.

"No canned corn."

Chapter 21

Joanna tipped her bucket and watered the small apple tree she and Menno had planted last week. Rosie poured her pitcher of water over the top of the tree, and Lily meticulously sprinkled her small cup around the base.

"Look, *Mamm*," Rosie said. "It's almost as tall as me."

The tree wasn't any taller than it had been last week when they'd planted it, but if it made Rosie happy to think it was growing, Joanna wasn't going to argue with her. "In a few years, it will be taller than all of us."

"Taller than Dada?" Lily asked.

"*Jah*," Joanna said, bending over and giving Lily a kiss on the top of her head. "And we'll get beautiful apples to eat."

"Do goats like apples?" Rosie wanted to know.

"*Jah*. They love them."

"I want to give Smiley an apple from our tree."

"We'll make sure she gets the first one." Joanna peered down the road, her heart swelling in anticipation. Menno would be home soon, and she would rejoice in another day with the three people she loved most in the world. Lord willing, their home would always be full of love,

laughter, and life. How *wunderbarr* that she was finally
Menno's *fraa*.

Their wedding had been smaller than Amish weddings
in places like Ohio and Indiana, but it was the perfect size
for Joanna and Menno. Each guest received their own
beautifully decorated cupcake and a pen printed with the
names of the bride, the groom, the groom's two *dochters*,
the family dog, and the family's four goats.

Dat had put on a fireworks show when it got dark. Mary
and Clay had had fireworks at their wedding, and Dat
didn't want Joanna to feel left out, even though Dat said
fireworks drew too much attention and would probably
keep the whole family out of heaven.

The goats were not allowed at the wedding, but they
heard the whole thing. Joanna and Menno were married
under a large tent set up right next to the barn. Joanna
had sewn matching dresses for herself, Lily, and Rosie,
and the little girls were allowed to sit on the front row
with the attendants during the ceremony.

Cathy Larsen and Esther made Joanna a quilt of Sugar
Bowl quilt blocks, and Joanna felt only slightly guilty
that she hadn't finished her quilt blocks for Grossmammi
Beulah's birthday quilt. What with the goats and babysitting and falling in love with Menno, the quilt had been
the furthest thing from her mind. Poor Grossmammi
Beulah. Lord willing, she would live to see the quilt finished. Of course, Beth had changed her mind about her
blocks so many times, she hadn't even started yet, so
Joanna didn't feel quite so bad.

With her bucket draped over one arm, Joanna took
the girls' hands and strolled with them back to the house.
She had insisted on waiting to get married until the brace
was off and she could walk without a limp. The first week
in October worked out very nicely, and the day had been

sunny and warm. Surely Gotte smiled on their union.

Menno's parents couldn't bear to be separated from their granddaughters, and they moved to Byler right before the wedding, not four miles from Joanna and Menno. Joanna was surprised by how young his parents were. He had often talked about them and their health problems, and Joanna had expected they'd be much older. She'd mentioned it to Menno's *mamm*, and Rebecca had given Menno a not-so-gentle poke with her cane.

Joanna smiled at the memory. Menno's *mamm* was completely devoted to him, but she never let him get away with anything.

Joanna stopped on the front porch and turned to look out at her yard and the small start that would grow into a mighty apple tree. She savored the feel of the two little hands held in hers. Her love for these sweet girls and Menno would only grow deeper and wider through the years. What had started out as a list, a chance meeting, and more than a little annoyance had turned into a profound and beautiful relationship. Out of the small and simple moments of life came great and *wunderbarr* things. Their love was a testament to that. She was blessed beyond measure, and Menno would always have her heart.

A week after the wedding, they had planted the apple tree in the front yard, and Joanna had perfected three apple fry pie recipes in anticipation of all the apples they'd harvest in the years to come.

She still made fry pies every week for the bakery, and Menno ate more than his fair share, reminding her that she had once assured him she would make her husband a fry pie every day if he killed all the spiders and if she loved him very much.

Which she did.

As a joke, Ada had given them a whole case of canned

corn for their wedding, and as a gesture of his commitment to Joanna, Menno had taken it outside and buried it in the backyard the day after the wedding.

Joanna smiled to herself. The man who memorized whole books of scripture never did anything halfway.

Glossary of Amish Words and Phrases

ach:	oh
Ach, du lieva:	Oh, my goodness
ach, vell:	oh, well
aendi:	aunt
appeditlich:	delicious
bruder, bruderen:	brother, brothers
bu, buwe:	boy, boys
buplie:	baby
Cum reu:	Come in
cum:	come
Dat:	Dad
Dawdi:	Grandpa
deerich:	foolish
denki:	thank you
Derr Herr:	The Lord
die buwe:	the boys
die kinner:	the children
die youngie:	the young people
dochter, dochters:	daughter, daughters
du bischt wilkumm:	you're welcome
dumm:	dumb
dummkoff:	dummy
Englisch, Englischer:	a non-Amish person
fater:	father
ferhoodle:	to confuse or mix up
fraa, fraaen:	wife, wives
froh:	glad

gmay:	church services
gmayna:	the Church
Gotte:	God
grossmammi:	grandmother
gute:	good
Guter mariye:	Good morning
hallo:	hello
Handt nunna:	Hands down (for prayer)
heartzley:	sweetheart
hinnerdale:	backside
jah:	yes
kaffee:	coffee
kapp:	prayer cap
Mamm:	Mom
Mammi:	Grandma
maedel:	girl, maiden
mater:	mother
nae:	no
Oh, *sis yuscht*:	Oh, this is just . . . (an expression of frustration or surprise)
onkel:	uncle
redd:	to clean
rumschpringe:	running around time
schwester:	sister
shwesteren:	sisters
sie so gute:	please
Vie gehts?:	How is it going?
wunderbarr:	wonderful